I0684917

COFFEE

IN

MANILA

A Novel

Written by
Patrick Higgins
(A Concerned American)

Coffee in Manila

Published by
www.ForHisGloryProductionCompany.com
www.CoffeeInManila.com

Library of Congress
Cataloging in Publication Data
Paperback ISBN 0-978-0-9658978-6-0

Patrick Higgins' books,

"I Never Knew You",

"The Unannounced Christmas Visitor",

and "The Pelican Trees"

are now available in audiobook format...

1

"LADIES AND GENTLEMAN, AS you can see the captain has turned on the fasten seat belt sign, as we are on final approach into the Metro Manila area," the flight attendant on board Japan Airlines Flight #734 announced, in a professional tone. "Please make sure that your seat belts are securely fastened, and your seat backs and tray tables are in their full and upright positions. Also, please turn off and stow all electronic devices. We should be on the ground shortly. Thank you."

Seated in row 42 on a nearly full flight, on this the third leg of a long and tedious flight, was Ryan Tipton. His trip began 24 hours earlier at Des Moines International Airport, in Tipton's home state of Iowa. From there, he flew to San Francisco International Airport, before boarding a Boeing 777 jumbo jet for the grueling eleven-hour nonstop flight to Tokyo, Japan. He left Tokyo four and a half hours ago, and was now moments away from landing at Ninoy Aquino International Airport, in Manila, Philippines.

Though Tipton had spent much of the past 24 hours flying on airplanes 40,000 feet above the earth's surface—mostly over water—he was too excited, mixed with an equal measure of anxiety, to feel the sheer exhaustion that would attack his insides once he landed and checked into his hotel room.

Based on what others who'd already made the long journey had told him, he would need a day or two to adjust to the jet lag he was sure to suffer, and at least that much time to adjust to the twelve-hour time zone difference.

But none of that mattered to him at present. As the plane continued its slow descent, Tipton could hardly contain himself. Excitement pulsated through his veins, knowing he was just moments away from meeting Maricel Arcamo, a young Filipino woman he met online six months ago, on an Asian dating site.

Forty-five and divorced, the Iowa native stood 5'7" in height and was noticeably overweight by at least 70 pounds. His skin was pale white; his soft blue eyes were always hidden behind thick eyeglasses. He had a full head of brown hair which was starting to turn gray in some places. His sideburns were completely gray.

The two words Ryan Tipton often used to describe his overall appearance were "nothing special." Because of this, his hope was that Maricel wouldn't take one glance at him and head for the terminal exits as quickly as she could, without ever looking back.

If so, it wouldn't come as a major surprise. It would be just another day at the office for him, that office being the always turbulent and unpredictable world of dating women.

But after chatting with the younger Filipino woman for six consecutive months—oftentimes into the wee hours of the night—he felt pretty good about his chances this time, making this a miraculous occasion of sorts for him.

Tipton had a reservation at the Bayview Park Hotel in downtown Manila, for the next seven nights. After hearing good things about two particular tourist hot-spots—the island of Palawan; the other a place called Tagaytay, which boasted one of the cooler climates in the Philippines—Ryan wanted to take Maricel to one of those two places for a day or two.

Despite how exciting it all sounded, she reminded him that she was saving herself for marriage before doing such things She had no trouble meeting him at his hotel each day, but made it crystal clear that she wouldn't sleep there. Nor would she go to those other places with him, unless accompanied by her best friend, Rosalyn.

Though disappointed, Ryan acquiesced to her wishes. Why rock the boat and muddy the waters by forcing the issue before they even met in person? Besides, there was plenty to do in Manila to keep them busy all week.

If there was one thing Ryan knew about Maricel Arcamo, it was that she found most men online to be too aggressive, rude even, which meant they were probably a hundred times worse in person.

With so much dishonesty on the internet, Maricel refused to post her personal information online for all to see. According to her, doing such things wasn't only desperate, it was foolish, because it opened the door to potential danger.

As it was, it took two weeks of numerous e-mail exchanges on the Asian dating site on which Ryan and Maricel had met, before she felt comfortable enough to chat with him on Skype.

But if she knew her American friend was chatting fairly-regularly with two other Filipino women he'd met on the same dating site they'd met on, her feelings for him would quickly change. Especially if she knew he would be spending two weeks in her country, instead of just one, as she believed was the case.

After this week, Ryan would travel to Cebu for four days to meet a girl named Jenny. After that, it was off to Davao City, in the southern part of the country, for a brief three-day visit with another young girl named Liezel.

Maricel had no idea…

Tipton looked out the airplane window trying his best to comprehend how someone possessing below average looks, wavering self-confidence, low self-esteem at times, and a menial job as a security guard in a shopping mall, could be so fortunate to find himself in this most enviable predicament.

Not only were all three women extremely attractive, they were much younger than he was—the youngest was a whopping 21 years younger! The very thought of it blew his mind.

Since most women back in Iowa blinked him away like he didn't exist, this was a whole new experience for Tipton on every level. Was it possible that Maricel would be so sickened by his appearance that the kindness she had always shown him online would quickly evaporate, when they stood face to face? Would she refuse to see him after today?

It couldn't be ruled out. But if it didn't work out with her, for the first time in his life, the American traveler had an insurance policy to fall back on. Two, in fact!

On top of that, Tipton sensed Jenny and Liezel were more liberated than Maricel was—Jenny especially—which meant he didn't know what to expect with either of them. He was gripped with anticipation just thinking about the many possibilities.

In just six months, although nothing had changed with his physical appearance, it was finally up to Ryan to choose who he wanted to be with, instead of being forced to settle for anyone desperate enough to show an interest in him.

The very thought of finally being in control was empowering...

Without a doubt, of the three women, Maricel Arcamo was the one Tipton felt the closest to. Even though 8,000 miles had separated them, whenever she flashed one of her brilliant smiles on his phone screen, part of him would melt inside.

She had a calming presence that always put his mind at ease, especially after a long day at work. No one had the ability to soothe his weary senses like she could.

Even so, she often said it was next to impossible to get to know others online, especially when looking for a lifetime partner. The instant someone started making various promises to her, she would roll her eyes, especially knowing most men made the very same bogus promises to other women as well, in the highly competitive and cutthroat world of online dating.

According to Maricel, it all came down to meeting in person and spending quality time together, before two people could ever proclaim to know each other well. Until then, she refused to invest too much of her heart into online profiles, regardless of how sincere someone proclaimed to be on the surface.

Tipton understood this full well. But what he didn't understand was why a woman of her stature would show an interest in someone like him in the first place? Maricel was the type of woman who would have little trouble meeting scores of handsome, more dignified men than him anywhere in the world, if she so chose.

So why me? Whatever the reason, Tipton knew so much was riding on this trip. They both seemed eager to take their "friendship" to the next level, whatever that next level was.

Hence, the nervous stomach.

Is Maricel truly the one for me, Tipton thought for the millionth time, as the plane he was traveling on gently touched down in Manila. He would soon find out...

By the time the pilot skillfully guided the immense aircraft up to the jet way, it was 6:53 p.m.

Tipton's heart throbbed in his chest. He turned on his cell phone and sent Maricel a text message: *Just landed...The day we've both been longing for is finally upon us...See you in a few minutes! Mwah!*

Maricel quickly replied: *Already here waiting for you. I'm so excited I can hardly catch my breath. Can't wait to see you. Look for me wearing a yellow shirt. Mwah!*

2

AN HOUR LATER, AFTER being cleared through customs, the moment was finally upon them.

Ryan Tipton felt himself trembling inside. His mouth was dry as cotton, and his palms were sweaty, along with the rest of him. The denim blue jeans and black, long sleeve button down shirt he had on only made it worse. He sighed. *Should've worn shorts and a tee-shirt instead!*

But wearing those things would have exposed even more of his overweight body to Maricel. Then again, regardless of what he wore, trying to look thinner in any capacity was merely wishful thinking on his part, a hopeless endeavor, really.

"Soon as I get home, the diet starts," Tipton chided himself under his breath. This wasn't the first time he'd said it, and it wouldn't be the last either. They were words only, with no motivation whatsoever behind them.

Eyes darting left and right throughout the throngs of people milling about the bustling airport, Tipton spotted a young woman wearing a yellow shirt leaning against a wall 50-feet to his left.

Their eyes met. It was Maricel. She squinted to make sure it really was him, then flashed one of the warmest smiles Ryan had ever seen before. Having never been on the receiving end of something so endearing—at least not in person—air got stuck in Tipton's throat. His heart pounded through his chest. It was like she knew something wonderfully amazing that no one else knew.

She's even more attractive in person! Tipton walked toward her. "So nice to finally meet you in person, Maricel!"

"Welcome to the Philippines! Mabuhay!"

"Mabuhay!" came the reply in a distinctive American accent. It was the official welcome to the Philippines. It meant "long life".

Tipton placed his carry-on bag on a vacant chair and they embraced. "I can't tell you how happy I am to be here."

Maricel blushed shyly, cutely. "Me too."

Tipton took a few prolonged deep breaths to calm his nerves, all the while trying not to gawk at her too much.

At 28, Maricel Arcamo was blessed with a natural beauty that seldom needed make-up or grooming. Standing 5'3" in height, she had a near-perfect build that would appeal to most men, and a head full of long black, silky straight hair which seemingly flowed forever down her back.

Her two most distinguishing features up close and personal were her gorgeous brown eyes, which were even more vibrant in person, and her captivating smile. Along with her high cheek bones, the overall combination helped proportion her face rather nicely.

Without a doubt, she was the most beautiful woman Ryan Tipton had ever laid eyes on before.

Though extremely shy, Maricel was a polite and engaging woman, who always seemed to enjoy whatever she was doing. Her life was simple, which was just how she liked it.

When it came to finding a life partner, she wasn't overly concerned with what a man possessed in life, materialistically speaking. She was more interested in his overall character and trustworthiness than anything else. Social status had little to do with it. "How was your flight?"

Ryan let out a loud sigh. "Long!"

Maricel giggled softly. "You must be tired."

"Yes, but seeing you makes the jet lag I'm sure to suffer well worth it. I still can't believe we're finally standing face to face."

"I know," Maricel said, looking down at her feet. "We've waited so long for this day to finally arrive, and now it's here."

When they locked eyes again, Ryan found it difficult to hold her gaze without going blank. In this surreal environment, at least to him, even just one glimpse from her rocked his world more than he cared to admit.

He took a few deep breaths and exhaled. "What do you say we get my luggage, exchange some American dollars for pesos, and get out of here. I don't want to see another airport until I leave next week!"

"Sure, whatever you say," came the reply, warmly.

"And don't worry, I didn't forget your pasalubong." Tipton was referring to a Filipino tradition adopted over the years where, essentially, visitors to their country—native and foreigner alike—were expected to bring gifts for each person they would visit.

Maricel smiled, flashing two perfect rows of white teeth. "I can't wait to see it!"

"Once we get to the hotel, I'll give it to you. Shall we?"

Maricel smiled again and nodded yes.

They arrived at Bayview Park Hotel 90 minutes later, on Roxas Boulevard, in downtown Manila. Tipton felt like the luckiest man on the planet entering this establishment, with an exotic beauty the likes of Maricel Arcamo by his side.

Fifth in line at the registration desk, the exhausted American yawned into his right fist and studied the faces of the people in front of them.

Of the three couples, two were older foreign Caucasian men standing alongside Filipino women, who were much younger than themselves, much like Ryan and Maricel.

The other foreigner was a businessman Tipton guessed was from Korea. He couldn't help but wonder how many foreigners were in the Philippines meeting with their "special someone" this night? He kept this peculiar thought to himself.

"Enjoy your stay with us at Bayview Park Hotel, Mister Tipton. If there's anything we can do to make your visit any more pleasant, please do not hesitate to let us know," the woman behind the large check-in desk declared warmly.

Her smile quickly faded when her gaze shifted to Maricel. Charm was replaced with a silent scorn.

Ryan was too busy trying to suppress another exhausted yawn to notice what had just transpired between the two women.

Ryan and Maricel walked to the bank of elevators and waited for the elevator to reach the lobby floor.

Maricel glanced at the vast expanse of the hotel lobby. Perhaps it was just her imagination, but it seemed many kept showering her with condescending looks. She gulped hard. *Do these people think I'm a prostitute? A player? A scammer?*

Whether it was real or imagined on her part, this was the first time she'd ever been stereotyped like this. The very thought left her feeling nauseous, since nothing could be further from the truth.

When the elevator door opened Ryan boarded, pulling his luggage behind him. When Maricel remained frozen in her tracks, Tipton's pulse raced in his ears. "What's wrong, Maricel?"

Maricel frowned. "I can't come up to your room, sorry."

Ryan shot her a sideways look. "Why not?"

Maricel became even more fidgety and played with her hair to try calming her nerves. It didn't work. "Perhaps next time."

Ryan grew long faced. "Did I do something wrong?"

"No. It's not you, promise!"

"What is it then?"

"I'll tell you later. Now isn't the right time. Sorry."

Apparently, her American visitor knew nothing about the growing problem in her country, regarding the countless Filipino women who loitered places like this looking for wealthy foreigners to latch onto.

Many younger women, especially, were willing to do almost anything, if it meant being rescued out from beneath the stark poverty found throughout much of the Philippine Islands, and being taken to some magnificent place far, far away.

Desperation filled his voice. "What about your pasalubong?"

"Next time," she replied. The tension on her face was evident. Having men gawking at her in public places was nothing new to her, but this was a whole new ball game. Even if their words were unspoken, they were starting to devour Maricel from within.

She needed to leave this place at once, before her body was completely doused in the flames of their unwarranted criticism.

Ryan stepped off the elevator car feeling completely dejected. His head was down, too afraid to make eye contact with her.

Maricel leaned into him and whispered softly in his ear, "I'll explain everything later. Promise." She kissed him softly on the cheek, lowered her head and left the hotel without ever looking back.

Her heart broke a little more for Ryan with each step she took...

Tipton rode the elevator up to the eighth floor, feeling sick to his stomach. *Perhaps I was wrong about her after all...*

He opened the door leading to his hotel room. Though desperate to speak to Maricel, he willed himself not to call her. He opted instead for a hot shower. If he didn't hear from her come daybreak, he would chalk it up as history merely repeating itself again.

As the warm water washed over his fatigued body, his mind raced with a million thoughts, none of them good. Had Maricel already lost interest in him? Was this her best way of breaking it to him softly? Tipton believed the answer was yes. After what had just happened, how could he possibly think otherwise?

After his shower, though completely exhausted, Ryan turned on his laptop computer and logged onto the Asian dating site that was responsible for his flying halfway around the globe in the first place.

If Maricel was no longer interested in him, perhaps he could find someone else to hang out with in Manila. If it wasn't too expensive to change his flight date, his other option would be to travel to Cebu to meet Jenny a few days earlier than he had planned.

Ryan viewed the profile of a 30-year-old woman from Manila and sent her a message saying he would be in Manila for the week, and perhaps they could meet for coffee.

She wasn't in the same league as Maricel, but she was a whole lot better than being alone.

A few moments later the woman replied, saying she would love to meet with him.

Her quick response breathed new life back into Ryan, replacing the life Maricel had just sucked out of him a short while ago.

Tipton sent a few more e-mails to a handful of local women in Manila, just in case, as he chatted with Jenny in Cebu and Liezel in Davao City.

During that time, he received replies from three other women, all of whom Tipton made tentative plans to meet with this week.

One was even willing to meet him at his hotel at this late hour. Mostly due to sheer exhaustion, he declined her rather tempting offer.

At 4:15 a.m., Ryan could no longer keep his eyes open. He fell asleep totally unaware that he had totally misread the situation down in the lobby earlier. Everything he did following Maricel's sudden departure was nothing more than his imagination—mixed with an unhealthy portion of paranoia—playing cruel tricks on him.

Maricel, on the other hand, kept tossing and turning on her bed, wondering if her actions had put a sizable gap between them that perhaps one week could never fully bridge. She hoped not.

She had every intention of calling or texting Ryan when she got home. But after being stuck in traffic, due to a fatal accident on the highway, what normally took an hour took nearly three. Her phone battery had died and she forgot to bring her power bank with her.

When she finally made it home, she figured Ryan would already be sleeping. After flying on airplanes all day, the last thing she wanted was to wake him.

"I should have at least texted him," Maricel grunted wearily, under her breath. *Too late for that now...*

By the time she finally fell asleep, the roosters were already crowing, as the sky slowly brightened and changed colors, filling the atmosphere with radiant light...

3

"MAGANDANG UMAGA, RYAN! KUMUSTA ka?"

"Hmm, I understand the 'Kumusta ka' part," Tipton said, rubbing his eyes. He looked at the clock on the small table next to the bed: 8:13 a.m. He had a splitting headache from a lack of sleep.

Instead of hounding Maricel right off the bat, he decided to play it cool. "If you asked how I'm doing, my answer is, 'mabuti!' I'm trying to remember the first part. I think it means, 'good morning'. Am I right?"

"Very good, Ryan! Or as we say here in the Philippines, 'magaling.' Did you sleep good?"

Even this early in the morning, her voice was lively and full of anticipation. "Not so," came the reply. "How about you?"

"No. I wanted to call you when I got home last night, to explain why I left so abruptly, but I was stuck in traffic and didn't get home until very late. I knew you were exhausted from the long flight and I didn't want to disturb you."

Ryan ran his fingers through his sweaty hair. "That's very thoughtful, Maricel, but I wish you would have texted me when you got home. When I didn't hear from you, part of me figured you were no longer interested."

"Sorry for that…" Maricel looked down at the floor. "But like I said last night, it had nothing to do with you."

"If it had nothing to do with me, why'd you do it then?"

"Would you like me to tell you on the phone, or in person?"

Ryan's eyes widened. "You still plan to meet me today?"

"Of course! That is, if you still want to."

Yes! "Tell me in person then. When can you be here?"

"If I leave now, I can be there in an hour, depending on traffic."

"Sounds like a plan. Let me know when you're close, and I'll meet you down in the lobby. We can have breakfast together."

A smiled crossed Maricel's face that Ryan couldn't see. "Okay. See you soon."

The call ended. A new burst of adrenaline kicked in. Tipton lowered his legs off the bed and hit the shower.

Less than an hour later, Ryan was riveted by the sight that met his eyes, as Maricel gracefully and effortlessly strolled through the massive lobby of the Bayview Park Hotel, wearing a simple green summer dress and white sandals. He wasn't the only one admiring her beauty. There were plenty of others.

Their eyes locked. Maricel flashed her trademark smile, then accelerated her pace in his direction.

Just seeing her again rendered Tipton breathless. "Nice to see you again."

"You too, Ryan," she said shyly, glancing down at the floor.

Not knowing what else to say, he asked, "Shall we?"

Maricel tipped her eyes up at him. "Sure."

They went inside the hotel restaurant and were seated.

After the waitress left them, Maricel said, "Okay, so here it goes; I don't know if you're aware of it or not, but some women in my country are notorious for hanging at places like this, for the sole purpose of finding rich foreigners."

Tipton looked surprised hearing this. "Wow! Really?"

Maricel nodded. "Not all Filipino women are like that. In fact, most of us aren't. But because of the few bad ones, some working at places like this tend to treat all of us as scammers or prostitutes. Didn't you notice the look on the woman's face who checked you into your room last night?"

"No, why?"

Maricel grimaced and her shoulders slumped. "I'm convinced she thought I was a scammer or a prostitute. I never experienced anything like that before. I must say I was quite offended."

Ryan sighed. "So would I, if I were you."

Maricel looked down at the table. "Chances are good she thought you were a player too. But since you paid for the room, you were treated like royalty."

When Ryan remained silent, she went on, "Even when we were walking to the elevators, I noticed many were staring at me for all the wrong reasons. I was mortified and wanted to run from this place as quickly as I could."

Tipton felt foolish for not giving her the benefit of the doubt. The look on his face conveyed that much. "Would you like me to file a complaint with management?"

"No need. Perhaps she was just having a bad day."

"That may be the case, but it still bothers me."

"I can assure you it bothers me even more."

The waitress appeared with their breakfasts.

Ryan observed as Maricel bowed her head to give thanks for the food she was about to eat. As she quietly prayed, he was deeply touched by her selfless gesture.

He couldn't help but wonder how many who proclaimed to be Christians online really were true believers? Was their faith in God genuine like the one whose presence he was in?

Or did they throw the word "Christian" around loosely, as if they were part of a country club or something?

Ryan grimaced, knowing he was part of that unflattering group. While Christianity was his religion of choice, if he was ever put on trial for his faith in God, he seriously doubted there would be enough evidence to convict him, as the saying went.

For someone who professed faith in Christ, Tipton was presently stuck in a spiritual rut. As it was, it had been many months since he last went to church, which he attributed to his hectic work schedule. And he couldn't remember the last time he read the Word of God, really read it.

But Maricel was the real deal. It was refreshing to see her living out her faith in front of him, especially after just meeting for the first time. Tipton couldn't help but be impressed by her. When she finished praying, she took a bite of her French toast. "Masarap!" Thanks to her, Ryan knew it meant, "yummy." She put another fork full in her mouth and swallowed. "My family is eager to meet you. Mama was busy all day yesterday preparing the meal. I just hope you like Filipino foods."

"I'm sure I will. What time's dinner again?"

"Whenever we arrive. After all, you're the guest of honor."

Ryan sighed. "I won't deny I'm a little nervous. What if they don't like me?"

"They will. Just be yourself."

"So, when would you like your pasalubong?"

Maricel broke into a smile that was reminiscent of a little girl on Christmas morning. "How about after breakfast?"

"Sure. Would you like me to bring it down to the lobby?"

"No. It's okay. Now that you're already checked-in, I no longer feel the pressure I felt last night. Besides, I'd love to see what the rooms here look like."

"As you wish," Tipton said.

After breakfast, they walked to the bank of elevators. Seeing that Maricel was nervous, Ryan reached for her hand when the elevator doors closed and gave it a comforting squeeze. He wanted her to always feel safe in his presence.

The first thing she saw when Ryan opened the door to his room, was a pink bag sitting on a table next to the TV.

"Is that it?"

Tipton nodded yes.

Maricel's face lit up. She sat on the couch and pulled the items out of the bag one at a time—her favorite perfume, chocolates, hand lotion and facial cream, three American T-shirts, a key chain and two colorful summer dresses.

She stood and faced him. "Thanks, so much, Ryan. I love everything you gave me."

"Glad you like it." There was an awkward silence. Ryan was unable to maintain steady eye contact with her. He looked down at the floor. He wanted to kiss her but wasn't sure how she would respond to his advance. Finally, he thought better of it and said, "Why don't we go for a walk and see some of your city?"

Maricel smiled cutely at him. "Sure. Whatever."

4

RYAN AND MARICEL STROLLED through the vast lobby of Bayview Park Hotel, hand in hand, and made their way outside. Despite the severe jet lag and still-throbbing headache, just feeling her hand in his—especially out in public—bolstered his pride and made Tipton walk with a little more spring in his step.

"What would you like to see first?" Maricel asked.

"Beats me. I'm new here."

The way he said it made her laugh. "The Manila Zoo isn't too far from here. It's located on Adriatico Street."

Ryan yawned into his fist. "We have plenty of zoos back in the States. I'd rather see some of your country's culture, if you wouldn't mind."

"Why don't we just start walking and see what happens?"

"Sounds like a plan," Tipton said. "But let's not overdo it. I feel like I was hit by a train. Perhaps just some local sightseeing for now."

They strolled Roxas Boulevard. Across the street from the hotel was the U.S. Embassy. Maricel glanced up and saw the American flag flying proudly above the building in the bright blue sky. "Hmm…"

Ryan heard her. "What?"

Maricel blushed. "Wala!"

"What's 'wala' mean?"

"It means, 'nothing.' I was just daydreaming." came the reply.

When Maricel glanced up at the American flag again, Ryan caught on and tightened his grip on her hand.

A smile curled onto her lips. It felt good.

They spent the next couple hours walking the busy streets of Manila. The air was hot and humid. Other than that, it was a picture-perfect day. Maricel made sure to take plenty of selfies of the two of them, using her cellphone.

Tipton felt uncomfortable at first. He never considered himself to be a photogenic person by any stretch of the imagination. But Maricel had this calming presence that instantly relaxed him.

At 1 p.m., they stopped for lunch at the most popular fast food restaurant in the Philippines—Jollibee.

After hearing so much about it the past six months, Ryan often ended his nightly online chats with Maricel by saying, "I can't wait to eat at Jollibee with you someday."

Today was that day. Instead of dining in, they took their food to Rizal Park and ate it near the musical dancing fountains.

Taking a bite of his burger Tipton said, "Finally!"

Maricel knew what he meant and smiled at him. She took a small bite of her chicken sandwich and swallowed. "You should see the fountain at night when it's lit up."

"We have all week. Perhaps we can see it before I leave."

"Sure, whatever you want."

After lunch, they resumed their strolling. They saw many sights and did plenty of window shopping along the way.

But Ryan was usually too busy staring at Maricel to give anything else his full, undivided attention. As far as he was concerned, she was the only attraction he wanted to see.

As lovely as she appeared on his phone or laptop screen 8,000 miles away, she was even more adorable in person. Whenever she smiled, her deep-set dimples would always surface. Her facial expressions were colorful and defined with perfect clarity.

And then there was the smell of her just-washed hair; yet another sensation Tipton never got to experience online.

Trying to compare the two was like trying to compare snail mail to e-mail. There simply was no comparison.

Maricel stopped in front of a clothing store and fixed her gaze on a mannequin proudly displaying one of the store's newest fashion designs. Seeing Ryan's reflection staring at her in the pane glass window, she said, "Isn't it beautiful?"

"Yes, you are."

Maricel stuck out her tongue. "Not me, silly, the dress."

"Yes, but it can't compare to your beauty."

Maricel grew more serious. "Really?"

Ryan nodded yes, but found it impossible to hold her gaze again. He needed a diversion. "Do you really like it?"

"I love it!" Her words were charged with excitement.

"It would be my pleasure to buy it for you, Maricel."

Maricel's cheeks turned red. "Aww, thank you, Ryan!"

They went inside. Maricel tried it on. "So, what do you think?"

"Wow! Whoever made that dress clearly had you in mind."

Maricel giggled. "Really?"

"Absolutely! I mean, look at you! You were born to wear it!"

Ryan made the purchase and they left the store.

At 3 p.m. Tipton was sweating profusely. The tropical heat was starting to get to him. "Would it be okay if we crossed the street and walked in the shade for a while?"

Maricel nodded yes. She was thinking similar thoughts. Like many other Filipino women in her country, she didn't like spending too much time in the sun, for fear that her skin would get too dark.

They came upon a quaint coffee and pastry shop roughly a quarter mile away from the hotel. The outside of the building was painted coral. A forest green colored awning hung above the front door and windows, protecting them from wind and rain.

A wooden sign hung on a steel bar jutting out from the wall advertising the cozy establishment. It read: *Agape Coffee and Pastry Shoppe. Everyone welcome!*

Ryan asked Maricel, "How does coffee sound?"

"Sounds good, actually."

"In this heat, what I really need is water. But after that long flight, I need an adrenaline boost."

Maricel shrugged her shoulders. "Whatever you want..."

"Shall we?"

Maricel nodded and they went inside. The transition from full sunlight to the dim lighting momentarily assaulted their vision. After their eyes had time to adjust, they settled upon a kind Filipino man who appeared to be in his late 60's.

His eyes were fully alive and blazing with goodness; his smile was downright comforting. His skin was dark and wrinkled, as if all the moisture had been wrung from his body.

His facial features were strong but noticeably kind. He had a short plump nose and a head full of salt and pepper hair.

"Welcome to Agape Coffee and Pastry Shoppe! My name's Ernesto. What can I get for you?" Ernesto wore a dark brown, knee-length apron proudly displaying the name of the coffee shop in bold yellow print across the chest.

"May we have two cups of your strongest coffee?" Ryan said, his mouth stretched in another yawn.

The way Tipton said it made the Filipino man chuckle, causing the twinkle in his eye to radiate even more. "Looks like someone didn't sleep much last night..."

"That would be correct."

Ernesto glanced at the young Filipino woman standing alongside him, and realized his comment had offended her. She looked down at the floor. What he didn't know was that it caused the many not-so-pleasant memories in the hotel lobby the night before to resurface in her mind. *Does this man think I spent the night with Ryan?*

Think, think, the kind old man thought to himself. "Just getting into town, young man?"

"Yes. Just last night."

"Well then, that explains the need for strong coffee," came the reply. His tone of voice couldn't have been any more welcoming.

Maricel tipped her eyes up and smiled politely at him.

Right then and there, Ernesto Angeles, co-owner of Agape Coffee and Pastry Shoppe, knew the woman standing alongside the Caucasian man was one of the good girls. "What do you take in your coffee, young lady?"

Maricel glanced up at the menu on the wall above the man's head. "Actually, may I have a mochaccino instead?"

"Certainly. What do you take in your coffee, sir?"

"Cream and two sugars, please."

"Will that be for here or to go?"

"To go," Tipton replied.

Ernesto smiled warmly at them again. "Be right back with your beverages."

As the old man got busy adding the right ingredients into both cups, Ryan let his eyes wander over the establishment. The counter he stood behind was off to the right of two swinging doors. There was a slight gap between them. Four of the six counter seats were occupied by customers enjoying their coffees and pastries.

To the left of the doors leading to the kitchen was a glass-covered display case, featuring a wide assortment of fresh-baked breads, pastries, and various other mouth-watering desserts.

The aroma permeated the entire shop, quickly seducing the nostrils of each person—employee and customer alike.

Four large plants stood in each corner like sentries protecting the establishment. The walls were painted a soft yellow. The wooden floor was light brown in color. But what stood out most to Ryan were the hundreds of photographs hanging on three of the shop's four walls. Varying in size, most displayed Filipino women standing alongside foreign men. Everyone looked joyfully happy.

"What's with all the pictures? Satisfied customers?"

"You could say that, young man," the coffee shop owner replied, without taking his eyes off the two beverages in front of him.

Tipton raised an eyebrow. "Everyone looks so happy. Coffee must be really good here."

The way he said it caused Ernesto Angeles to burst into laughter.

Maricel chuckled, too, but in a much softer tone.

"Guess you'll find out soon enough," Ernesto said.

A young woman emerged from the small kitchen carrying a tray full of apple pastries. After carefully placing them inside the display case, she quickly retreated to the kitchen.

A moment later, she emerged again, this time carrying a tray full of just baked leche flans.

Following closely behind her, an older Filipino woman carried a wicker basket full of freshly baked breads wrapped in cellophane, ready for purchase. She appeared to be in her late 60's and was about the same height as the man preparing their beverages.

Much like him, her eyes were radiant and fully alive, her smile, captivating. And she had the same angelic glow on her face as the old man. A little on the heavy side, she had short cropped gray hair, a plump nose, and chubby cheeks.

When she squeezed past Ernesto, he gave her a quick peck on the cheek. "My wife of forty-eight years," he said to his customers. "She's even more beautiful now than when I married her."

"Aww, how sweet." Maricel was astonished that this man still made his wife blush after nearly 50 years of marriage. They reminded her of her parents. "That's the kind of love I want," she whispered softly to herself.

Ryan heard it and tightened his grip on her hand.

A moment later, their beverages were ready. "Would you like fresh-baked bread or pastries to complete your order?"

Maricel shrugged her shoulders. "Up to you," she said to Ryan, cutely, shyly.

"No thanks. Still full from Jollibee. I'm saving my appetite for the feast later."

The coffee shop proprietor inquired, "Feast?"

"Opo, sa bahay ko," Maricel said. Then to Ryan: "I told him it's at my house."

"I see."

"Hope you enjoy the feast," the older Filipino man said.

"Salamat, po." Ryan knew what that meant, "Thank you."

"Walang anuman, young lady," Ernesto said, warmly.

Thanks to Maricel, Ryan also knew what that meant, "You're welcome."

"May I know your name?"

"Maricel, po."

"My name's Ernesto. And this is my lovely wife, Gloria."

"Nice to meet you both."

"And you, young man?"

"Name's Ryan Tipton."

"Welcome to the Philippines, Ryan!"

"Thanks. Happy to be here." Ryan reached into his pants pocket to retrieve his money. "Would you prefer U.S. dollars or pesos?"

"Neither actually. It's on the house."

Ryan shot a quick glance at Maricel before glancing back at Ernesto. "Are you the owner of this place?"

"Indeed, I am, Ryan, along with my wife."

"Now I see why everyone's smiling in the pictures. Did you give them free coffee too? If so, you must be very wealthy!"

Ernesto burst into laughter again. "I see someone has a good sense of humor."

"I have my moments." Tipton was thoroughly enjoying the laughs his comment had elicited from Maricel and Ernesto.

"I appreciate a man with a good sense of humor. And I hope you appreciate that it's our pleasure to treat you both to coffee."

"Of course, I appreciate it, sir, but it's not necessary."

Gloria stood alongside her spouse. "Like my husband said, it's on the house. Consider it our way of officially welcoming you to our beautiful country." Gloria glanced briefly at Maricel with a certain sparkle in her eyes, and went on, "The only thing we ask in return is that you treat Maricel with the respect she deserves."

Ryan winced then gulped hard, as Jenny's and Liezel's faces surfaced in his mind. "I will. Thanks for the coffee."

His brief change of expression didn't go unnoticed by Gloria. "Hope you enjoy it. Please take one of my homemade mango float desserts with you, to help take the edge off before dinner."

"That's very kind of you, Gloria," Ryan said.

Just then, Ryan felt a warm sensation rising from the floorboards, which quickly washed over him. He thought he felt something similar when they first entered inside, but now it was unmistakable. He didn't know what it was or from where it came.

Ryan wanted to ask Maricel if she felt it too, but he didn't want his inquiry to cause her to think he was a little off. *Probably just the jet lag*, he reasoned.

"Maraming salamat, po, sa kape at sa mango float," Maricel said to the coffee shop owners. Then to Ryan: "I thanked him for the coffee and mango float."

"Walang anuman, Maricel," said Ernesto, in reply.

Gloria glanced at Ryan. "Enjoy your visit to the Philippines."

"Thank you. Or should I say, 'Salamat!'"

Gloria smiled cordially. "Either is fine. We understand both."

Tipton didn't know what it was, but something about this couple and their establishment comforted him greatly.

Ernesto said, "Please stop in and see us again."

Ryan took a small sip from his coffee cup. "Okay, but under one condition…"

"What's that?"

"That you let me pay for the coffee next time."

Gloria chuckled. "Yes, of course."

"Okay, then it's a deal."

Gloria excused herself to assist another customer.

"Ingatan mo sarili mo, Maricel," Ernesto said, "at pagpalain ka ng Diyos."

"Maraming Salamat, po. Ikaw din."

At that, Ryan and Maricel left Agape Coffee and Pastry Shoppe, both feeling that the establishment they had just left was so much more than a quaint little coffee shop.

Tipton craned his neck back and watched a teenage employee, identified by his dark-brown apron, cleaning a table by the window for three waiting customers holding their coffees and pandesal— which was a fresh-baked bread many Filipinos enjoyed with their morning beverages. He, too, seemed fully aglow.

Ryan was still convinced that something strangely invisible had risen through the floorboards, especially when the owners refused to take his money for the beverages. Whatever it was, it quickly enveloped him, making him feel completely safe and protected. It was a warmth he had never felt before.

Walking back to Bayview Park Hotel, Maricel explained to Ryan what Ernesto said just before they left, "'Ingatan mo sarili mo' means take care of yourself. 'Pagpalain ka ng Diyos' means God bless you."

"Salamat, Maricel, but I don't think I'll remember that thirty seconds from now."

Maricel smiled. Sure enough, she felt the same sensation rising through the floorboards of the establishment they'd just left.

Whatever it was, it had nothing to do with the rich aroma from the coffee and delicious homemade pastries they sold. This sensation stretched far beyond smell and taste, touching all five of her senses. Yes, there was just something about that place...

But what in the world was it? Much like Ryan, she had no idea...

5

AN HOUR LATER, THE taxicab that Ryan and Maricel were riding in pulled up to a yellow and white stucco house, in Quezon City. She said, "Here we are. It may be small, but it's home to us."

"Nice house," Ryan said, meaning it. Now just moments away from meeting her family, Tipton became increasingly fidgety.

Maricel noticed. "Relax" she said, "everything will be fine."

"I'm fine, really; excited to meet everyone." But Ryan's face betrayed his words.

Tipton paid the cab fare, and they walked up three small steps leading to a wooden door forming the main entrance to the Arcamo residence. They weren't holding hands this time. First impressions and all. Then again, even if Ryan wanted to hold her hand, he couldn't. His hands were full of bags—Maricel's pasalubong in one hand; the dress he purchased for her earlier in the other.

Hazel Arcamo had been peeking through the window the past few minutes, waiting with bated breath for her daughter and the American visitor to arrive. Spotting them, she dashed to the front door. "Welcome to our home, Ryan! We've been looking forward to this day for a very long time."

At 47, which Tipton was painfully aware was only two years older than his own age, Hazel didn't necessarily look younger than her age, but much like Maricel, she looked even more attractive in person. "Me too. I see where Maricel gets her beautiful smile."

Hazel beamed from ear to ear. "Please come in and meet everyone."

Ryan saw Maricel's father Francisco sitting on the couch in the small living room. He knew what he looked like from seeing his photos on social media, and from occasionally seeing him when he was videochatting with Maricel. "Nice to finally meet you in person."

"How was the flight?" the 51-year-old man asked, his friendly eyes probing, wondering if he really was the one for his daughter.

Ryan suppressed a yawn. "Long and grueling. Just glad to finally be here."

Francisco got up off the couch, and the two men shook hands. "Welcome to our humble abode. Make yourself comfortable."

Hazel went on with the introductions. "This is our son, Miguel, and our daughter, Vivian."

Tipton cleared his throat. "Nice meeting you both."

"You too," said Miguel, shaking Ryan's hand.

Vivian smiled shyly at him but remained silent.

Whereas Ryan had frequently seen Maricel's parents on his phone screen back in Iowa, her siblings were usually too caught up in their own little worlds to pay much attention to who their sister chatted with.

And whereas Maricel resembled both of her parents—mostly her mother—Miguel, now 25, was a spitting image of his father, possessing Francisco's same height—5'6"—and good looks.

Vivian, on the other hand, looked just like her mother. She was 22, quite beautiful and painfully shy. Maricel feared if her younger sister didn't find a way to break out of her cocoon, it might prevent her from getting married someday.

Hazel asked, "Where's Rosalyn?"

"She just called, Mama," Maricel said. "She'll be here soon."

Hazel wasn't surprised that her eldest daughter's best friend was late. Rosalyn was always late. "Are you hungry, Ryan?"

"A little, I suppose." Seeing his bloated reflection in a mirror hanging on a living room wall, Tipton ignored his grumbling stomach for the time being. Perhaps it was the colorful, XXL Hawaiian-style shirt he wore, but it made him look 350 pounds instead of 250. At least in his estimation.

Maricel glanced at him as if to say, "You're safe here," before shifting her focus to her mother: "We're both hungry, Mama. We haven't eaten since lunch."

"Everything is ready. Just waiting for Rosa to arrive."

Tipton took a seat and did a quick study of everyone. Amazingly, no one seemed concerned with his obvious weight problem. Either that or they were very good actors, which Ryan seriously doubted was the case. He breathed a sigh of relief and relaxed a little more.

There was a knock on the door. Before anyone could open it, Rosalyn came barreling through wearing a simple blue cotton dress, with enough energy inside to power a small village. "I'm here!" she shouted.

"Welcome back, Typhoon Rosalyn," Francisco said, causing Miguel and Vivian to burst out in laughter. But with Ryan among them, it was quickly muffled.

Rosalyn snorted a laugh. "Ha ha ha, very funny, po!"

From a physical standpoint, apart from her luminous smile, most might think there was nothing else remarkable about the 28-year-old woman. But what Rosalyn lacked in physical beauty, she more than made up for with limitless amounts of charm and charisma. Despite her nondescript features, this was someone who felt quite comfortable in her own skin.

Before Ryan could ask why Francisco had called her by that name, Rosalyn answered the question by sheer demonstration.

"Nice to meet you, Ryan. I'm Rosalyn. Call me Rosa for short."

"Nice to meet you, Ro..."

Rosalyn cut him off in a way that was more humorous than rude. "Welcome to the Philippines! What do you think of my country so far?"

"So far, so good," Tipton said as quickly as he could. If he tried keeping pace with her, he'd be dizzy in no time.

With a curious expression on her face, Rosa probed on, "What do you think of my best friend? Isn't she beautiful?! Quite the catch, don't you think?"

Ryan blushed. *She really is like a typhoon!*

Before he could utter a reply, Rosalyn saved him. "Just kidding."

Maricel shot Rosalyn a quick telepathic glance that screamed, "You're embarrassing him, sis! Calm down! Let him breathe."

Rosalyn replied with a telepathic expression of her own; "Sorry, girlfriend," and backed off without finishing her customary full-blown interrogation, before the poor guy even had a chance to eat.

Maricel often wished she was born with the same dynamic personality her best friend was blessed with at birth. For better or worse—regardless of topic—the moment Rosa opened her mouth, everyone was sucked into her highly energized and slightly chaotic orbit. She wasn't the type to hold back on much, if anything.

Rosa always told it like it was. To those who knew and loved her, it was just Rosalyn being Rosalyn.

Miguel and Vivian couldn't get enough of her magnetic personality. She always kept things lively and entertaining. They loved living vicariously through their ate's (elder sister's) best friend, especially when Rosa asked the challenging questions they always wanted to ask, but they were too shy and afraid to.

"Time to eat everyone," Hazel announced.

Everyone gathered around a table loaded with bowls full of freshly prepared Filipino foods. The aroma was heavenly.

Ryan noticed there were no chairs around the table. It was a buffet-style meal, which suited him just fine.

Hazel glanced at her husband. "Dear?"

Everyone held hands and bowed their heads, as Francisco offered up a prayer of thanksgiving to their Maker for the meal. The man of the house ended with, "We ask these things in Jesus' mighty name, Amen!"

"Amen," came the reply from everyone else in unison.

"Ryan, please help yourself first."

"Salamat, Hazel." Tipton grabbed a plate. Before digging in, he did another quick scan to see if anyone was staring at him. They were looking at him, yes, but certainly not staring at him or judging him with their eyes. He relaxed a little more and filled his plate with a little bit of everything. "Where shall I sit?"

"Anywhere you'd like. Make yourself comfortable," Hazel said.

The first thing Tipton tried was a noodle dish. "M-m-m, delicious! What's it called?"

"Pancit," Hazel said. "It's one of our most common dishes here in the Philippines."

"I remember seeing it at Jollibee earlier, but I didn't try it. Glad I waited—yours looks so much better."

Hazel's face lit up. She glanced at Francisco, and saw him smiling, then shifted back to Ryan, "So nice of you to say…"

"It's true!" Ryan stabbed his fork into what he believed either was chicken or pork. "What's this called?"

Maricel said, "Adobong baboy or pork adobo in English."

"It's my favorite," Rosalyn opined, without being asked.

It wasn't the words she spoke that caused Miguel and Vivian to burst into laughter again, it was *how* she said it, without being asked. Rosa really was over-the-top hilarious. At least to them, she was.

Ryan took a bite and the robust flavor instantly exploded in his mouth. "Now, that's tasty!"

Hazel beamed again. "Glad you like it."

Tipton stuffed three more forks full of pork adobo inside his mouth, before venturing onto the next item on his plate. "What's this called? Looks like beef stew."

"Close," Maricel said. "It's kalderetang manok or chicken caldereta in English…"

Rosalyn took over, "It's made with chicken, potatoes, carrots and peas in a thick tomato sauce." The way she described it, so vividly, one might think Rosa had prepared it herself.

Once again, Miguel and Vivian broke out in laughter.

Most of the things Tipton tried he liked. But his taste buds didn't necessarily agree with two items in particular; the first was bagoong. Widely used in the Philippines as a condiment consisting of raw fish—anchovies and other small fish—it was salt cured then left to ferment for many weeks, before finally being served.

The finished product looked more like dead worms than fish.

The other item Tipton didn't care for was balut—18-day-old fertilized eggs containing partially developed duck or chicken embryos, which were boiled then eaten inside the shell. It looked disgusting. But out of respect for Hazel, Ryan made sure to swallow everything he put inside his mouth.

Conversation was lively as they ate. Even if Rosalyn did most of the talking, Ryan still couldn't help but like her. Yes, she was surely an attention seeker, but not in an arrogant way.

Tipton couldn't remember feeling any more comfortable, especially after meeting a group of individuals for the very first time. The Arcamos made him feel like he was already part of the family. Rosalyn too. He savored their company as much as the food.

At 11 p.m., the leftover food was wrapped in cellophane and placed inside the small refrigerator.

Ryan noticed that Francisco kept yawning.

"Five a.m. comes quite early," he said, apologetically.

It was time to go. Tipton called for a cab and was told someone would be there to fetch him in a few minutes.

"Is there anything I can do before I go, like help clean up?" the American visitor asked.

"No. Just having you here is good enough," Hazel replied.

Even exhausted, Francisco couldn't ignore what he saw on his daughter's face, as she sat on the couch next to Rosalyn. They weren't saying much—which was a minor miracle in itself—but he knew what they were thinking. It was written all over their faces.

34

Maricel's feelings for Ryan kept growing stronger. *Could this be the one*, the father of three thought to himself again, keeping it to himself.

Despite that his American guest was only six years younger than he was, he seemed like a perfect gentleman. Even so, it was difficult imagining any man kissing his two daughters.

Most fathers raising sons never worried much about who their sons dated, but raising daughters was entirely different.

It was a Daddy thing...

Francisco looked out the front window and breathed a sigh of relief. "I believe your taxi is here."

Ryan got up out of his chair. "It was a pleasure meeting you all."

"You're always welcome here, Ryan."

"Thanks, Francisco. Hope to see you all again before I go back to the States."

"Next time we'll sing karaoke."

"Sounds good. But I must warn you the moment I start singing, your neighbors may call the police. I'm that bad."

Francisco laughed. "Perfect! We can have a contest to determine who has the worst voice in all the land."

"Sounds like a contest where the odds are in my favor."

"We shall see," said Francisco. The two men shook hands.

Ryan turned to Hazel. "Thanks again for the delicious meal. I especially enjoyed the calderita and pork adobo," he opined. "The egg rolls were also yummy!"

"You mean fried lumpia," Hazel said, politely.

"Lumpia, sorry."

"Come back soon and I'll prepare those things again for you."

"Salamat, Hazel." Tipton took comfort knowing Maricel was so much like her mother. *The fruit really didn't fall far from the tree!*

"It was nice meeting you both," Ryan said to Miguel and Vivian.

"You too," they said at the same time. Both were sitting on the floor scrolling on their mobile phones. Miguel made brief eye contact with Ryan, before his eyes drifted back to his phone. But Vivian's eyes remained glued onto her phone screen.

Ryan didn't take it personally. He said to Rosalyn, "It was a pleasure meeting you. I wish I had half the energy you have."

Rosalyn chuckled softly. "Pleasure meeting you, too, po."

Maricel shot a nervous glance at her parents when Ryan wasn't looking. They both nodded their approval.

She then looked at Rosalyn, who gave her best friend a quick thumbs-up gesture. Satisfied with their silent assessments of her American visitor, Maricel walked him out to his waiting cab.

Ryan said to the driver, "Can you wait a second?"

"No problem," he said, turning the meter on.

But Ryan wasn't concerned about the running meter right now. He was too busy trying to slow his pulse to a more normal rate. "So, I'll see you in the morning for breakfast?"

Maricel smiled and nodded yes. "Nine a.m.?"

"Sounds good."

There was an awkward moment of silence, as they stared at each other rather expectantly.

Should I do it? Tipton glanced back at the house. Satisfied that no one was spying on them, he steeled himself to take the plunge and inched in a little closer.

Maricel reciprocated and did the same.

This gave Ryan the confidence to take another step toward her. He leaned in closer and tilted his head until their lips locked.

For a brief moment, they were frozen in time with only their lips touching. Then Maricel wrapped her arms around Ryan's neck and the rest of the world faded away. They were completely lost in each other, savoring every precious second.

The taxi driver gave a courtesy revving of the engine to remind them both that he was still there, disrupting this intimate moment.

The smitten couple pried themselves apart from one another and tried regaining their collective equilibrium. Gazing at each other in the darkness, now that the next step had been taken in their relationship, they both knew the way they would relate to one another from this moment on was forever changed.

It took every ounce of strength Tipton possessed to lower himself into the cab. He rolled his window down. "I can't wait to see you again in the morning."

"Me too." Maricel was surprised she could even speak.

As the driver pulled away, she became misty-eyed, as she tried harnessing what she felt inside. Was it love? It sure felt like it.

Maricel glanced back at the house. Sure enough, Rosa was glued to the window watching, a tender expression on her face, wishing she could find true love someday.

When it came to developing relationships, many women believed it came down to that all important first kiss. That's when most proclaimed to know for sure if they truly were in love or not.

But Maricel was raised to think differently. Though she'd greatly anticipated this moment all her life, she knew true love wasn't predicated on a physical gesture such as a kiss, but on a commitment, dedication, trust and loyalty toward the other person.

All of which were inside things...

Nevertheless, she always wondered what her first real kiss would feel like. Ryan Tipton didn't disappoint her. It wasn't the kiss itself that made her feel all tingly inside; it was the feeling behind his tender embrace.

Maricel Arcamo was finally introduced to the passion she'd always read about in paperback books and girlie magazines, but had yet to personally experience. This was, by far, the most romantic and passionate moment of her life so far. It was infinitely better than the million times she had imagined it inside her mind.

Rosalyn joined her outside. "Well?"

"Wala!"

Rosalyn laughed. "Come on, tell me!"

"What can I say? It was amazing."

"Waaaaa, selos ako," came the reply, with a grimace.

"Don't be jealous, sis, your time will come again."

"I wish Ryan had a brother for me."

Maricel didn't reply. She looked skyward and thanked God for finally blessing her with a good man to love. If she needed further proof that she was falling in love with Ryan Tipton, his kiss had just sealed it for her.

Riding back to the hotel, Tipton could hardly sit still. After suffering so many knockout blows from women in the past, he finally found the woman of his dreams.

He sent a text message to Maricel: *I can't believe how much I miss you. Sweet dreams. Mwah!*

A few moments later, Maricel replied to his text message: *Miss you too! Nite nite, sweetie...mwahhhhhh!*

Sweetie? Ryan looked outside the taxicab window. *Wow!*

Tipton showered back at the hotel, then e-mailed the four women he had made tentative plans to meet with this week. He apologized to each of them, saying something had come up and he wouldn't be able to meet with them after all.

Before logging out of the Asian dating site, he viewed Maricel's profile for the millionth time since joining a half year ago. Her last visit was three days ago. Staring at her profile picture on his laptop screen, his heart rate accelerated. *I can't believe I just kissed her!*

At 3 a.m., though still jetlagged, Tipton couldn't sleep. How could he with visions of Maricel Arcamo dancing in his head, each one ending at the same place—by the taxicab leading to their all-important first kiss?

What a difference 24-hours had made in his life. He went from battling a restless spirit inside, to suddenly feeling like he was in love with Maricel. One thing was certain: he never felt this way before. Not even his ex-wife made him feel this way. *Life is good!*

At that, Ryan Tipton finally drifted off to la-la land, already knowing that no matter how good his dream might be, it could never compete with his present reality...

6

"MAGANDANG UMAGA, RYAN!"

"Good morning, Maricel! Did you sleep good?"

"Yes, I did. How about you?"

"Eventually. But I tossed and turned for the longest time."

"Why?" Maricel asked, certain she already knew the answer.

Tipton chuckled into the phone. "How could I possibly sleep after the day we had? It was the best day ever!"

Maricel grinned to herself and left it at that. "Are we still going to Mall of Asia today?"

Ryan suppressed a yawn. "Yes. But you may want to bring a swimsuit in case we decide to go for a swim before we go 'malling', as you say here in the Philippines."

"Okay. I'm leaving now. See you soon."

An hour later, Maricel arrived and they moseyed into the hotel restaurant for breakfast. When the waiter brought their food, Ryan surprised her when he offered to say grace. She bowed her head and closed her eyes. She thought to herself, *If my parents could only see this, his stock would soar to even greater heights.*

They ate in silence until Maricel broke it, "I look forward to going to Enchanted Kingdom tomorrow."

Ryan put a piece of bacon in his mouth and took his time chewing on it, before swallowing. "How many times have you been there?"

"A few. But it's been a while."

"I'm sure it'll be fun. But I'm even more eager to go to Ocean Adventure Park the following day."

Whereas Enchanted Kingdom was an amusement park resembling your basic Six Flags parks in America, Ocean

Adventure Park at Subic Bay was the Philippines' toned-down version of Sea World.

Ryan took a sip of orange juice. "If we have enough time this week, I'd like to visit Corregidor Island. According to the brochure, the ferry departs daily at 8:00 a.m. and returns in the afternoon, so it won't take up the entire day."

Maricel chuckled under her breath at the way he mispronounced the word, *Corregidor*.

"Remember I told you my uncle Floyd fought here in World War two?" Maricel nodded yes. "Thankfully, he came home after the war. I'd like to go and pay my respects to the many Americans who didn't come home. With you, of course…"

"I would love to go there with you." The way she said it made Ryan's cheeks turn bright pink in color.

After breakfast, they changed into swimsuits and sat on adjoining chaise lounge chairs by the hotel pool.

Ryan wore a colorful knee-length swimsuit which exposed pale white legs below the knees that hadn't seen the sun in quite some time. He also wore a light blue T-shirt that was too big even for himself, which said something. Tipton had no intention of removing it at any point, not even in the swimming pool.

Maricel wore a stylish, one-piece, pink and black swimsuit that was hidden beneath a white, oversize beach dress. Mostly out of shyness, she had no plan of removing it.

"Okay, so let me get this straight," Ryan said, a determined expression on his face, "good morning, good afternoon and good evening all begin with the word, 'magandang'?"

Maricel nodded yes. She found his accent adorable; especially the way he pronounced the word *magandang*.

"Sounds simple enough. Just hope I remember it later."

"Just remember the word you always type online to describe me, 'maganda', then add the letters 'ng'."

"Since you put it that way, how can I forget? Now I just need to remember the other three words."

"Let's say them together—umaga, hapon, gabi."

Tipton did as he was instructed.

41

Maricel smiled at him. "Very good, Ryan."

"Salamat, teacher."

"Walang anuman, estudyante! You're off to a good start."

Ryan smiled at the compliment. "Can you teach me a little more each day? This way, I won't feel overwhelmed all at once."

Maricel nodded yes. "Okay, let's recap some of what you've learned so far."

"Okay, shoot."

"How do you say, 'thank you?'"

"That's an easy one, 'salamat.'"

"How about 'you're welcome?'"

"Walang anuman."

"How about, 'how are you?'"

"Kumusta ka, right?"

"Oo, magaling!" Maricel said, once again sounding like a proud teacher congratulating her student on a job well done.

"I think you said, 'Yes, very good,' right?"

"Oo, korek, which means, 'Yes, correct.' You can also say, 'tama', which means 'true.'"

"Got it. At least I think I do…"

"Good. Now give me two replies to 'kumusta ka.'"

"Okay, the first is, 'okay lang'. The second is 'mabuti.'"

"Wow, magaling ulit, Ryan."

"What is 'ulit?'"

"It means 'again,'" Maricel said. "Now, tell me again how to say, 'Good morning?'"

"Magandang umaga," came the reply. Even after chatting online for six months, and hearing Maricel say those words to him numerous times, he still had difficulty pronouncing the first word.

Maricel chuckled cutely more to herself than to him. "Very good. How about good afternoon?"

Ryan loved how she could laugh so easily, yet still listen to him with great interest. "Magandang hapon."

"What about good evening?"

"Magandang gabi."

"Bravo! Okay, now tell me I'm beautiful."

"Maganda ka!"

"How do you say, 'I love you?'"

"That's easy, 'Mahal kita.'"

Maricel grew more serious. Her face reddened. "Oo, pero bakit mahal mo ako?"

"What?"

"Wala," she said, looking down at her hands.

"What is 'wala' again?"

"It means 'nothing.'"

"Please tell me. I know it has something to do with love, because I heard you say 'mahal'. But that's all I understood."

Maricel looked him square in the eyes, "I asked, why do you love me?"

Her gaze froze Ryan dead in his tracks. Air got stuck in his lungs. After a brief pause, he cleared his throat and said, "Well, truth be told, it's easy to love someone like you."

"Talaga?"

"I think that means, 'really', right?"

"Oo."

"Okay then, my reply is, 'Oo' in return."

Maricel blushed and looked down at her feet.

"Why do you mahal me?" Ryan said, his voice cracking.

"Hmm, time will tell," she said, with a playful wink. "All I know is that I want to be married before I'm thirty, Lord willing, and a mother at thirty-one, which doesn't leave much time."

Tipton's pulse raced in his ears. He gasped and nearly lost his train of thought. "Care to join me for a swim in the pool?"

"Think I'll stay in the shade and watch you swim. Don't want to get too dark."

"Suit yourself." Tipton lowered himself into the pool using a mounted ladder. T-shirt on, the thought of exposing his shirtless body to anyone, especially Maricel, sickened him. "When I get back home, the diet begins," he said, submerging himself beneath the water. It was the tenth time he had uttered those words to himself since arriving in the Philippines.

At 1 p.m., they left the hotel for the SM Mall of Asia, in Pasay City. At times, Tipton thought he was in New York City. But instead of seeing yellow taxicabs crowding the streets, he saw Jeepneys, which more resembled buses, circa 1970, than jeeps.

As far as the eye could see, the drivers of these mass-transportation vehicles zigzagged and weaved in and out of traffic, as well as any New York City taxicab driver could ever hope to.

Maricel spotted the enormous steel globe out in the distance, which proudly greeted each visitor to the cavernous shopping mall, and knew they were getting close.

Before heading inside, Maricel took a few pictures of her boyfriend posing in front of the world-famous landmark.

From there, they strolled down to the water's edge for more selfies. A friendly passerby offered to take a few snapshots of her and Ryan, with Manila Bay shimmering brightly behind them.

They went inside. Though it was bigger than the mall Tipton worked at back home, SM Mall of Asia very much resembled your basic American malls. Even many of the stores were the same.

But what separated this place from Iowa was that Tipton now represented the minority race. But he felt perfectly comfortable in the presence of so many Filipinos. How could he not when most seemed genuinely happy for the mixed couple?

A smile broke across his face, as his mind raced back to all those times he was working, watching scores of happy couples slowly passing by. The goofy, love-struck looks on their faces he always thought was immature now made perfect sense to him.

Ryan pointed to Café Adriatico, located on the mall's second floor. "How's the food there?"

"Very good," came the reply.

"Why don't we have dinner there tonight?"

Maricel smiled brightly. "Sure, but they also have a location on Adriatico Street. The ambiance is so much better there."

Ryan asked, "Would you rather eat there instead?"

Maricel nodded yes.

"Let's do it then," Ryan said matter-of-factly.

Maricel wanted to shout, "Yippie!" at the top of her lungs, but she managed to control herself. She'd often dreamed of walking Adriatico Street with her boyfriend at her side.

She never quite understood why the man in her dream was always faceless until just now. It wasn't the face that mattered most. It all came down to the heart. And Ryan Tipton apparently had a very good ticker.

Despite what others may have thought about his outward appearance, her boyfriend was attractive on the inside, at least to her. Not only that, she felt safe being in Ryan's presence. Those things were far more important to her than physical appearance.

After three hours of walking and still not seeing everything, they shared a medium size Hawaiian pizza—which did nothing to quell Ryan's appetite—and decided to head back to the hotel to freshen up before dinner.

Taking the escalators down to the ground floor level, Tipton nearly gasped when he saw the huge steel globe silhouetted through the mall's large ceiling to floor plate glass windows.

He read somewhere online that 200,000 shoppers visited the mall each day. He silently wondered how many of them posed for selfies in front of the globe? *Probably most*, he concluded.

They arrived at Café Adriatico on the street bearing its name, a little before 6 p.m. They waited 90 minutes before finally being seated on the upper level.

"Welcome to Café Adriatico. My name is Nonoy. I'll be your server. Can I bring you something to drink from the bar?"

Ryan glanced at Maricel. "Glass of wine?"

She smiled sweetly. "Sure, why not?" she replied, knowing she would never finish it. She would only need one hand to count how many alcoholic beverages she had consumed in her life.

"What do you recommend, Nonoy?"

"The Sauvignon Blanc is one of our popular white wines, sir."

Ryan looked at Maricel again.

She shrugged her shoulders. "Never heard of it before."

"We'll both have that," said Ryan.

"Certainly sir. Be right back with your drinks."

A few minutes later, Nonoy was back. "Would you care to start with appetizers?"

Ryan glanced at Maricel and nodded for her to order first.

"I'll have the monggo soup," she said, which was a green bean bisque topped with smoked fish flakes.

"As for me, I'll have the Sinigang na Baboy sa Sampaloc."

The way Ryan said it—mispronouncing every word—caused Maricel to burst into laughter.

Somehow, Nonoy managed to control himself.

Ryan glanced across the table. "What?"

Maricel took a small sip of wine. "Cute!" she said, a playful smile on her face.

Nonoy said, "And for the main course?"

Ryan glanced at his date again. "Maricel?"

"Lola Ising's Adobo, please," she said, which was fried Spareribs served adobo style.

The waiter jotted her order on a piece of paper. "Good choice. And for you, sir?"

"I'll have the Teriyaki Steak grilled in a ginger marinade." Ryan stuck his tongue out at Maricel, knowing he had pronounced every word properly.

Nonoy wrote it down. "Very good choice, sir."

"Salamat. For dessert later, we'll have one leche flan, one slice of blueberry cheesecake, and two coffees."

"Very good, sir," Nonoy said, concealing a quizzical expression. He wasn't used to taking the entire order all at once.

Maricel was drinking it all in, doing all she could to suck the marrow out of this most enjoyable life moment.

By the time they finished eating, it was 9 p.m. Like most nights in Manila, it was hot and steamy. As they strolled down a very crowded Adriatico Street, Tipton's shirt was drenched with sweat.

But Maricel didn't seem to mind. She was too caught up in the moment. She looked up at the stillness of the moon and stars and mumbled a simple "thank you" to her Creator.

When they stopped at a cross section, Maricel stretched her hands high above her head. Her mouth was forced wide in a yawn.

It was time to go. Ryan was tempted to invite her back to his room, so they could watch a movie together, but he dismissed the idea and hailed a cab instead. He didn't want to push things.

"Where to?" the driver said matter-of-factly.

Ryan opened the door for Maricel. "Quezon City."

At first, she was startled. *Not even a hug?*

Then he climbed in behind her. "Did you think I was going to let my girl go home unescorted?"

"You don't have to, Ryan. We're so close to your hotel."

Ryan steadied his gaze on her. "I insist, Maricel."

Maricel was touched by her boyfriend's gentlemanly, chivalrous demeanor. She leaned into him, thankful that his left shoulder wasn't soaked with sweat like the rest of him.

Forty-five minutes later, the cab pulled up to the Arcamo residence in Quezon City.

"Can you wait a few minutes? I shouldn't be long."

"Sure," the cab driver said to Ryan, in reply. "Take your time."

"Feel free to keep the meter running."

He flashed a greedy smile. *Don't worry, I will!*

Hearing their voices outside, Hazel Arcamo peeked through the window and saw the happy couple approaching hand in hand.

Just like the night before, she met them at the front door. "Welcome back, Ryan! I didn't expect to see you tonight."

Ryan grinned. "Since your daughter was in my company all day, I felt it was my duty to make sure she arrived home safely."

The look on Hazel's face was worth a million words. *He really is a gentleman after all.*

"Please come in," the mother of three said warmly.

"Sure, but only for a few minutes. The meter's still running," Ryan said, pointing back to the waiting cab.

Francisco rose from the chair he was seated on. "Welcome back, Ryan!"

"Nice to see you again, Francisco."

"Likewise." He glanced at his daughter. "How was your day?"

"Simply perfect, Papa." There was a dreamy glint in her eye that was impossible to overlook.

Hazel asked, "Did you go to the Mall of Asia?"

"Yes. After that, we had dinner at Café Adriatico, in Malate."

Francisco nodded his head. "Sounds like you had a full day."

"Indeed, we did," Tipton said, "And I anticipate another full day tomorrow at Enchanted Kingdom, with lots of walking, which means we'll need all the rest we can get."

"I would think so," Francisco said.

"Where are Miguel and Vivian?"

Hazel answered, "Miguel is out with friends. Vivian is sleeping. They'll be sad they missed you."

"Please tell them I said hello…"

"I'll make sure to do that. Will we see you again before you head back to the States?"

"I hope so, Hazel. After all, your husband and I still need to have our singing contest."

Francisco belly laughed.

"Stop by, anytime," Hazel said to Ryan, "We're always here."

Tipton beamed from ear to ear. "Thanks for the open invite. Hope you all have a pleasant evening."

Maricel and Ryan went outside. After making sure her parents weren't spying on them, Tipton puckered up his lips and inched in a little more confidently this time. Gazing deep into his girlfriend's gorgeous round eyes, eyes that easily drank him in, his knees nearly buckled. His lungs screamed for oxygen.

The moment their lips met those same intense feelings he felt the night before resurfaced. For the first time ever, Tipton felt fully alive, weak knees and all!

Ryan opened the cab door. "Wait. I almost forgot..." He reached inside his pants pocket for money. "This should cover your transportation in the morning." Unemployed the past five months, he knew even cab fare was a big stretch for her.

Maricel was grateful for his kindness. "Salamat, Ryan."

"My pleasure, sweetie." Tipton leaned in for one last kiss, then lowered himself into the back of the cab. "See you bright and early tomorrow morning."

"I'll be there," Maricel said, still glowing.

The driver left for the Bayview Park Hotel.

Ryan asked, "Can you please turn the AC on full blast? I'm roasting back here."

"Sure thing," the driver said to his American passenger.

Maricel stood outside watching until her boyfriend's cab was completely out of sight. *I could easily get used to this!*

She went back inside the house eager to tell her parents about the wonderful day she had, which started when Ryan had insisted on praying at breakfast.

After that, she would call Rosa, who'd already texted her 23 times, pressing her for the juicy details.

Meanwhile, Tipton chuckled to himself in the backseat of the taxicab. In his wildest dreams, he never thought he'd see the day when the words "taxicab" and "romance" would combine to create the two most passion-filled moments of his life thus far.

Both incidents were forever seared into his mind, giving him a feeling inside that bordered on sheer ecstasy.

That is, until he arrived back at his hotel and turned on his laptop computer to e-mail Jenny and Liezel.

A knot formed in his throat. The game needed to continue.

The very thought of being so secretive behind Maricel's back now sickened him. Tipton sighed. *Why am I doing this!?* Everything suddenly seemed clouded again...

7

THREE DAYS LATER

"MAGANDANG UMAGA, MARICEL."

"Magandang umaga din sayo, Ryan! You're up early."

"Yeah, been awake since five. I was going to call you earlier, but figured I'd let you sleep. I feel the need to get out of Manila."

"What do you have in mind? The beach?"

"Not exactly. You know how badly I've been wanting to visit Tagaytay. Phillip, the concierge guy here at the hotel, told me it's a must-see place. Besides, I never saw a real live volcano before. Even if it's the world's smallest, I'd still like to see it."

"Last time I went there was for a high school trip."

"Let's go then!" Ryan paused a moment. "All of us."

"All?"

Mindful that Maricel wouldn't travel outside Manila without a chaperon, this represented the perfect solution. "I thought it might be good for your family to get out of the house for the day."

"Really?" An excited shock filled Maricel's face.

"Rosalyn can come too if she wants. Tell her it's my treat. I've already hired a private driver for the day. Wasn't too expensive."

"Papa has already left for work, but I can ask Mama..."

"Please do."

A moment later, Maricel said, "She would love to join us."

"Great!" Hearing the excitement in her voice satisfied Ryan immensely. But he also sensed a deep sadness creeping in on the other end of the phone. "Let's do our best to enjoy the moment, without thinking about two days from now."

Maricel sighed. "How did you know I'm feeling sad?"

"Because I'm sad too. But let's make the most of our remaining time together, fair enough?"

"Okay, sweetie."

"The driver will be here at ten, so please be here at nine-thirty at the latest." Ryan had a sudden thought. "Better yet, why don't you leave now so you can stay ahead of rush hour traffic? You can all shower here if you want. I'll ask the maid for extra soap and towels."

"What about Miguel and Vivian?"

Ryan checked his look in the mirror. "I'll be hurt if they don't come."

"You should see my mother. It's been a while since she's done anything spontaneous like this."

"Happy to hear that. We have less than three hours and counting. Time to get everyone motivated. If Rosa decides to join us, tell her I'll pay her cab fare."

"Thanks for doing this, Ryan."

"If you really want to thank me, you can do it by being on time. Rosa too! And don't forget to bring light jackets for Tagaytay."

"I already thought of that. See you soon."

An hour later, the four Arcamo family members arrived at the hotel.

Maricel was the first to get out of the cab. She hugged Ryan. "Rosa just texted me. She'll be here soon."

Ryan handed his girlfriend his room key. "Why don't you take your bags up to the room so you can get ready. The maid left plenty of towels. I'll wait here for Rosa."

Maricel kissed Ryan softly on the lips. "Okay, sweetie."

Marco and Nathaniel, the two bell men Ryan was always joking with, watched as they smooched. Noticing, Tipton shot them both a thumbs-up gesture. They smiled back warmly at him.

Ten minutes later, Rosalyn's cab pulled up to the hotel. "Thanks for the invite Ryan. It'll be nice breathing clean air for a change."

"Glad you decided to join us. Do you need to use the shower?"

"No. All set."

At 10 a.m., everyone was outside waiting, when a vehicle pulled up to the front entryway of Bayview Park Hotel.

"Mister Tipton?"

"That would be me."

"My name is Rodrigo. I'll be your driver for the day. Welcome to the Philippines," he said warmly. "Is there any particular route you'd like to take to Tagaytay?"

"Since this is my first time visiting your country, why don't we take the most scenic route?"

"Yes, sir," Rodrigo replied. "I would suggest the coastal road through Imus, Dasmarinas and Cavite. It will take a little longer than the South Superhighway, and we'll surely encounter traffic along the way, but it offers many beautiful sights to see. We can always take the SSH coming back."

Ryan nodded agreement. "Sounds like a plan, Rodrigo."

Once everyone was buckled in their seats, Rodrigo pulled away from Bayview Park Hotel.

Rosa asked Ryan, "Did you know Tagaytay is known as the second summer capital of the Philippines, because of its clean air and cool climate all year long?"

Ryan raised an eyebrow. "I did not know that."

Rosalyn smiled warmly. "It's true. Baguio is number one…"

"Thanks for the geography lesson, Rosa. Sounds like the perfect place to visit. I could use a break from all this heat."

Hailing from the very flat state of Iowa, the many steep inclines along the way surprised Tipton, especially as they inched closer to Tagaytay, parting pineapple groves along the way.

Most of the roads were smooth. But at one point the incline was so steep, it felt for a moment like they were falling off a cliff.

Just before noon, they arrived in Tagaytay City. Rodrigo craned his neck back. "Where to first, Mister Tipton?"

"What do you suggest, Rodrigo? And please, call me Ryan."

"Well, since this is your first time here, I would suggest the park overlooking Taal Volcano. If you're hungry, they have a concession stand offering your basic fast-food items like burgers and fries. Or I can take you to the city market for fresh fruits and vegetables."

When Ryan couldn't decide, Maricel said, "Let's go to the city market for some fruit."

Tipton nodded yes. "Sounds good to me."

Rodrigo nodded at them and drove off in that direction.

Ryan never thought he'd see the day when he could purchase five fresh pineapples for the equivalent of one U.S. dollar. He purchased five bags full of fresh produce, knowing Hazel would let none of it go to waste.

Everyone piled back in the vehicle and Rodrigo took them to the park overlooking Taal Volcano, located in neighboring Batangas.

They found a wooden picnic table and claimed it as their own. Hazel wasted no time cutting open a pineapple, as Maricel, Rosalyn and Vivian posed for selfies with Taal Volcano in the background.

Ryan took a bite of the pineapple, then motioned for Rodrigo to join them. "Consider yourself part of the family today."

Rodrigo was deeply moved by his American passenger's kindness. "Gosh, I don't know what to say."

"No need to say anything. Just join us." Ryan ate another slice of pineapple. "Now I see why it's the world's smallest volcano. Looks so tiny down there. But what a spectacular view!"

"Yeah, I never grow tired of coming here," Rodrigo said.

Tipton had a thought. "Can we go to the crater?"

"Yes, by boat. But be prepared to negotiate the price."

"Are you a good negotiator, Rodrigo?"

"Pretty good, I suppose."

"Good, because I'm not."

"I'll do my best, Ryan." They went down by the water, to find scores of vendors all advertising their so-called "special" prices. Rodrigo already knew the going rate and was able to effectively negotiate what he believed was a fair price.

Ryan paid the man, and everyone boarded a boat for the 30-minute ride to Taal Volcano.

Once they reached the other side, Rodrigo started negotiating again, and they mounted six malnourished-looking horses for the 30-minute trek to the top of the crater. Each rider was led by a local guide who mounted the horse half-way up the trail.

Upon reaching the crater's edge, Ryan let his eyes wander off in all directions. He was completely mesmerized by the stunning view it offered. He took a few moments to drink it all in, as Maricel, Vivian and Rosalyn took selfies.

After everyone had seen enough, they began the 30-minute trek back down the crater. Once there, Tipton purchased T-shirts for everyone, including Rodrigo.

Rosalyn ordered everyone to put them on, then asked the vendor who had sold them the shirts to take a few photos of them using her cellphone.

After just selling them six shirts, he was happy to do it.

From there, Rosalyn, Miguel and Vivian rode the zipline. Maricel wanted to join them but knew Ryan would never try it. She remained on the ground with her boyfriend taking video, as the three soared high above them on steel cables.

Once they were back inside the vehicle, Ryan said to Rodrigo, "Where would you suggest we go for dinner?"

"My favorite place is Josephine's. It's a little pricey, but the food's delicious."

Ryan glanced at Maricel. She shrugged her shoulders. "Sounds good to me."

"Okay then, Josephine's it is!" Ryan leaned up in his seat. "Would you like to join us for dinner, Rodrigo?"

Rodrigo looked in his rearview mirror. "If you're inviting me, I proudly accept."

Tipton flashed a smile at his driver. "Indeed, I am…"

They arrived at Josephine's just before 6 p.m.

"Good choice, Rodrigo!" Ryan said, in between bites of food. "So far, you're batting a thousand."

Rodrigo rubbed his chin with two fingers. "I've never had a complaint about this place from any of my customers."

"I can see why. The food's delicious!"

Rosalyn broadcasted live on Facebook so her online friends could watch. In between bites of food, she thanked her many viewers for watching and introduced them all to Ryan.

After the meal, Tipton paid the bill, and was pleasantly surprised that what Rodrigo had called a little pricey wasn't so pricey after all. Everyone ate and drank to their heart's content for only U.S. $80, which included a generous tip.

As Maricel, Rosalyn and Vivian posed for more selfies outside the restaurant, Ryan could only smile.

Just seeing Vivian so energized and full of life put a smile on his face. If her "comfort people" weren't there to protect her, she would no doubt still be buried deep inside her shell.

At 8 p.m., they were en route back to Manila. Miguel and Vivian were both sound asleep.

For the first hour or so, Maricel taught Ryan a few more Tagalog words. She was pleased with his progress so far.

Whenever he mispronounced a word, which was often, Hazel chuckled softly to herself in the front seat.

Rosalyn was in the back row of seats with Miquel and Vivian, chatting with friends and uploading photos onto Facebook and Instagram. Every few seconds, she would burst into laughter, momentarily jolting Miguel and Vivian from their sleep.

As always, Rosa was too absorbed inside her highly energized universe to realize how loud she was being.

Hazel's eyes were closed, but she wasn't sleeping. She had the most satisfying expression on her face: it made her look 10 years younger than her actual age. Tipton quietly surmised that would make her eight years younger than himself.

Ryan and Maricel had the middle row all to themselves. Awesome as the day had already been, feeling Maricel's head resting on his left shoulder was the icing on the cake for him.

As much as he would have loved to spend the night with Maricel at a hotel overlooking Taal volcano, then enjoying morning coffee together on their own private balcony, breathing in the crisp morning air, a blanket wrapped around them for warmth, he knew it wouldn't happen.

Now more than ever, having spent five days with her, he respected that she was saving herself for marriage before doing such things. This was more than good enough for now...

At 9:30 p.m., Rodrigo slowly pulled up to the front entryway of Bayview Park Hotel, in downtown Manila.

Everyone piled out of the vehicle looking exhausted.

Maricel stretched her hands behind her back and slid them upward, lifting her long black silky hair through her fingers, releasing a pleasant aroma of shampoo and nature into the atmosphere. She glanced up at the American flag flying atop the U.S. Embassy building, across the street. "Hmm…"

Ryan was comforted by the gesture, until Jenny and Liezel invaded his mind. The more time he spent with the Arcamos, the guiltier he felt about the secret he was keeping from them.

Tipton sighed, then whispered to himself, "Why am I doing this?"

Maricel asked, "What sweetie?"

"Oh, nothing." Needing a diversion, he said to Rodrigo, "This is for you. Thanks for the great service."

The driver's face lit up. "Part of me doesn't want to accept this money from you. You've already been so generous to me."

"Take it. You've earned it, Rodrigo. Besides, we enjoyed your company as much as you enjoyed ours."

Rodrigo looked deep into Ryan's eyes; he couldn't ignore the genuine sincerity there. "Hope you enjoy the remainder of your time here in Manila."

The two men shook hands and Rodrigo drove off.

Ryan asked Hazel, "I've been thinking, why don't you all stay here tonight?"

Hazel's face lit up like a Christmas tree displaying a thousand lights. "That isn't necessary, Ryan."

"It'll be my pleasure to reserve an extra room for you."

"Let me call my husband. If he doesn't object, we'll stay."

Ryan asked, "Why don't you ask him to join us?"

Hazel retrieved her mobile phone from inside her handbag. "He's off the next two days, so perhaps he'll agree to come."

"Great! The boys can stay in one room, the girls in the other." Ryan shifted his gaze to Miguel. "That is, if you wouldn't mind shacking up with me…"

"Sure," came the reply.

Ryan glanced at Maricel. She was nearly in tears. "You okay?"

The expression on her face exposed a deeper, more tender side Ryan had yet to see. "Wala akong masabi," she whispered softly.

"What does that mean?"

"It means, I'm speechless."

Hazel broke the moment. "Francisco would love to join us!"

"Awesome! Now let's hope they have an extra room for us."

Not only did they have vacancies, the room on the eighth floor next to his was also available. Tipton quickly reserved it. "I may need it for two nights. Would that be okay?"

"Absolutely, sir," came the reply, from the friendly man behind the desk.

Hazel called Francisco again. In quick Tagalog, she instructed her husband to bring the things she didn't pack earlier, because she didn't know they would be spending the night away from home.

Ryan had no idea what Hazel was saying, but her excitement level was so high, he thought she might burst wide open.

When the call ended, Tipton said, "Why don't you ladies get settled into your room. Miguel and I will wait for Francisco to arrive. That is, if you wouldn't mind?"

"Okay, po," Miguel said, maintaining steady eye contact this time, which Ryan took as a step in the right direction.

Maricel scanned the hotel lobby looking for the female employee who caused her to flee from this place the other night.

She didn't see her. But even if she did, she was no longer concerned with what she, or anyone else working there, thought about her—not after the amazing week she was having...

But knowing they only had one more full day together, a mounting sadness kept brewing just beneath the surface.

Maricel leaned into her boyfriend and clung to him for dear life. *Why can't he remain in the Philippines forever?*

She never thought it could be possible to fall in love with someone so easily, especially after just meeting for the first time. But as she basked in the warmth of Ryan's embrace, she was convinced that what she felt for him was genuine and true.

And that meant she would never entertain another man ever again. Her heart was sold out to Jesus first, then to Ryan and only him. "I love you, Ryan," she said, loud enough for everyone to hear.

Ryan's eyes widened. His cheeks turned deep red. He had difficulty gulping in air. "Love you, too, Maricel."

Tears flooded her eyes. At that, Maricel, Hazel, Vivian and Rosalyn left for the elevators. All four were giddy with laughter.

Waiting for the elevator car to reach the lobby floor, Rosalyn said something that caused the three Arcamo women to burst into laughter. Their voices echoed throughout the massive lobby.

The more Rosa spoke, the more her audience of three roared with laughter. Her body may have been exhausted, but certainly not her mouth.

Did her mouth ever get tired? Ryan wondered...

Just before the elevator door closed, Maricel peeked out one last time at Ryan. Their eyes met.

Miguel saw Ryan's face turn bright pink again. *He really does love my sister!*

Francisco arrived a few moments later, looking completely exhausted, after a busy day at work. The three men went up to the eighth floor and spent an hour or so inside the girls' room before calling it a night.

As everyone settled into bed for the night, Ryan no longer wished to be spending the night in Tagaytay with Maricel. To have the privilege of spending quality time with her family in Manila was infinitely better than that.

In the darkness, Tipton couldn't wipe the smile off his face. Nor did he want to. As far as he was concerned, this was the perfect way to end what had already been an awesome day...

8

"MAGANDANG UMAGA, RYAN!"

"Magandang umaga, Maricel! Did you sleep good?"

"Yes. And you?"

"When I finally fell asleep, I slept soundly. But we heard you laughing until two in the morning."

"Sorry for that."

"No need to apologize, Maricel. You kept us entertained." Ryan scratched his forehead. "Your father and Miguel want to go for a swim before breakfast. Think I'll join them."

"Can we come? Or is it a boys-only swim?"

"Not at all. Please join us. By the way, after discussing it with your father, I've decided to reserve your room for one more night. So no need to pack your things just yet."

"Ikaw ang mabait, Ryan."

"Hmm, I know you said it yesterday, but I can't remember what it means, sorry."

"It means you're nice."

"What can I say, I enjoy being with your family. Anyway, we're headed to the pool now. Feel free to join us whenever."

Maricel asked, "Want me to bring some of the fruit we purchased in Tagaytay, to snack on before breakfast?"

"Sounds good. I'm sure everyone would enjoy that."

"Okay. See you shortly."

A few minutes later, everyone was poolside eating fresh mango and pineapple. They swam in the pool for nearly an hour, before heading back up to their rooms to get changed for breakfast.

Once they were seated, a waiter took their drink orders, and everyone got in the buffet line.

Before eating their meals, everyone bowed their heads as Francisco led them all in the saying of grace.

"I'm sad to think this is your last day," Hazel said, in between bites of food. The mounting sadness in her eyes was evident.

Ryan sighed. "Me too. This has been the best week of my life. I'd stay another week if I could, a month even, but I can't…".

Maricel did her best to avoid looking at her mother. Just one glance would cause more of her own tears to surface. She already sensed she would be fit for a straight-jacket 24 hours from now.

Rosalyn took a sip of coffee. "So, what's the plan for today?"

Ryan looked at his watch: 8:07 a.m. "The ferry to Corregidor Island left seven minutes ago, so we can scratch that off the list."

"Sorry sweetie," Maricel replied, sadly.

"It's okay. It gives us something to look forward to next time I come back, right?"

Maricel laid her head on her boyfriend's right shoulder. "We can go to the American Cemetery if you'd like. It's not too far from here, so it won't take up too much of our time."

"I've always wanted to visit there myself," said Francisco.

Ryan kissed the top of Maricel's head. "Let's go after breakfast then."

"And after that?" asked Rosalyn.

"Perhaps we can go to Star City," Hazel replied. "They've recently reopened after a fire destroyed the park. Or we can go sightseeing in Makati."

Rosalyn said, "Let's take a vote. Who wants to go to Star City?"

Miguel raised his hand then sheepishly lowered it, after realizing he was the only one.

Rosa said, "It's settled then. Looks like we're going to Makati.

Ryan interjected, "Just no more shopping malls, please!"

Maricel and Rosalyn both laughed.

Francisco said to Ryan, "Maricel told me you're interested in seeing some of our country's rich history. There are plenty of museums in Makati. That might be a good place to start."

"Sounds like a winner, Francisco. Which one's the best?"

"Personally, I prefer Ayala Museum."

"Okay, Ayala Museum it is. After we visit the cemetery, we'll go there."

All eyes settled on Maricel when she started sniffling. She dabbed at her moist eyes with a napkin. "I'm fine, really I am."

But everyone knew she was nothing close to being fine.

After breakfast, they took a taxi to the American Cemetery in Manila. Ryan was both touched and impressed at how the workers had honored his country, by maintaining the memorial all these years, as if caring for their fellow countrymen instead of foreigners.

"Uncle Floyd would be proud," Tipton said somberly, taking one last look at the sprawling grounds.

From there they took a cab to Makati. In the three hours they spent at Ayala Museum, Ryan was given a brief education on the history of the Philippines, including some of its most troubling parts. After that, they ate lunch at a local restaurant.

At 6 p.m., they were back at the hotel enjoying an early evening swim. Ryan still couldn't bring himself to remove his shirt. But no one asked him to. Shirt or no shirt, they accepted him just the way he was.

At 7:30, Ryan and Maricel walked the short distance to Yellow Cab Pizza for the two pizzas they had ordered—one pepperoni and mushroom and one Hawaiian. They ate them in the girls' room.

Hazel grabbed a slice of Hawaiian pizza. Before taking a bite, she said, "After we finish eating, why don't we go to Rizal Park to watch the musical dancing fountain show? After that, we can come back and watch a movie."

"Good idea," Ryan replied. "Been wanting to see it all week."

At 8:45 they made the short stroll to Rizal Park.

Maricel remained nestled in her boyfriend's arms the entire time. Without even looking, Ryan knew she was crying again. The small pockets of moisture he felt seeping through his shirt wasn't his own perspiration this time. It was his girlfriend's teardrops.

He squeezed her a little tighter, doing all he could to hold back his own tears.

They arrived back at the hotel just before 10 p.m. The movie ended just before midnight. Everyone was tired.

Ryan desperately wanted to kiss Maricel on the lips before calling it a night. But out of respect for her family, he kissed her right cheek instead. "See you in the morning, sweetie."

"Tulog ng mahimbing, Ryan," came the reply softly, sadly.

Before Ryan could inquire, Maricel said, "It means sweet dreams." She was clearly on the verge of tears again.

It was torturous looking into her sad, puffy eyes. "Hey, come on, you know I have every intention of coming back again, okay?" When she didn't reply, he said, "I promise!"

Maricel smiled wearily as her boyfriend followed her father and brother back to their room, knowing she wouldn't laugh herself to sleep again like she did the night before.

Lying in bed next to Rosalyn, she did her best to keep her sniffling to a low decibel level.

But it was impossible. Everyone heard her.

Rosa wrapped an arm around her best friend to comfort her. Maricel appreciated it but, more than anything, she wanted Ryan to hold her instead. But he was in the room next door.

In the darkness, Maricel thanked God again for blessing her with a good man to love. She then asked her Maker to remove the deep sadness she felt, which only intensified as the minutes passed.

At 2:30 a.m., she was finally able to fall asleep.

AT 7:15 THE NEXT morning, Maricel was awakened by the ringing of the phone inside her room. "Hello?"

"Good morning, sweetie. Did I wake you?"

"Not really," Maricel said softly, sadly.

"I think your father and Miguel are going for one last swim in the pool before breakfast."

"Will you join them?"

Ryan massaged his chin with two fingers. "No. Think I'll stop by the coffee shop we went to the first day I was here, to see Ernesto and Gloria one last time. Care to join me?"

"I'd love to." There was a pause. "I would give anything if you could stay a little longer."

The way she said it, desperation dripping from her voice, caused tears to surface in Tipton's eyes. He grimaced. "Me too, but you know I can't," he said, remorsefully. *Why am I doing this?*

"Just wishful thinking. I'll be ready in twenty minutes."

"See you soon, sweetie," Tipton said, suppressing more guilt.

A half hour later, everyone rode the elevator down to the lobby floor. The mood was increasingly somber.

Ryan said to Francisco, "We'll be back in plenty of time for breakfast."

"Have fun," Rosa said, answering for him. She, too, could no longer conceal her own mounting sadness. She followed the Arcamos out to the pool area with her head down.

Ryan reached for Maricel's hand, and they left at once for Agape Coffee and Pastry Shoppe. Halfway there, he silently panicked, after realizing he had forgotten to lock his suitcase.

How would he explain himself to Maricel if Francisco or Miguel accidentally knocked it over, exposing the gifts he had stashed inside for Jenny and Liezel? He pushed that dreadful thought out of his mind. *Dummy!* Guilt twisted through him.

A few moments later they arrived at the coffee shop, to find Ernesto Angeles waiting on a customer. "Well, hello there, Ryan and Maricel!" the Godly Filipino man with the radiant smile said. "Nice to see you both again! It's been a few days."

"We've been busy." Ryan was impressed that he remembered their names. "I'm sad to say this is my last day here. But I wanted to have my last cup of coffee in Manila here at your place."

Ernesto asked, "Don't they have coffee at your hotel?"

Ryan's face lit up. "Of course, they do! But what they don't have are the two of you."

Gloria was deeply touched by the gesture. "Kind of you to say that, Ryan."

Ryan shrugged his shoulders. "It's true."

Ernesto noticed Ryan's change of posture and shot his wife a certain look she knew all too well—he wanted to be alone with Ryan.

"Teresa, would you mind watching the register?"

"Opo," said the young female employee.

Ryan grabbed his coffee and followed Ernesto to an empty corner table.

The older Filipino man wasted no time. "Gloria and I think you and Maricel make a lovely couple. We wish you both the best in your new relationship."

Ryan smiled wearily. "She really is an amazing woman."

"Indeed, she is. Do you plan to visit her again?"

"Absolutely. If I were rich like you, I'd come back once a month."

Ernesto cracked up. "I think what I'll miss most about you is your lively sense of humor."

"It would be nice if we all lived closer together. There's just something about this place..."

The coffee shop owner's ears perked up. "Yeah? What is it?"

Ryan sighed. "Hmm, I don't know how to properly describe it. Except to say I believe the overwhelming energy I feel in this place has nothing to do with the great coffee you serve..."

Ernesto leaned up in his seat. "What exactly do you mean, Ryan?"

"Not sure, actually. All I can say is the joyful faces in all those pictures on your walls resemble the way I feel when I'm here."

Tipton stopped there. As much as he wanted to talk about the warm sensation he was convinced was rising-up through the floorboards of this place, he felt uneasy discussing it. Whatever it was, it could no longer be considered jet lag. That unpleasant sensation passed days ago. This sensation only intensified.

Ernesto nodded thoughtfully. "Perhaps in time you'll be able to better explain whatever it is you're feeling."

The one rule Ernesto and Gloria Angeles both had was that they never shared the *Source* behind the warm sensation with anyone, not until someone first inquired. Since his American visitor didn't mention it specifically, the old man changed the topic. "Do you mind if I ask you a personal question?"

"Sure," Ryan said, "go right ahead."

Ernesto waited patiently, as Ryan took another sip of coffee, then asked, "What are your true intentions with Maricel?"

Ryan felt like he had just been sucker-punched in the nose. His expression changed as he considered the question. Soon to be in the presence of another Filipino woman—with another girl waiting after Jenny—he was trying to suppress his growing feelings for the woman in Manila, whose heart now beat strongly for him.

He gulped hard and momentarily looked away, before regaining eye contact with the coffee shop proprietor.

To make matters worse, it seemed the many couples in the pictures hanging on the walls were all glaring at him, waiting for a satisfactory answer to their Godly leader's question.

Tipton cleared his throat. "Well, all I can say for now is that my feelings for her keep growing."

Ryan knew his answer had disappointed Ernesto. He expected the faces on the three walls to suddenly materialize and heckle him, for giving such a lame answer to a fair question, "What are your intentions with Maricel? Tell us Tipton! Tell us now!"

It was like one of those torturous jingles that enters through the ear canal then ricochets around the brain looking for someplace to escape, but never finding one.

But in this case, it wasn't some mindless jingle; it was a thousand accusations being hurled at him all at once.

Tipton's brow furrowed with uncertainty. *You really are lame*, he thought, guilt gnawing away at him again.

Ernesto saw the deep confusion on his American visitor's face. Clearly, something was bothering him, something that went far beyond the sadness he felt for leaving the Philippines. But now wasn't the time to push him for answers. "If you ever come back to my country, please stop in and see us again," he said.

Tipton said, "That goes without saying."

"Please take one of our business cards with you. In fact, let me write our home number and e-mail address on the back, in case you ever need us for anything, including prayer."

"That's very kind of you." Ryan took the card from Ernesto and stuffed it inside his pants pocket. He removed his eyeglasses to clean them, allowing the coffee shop owner the first real glimpse into his eyes.

What Ernesto saw behind the sadness and confusion was a gentle kindness in the American man's eyes. "Something tells me this won't be the last time we'll see each other."

Ryan nodded in agreement with him. "I have that same feeling myself." He looked at his watch. "Time to head back to the hotel so we can have breakfast with Maricel's family, before heading to the airport."

Ernesto said, "I understand. Thanks again for stopping by. Hope you have a safe flight home."

Tipton downed the rest of his coffee. "It was a pleasure meeting you and Gloria. Thanks for making me feel so welcome in your country."

"You're welcome, Ryan."

Ryan stood to leave. Maricel was seated at the counter with Gloria. The moment eye contact was made, Ryan knew she had been crying again. "Shall we, sweetie?"

Maricel dabbed at her eyes with a tissue, and nodded yes.

Ryan knew it would only get worse later at the airport.

Upon arriving back at Bayview Park Hotel, everyone met in the lobby restaurant for one last meal together.

After breakfast, a shuttle van took them to the airport.

Less than an hour later, the driver pulled up to the departures gate for Japan Airlines, located at terminal one at Ninoy Aquino International Airport. Everyone piled out of the van.

Once the Arcamos were out of sight, Tipton would hightail it straight to the Cebu-Pacific Airlines in terminal three, for his domestic flight to Cebu City.

"Well, here we are," Ryan said.

Maricel lowered her head and started weeping. Ryan looked away to avoid losing it himself. His eyes drifted to Hazel. It was a big mistake. She was sobbing just as hard as her daughter was.

It was the straw that broke the camel's back. Tipton placed his carry-on bag on the ground and removed his thick bifocal glasses, so he could wipe his moist eyes with his long shirt sleeve.

Francisco held his wife hoping to comfort her. Miguel and Vivian remained silent. But the looks on their faces told Ryan all he needed to know; they, too, didn't want him to leave.

That went double for Rosalyn.

Tipton somehow managed to pull himself together. "I want to thank you all from the bottom of my heart, for taking me in and treating me so kindly." His lips started quivering. "I'm going to miss you all so much. It's amazing how close I feel to you."

"We should be thanking you for this brief two-day vacation," said Francisco. "It was a nice break for us."

Ryan sighed. "It was my pleasure, Francisco. I promise to come back just as soon as I can afford to."

COFFEE IN MANILA PATRICK HIGGINS

Hazel wiped her eyes with a tissue. "We already look forward to that day, Ryan. You're always welcome at our house."

Ryan nodded his reply, then placed his hands on Maricel's shoulders and looked deep into her eyes. "Are you okay, sweetie?"

All she could do was gape at him and shake her head from side to side, as a new batch of stinging tears streamed down her cheeks.

She would give anything if he could stay with her a little longer. But he was leaving and there was nothing she could do to stop it.

Ryan tightened his grip and felt her body shaking through her tears. This was even more difficult than he thought it would be.

They ached for each other.

Francisco watched sadly, but also proudly, like a father-in-law admiring a son-in-law for loving his daughter so much.

It was a look that touched Ryan deeply for the moment, but also one he knew would come back to haunt him in the days ahead.

Ryan took one final glimpse into Maricel's innocent eyes. The love he saw there was too awesome, too incredible, too sincere to try explaining to others. If there was one thing her eyes projected, it's that she loved him with all her heart.

Ryan felt like weeping. He went inside the terminal knowing the gut-wrenching pain now clutching her heart would be elevated to heights never before visited in her 28 years on this planet, if she ever caught on to what he was doing.

It would be enough to make the deep anguish she felt from her boyfriend leaving her feel like an annoying mosquito bite...

Ryan grimaced. *How could I betray them like this?* Just thinking about it caused his heart to sink even deeper into his chest.

70

9

THE FLIGHT FROM MANILA to Cebu was relatively short, and save for a few pesky air pockets, mostly turbulent free.

But inside Ryan Tipton's heart and mind, it was quite stormy. The tears hadn't even dried from his emotional departure with Maricel, yet here he was flying off to meet with someone else.

What in the world am I doing? No matter how hard he tried, he couldn't come up with a convincing answer to this rather simple question.

Adding to it all, aside from the few chats he had with Jenny and Liezel—when Maricel wasn't around—he barely gave the two women a passing thought. He needed this time on the plane to mentally prepare for the next four days in Cebu.

Only Maricel wasn't a lightbulb he could easily turn off with the flick of a switch. Try as he might, each time he looked forward, his mind always raced back to his girlfriend in Manila.

It's like his brain had been turned into a movie theater of sorts, each picture starring Maricel, and the priceless memories they'd created together. It was impossible to recall each blissful moment; there were so many from which to choose.

The movie presently playing inside his head occurred at Enchanted Kingdom four days ago, when Ryan bit into a cheeseburger and mustard, ketchup and hamburger grease fell out of the bun onto his shirt, instantly staining it.

Of the thousands of visitors to the park that day, some were taller than he was, but few were wider than him. The last thing he wanted was to stroll a busy theme park with food stains on his shirt. If he did, it would surely bring unwanted attention his way.

Tipton solved the problem by purchasing matching *Enchanted Kingdom* T-shirts for himself and Maricel.

Maricel appreciated the gesture. But even without the shirt, she was too busy enjoying the comical moment to be the slightest bit concerned with what others might have thought about her boyfriend. She laughed with Ryan, yes, but certainly not at him.

Then there was the childlike expression on her face the next day, as they watched the dolphins performing at Ocean Adventure Park. Toward the end of the show, it started pouring rain, and everyone ran for cover.

But Ryan and Maricel remained in their seats and kept watching, as if the sun was still shining brightly. Perhaps to some they were being foolish, but they didn't care. They were too focused on creating more priceless memories together to give a hoot about what others may have thought about them.

Ryan's favorite souvenir from that place was the selfie he took of Maricel, just as three dolphins burst out of the water, and soared ten feet skyward—in perfect synchronization—before landing back in the aquarium ever so gracefully.

The unbridled awe stenciled on her rain-splashed face at that precise moment, was well worth the price of admission.

It also garnered the most likes on his Facebook and Instagram accounts. In order to keep the lie going, he made sure to change his settings, so Jenny and Liezel couldn't see any of his posts in Manila.

Awesome as that day was, nothing compared to their first kiss. Even flying on a steel bird high above the earth, the very thought of it caused his heart rate to accelerate. It was one of those "beyond description" life moments that Ryan knew he would still think about when he was old and gray.

Without a doubt, this was the most incredible week of his life. He had every reason to believe Maricel felt the same way.

Which was why he felt so tortured inside now. If she truly was the one for him, what logical explanation could justify his flying to Cebu to meet with another woman?

If he truly loved Maricel, shouldn't he have canceled his plans and remained in Manila with her? Wouldn't the love they'd shared be all the explanation he would need to legitimize the lost airfare?

Tipton sighed. Maricel wasn't the only one he was leaving behind in Manila. He also left behind a wonderful family he felt so incredibly connected to, not to mention, Rosalyn, who was sort of like the crazy cousin he never had.

And then there was Ernesto and Gloria Angeles, and the cozy little coffee shop they owned. Tipton still couldn't properly describe, let alone explain, what he felt both times he was there.

Whatever it was, it felt good...

A new pang of guilt snaked through him. Suddenly, the question Ernesto asked before leaving the coffee shop popped into his mind again, "What are your true intentions with Maricel?"

Tipton gasped. *What are my intentions with her?* He pushed that thought out of his mind and turned on his laptop, looking for things to do in Cebu.

After a while, it seemed to do the trick. He was finally able to focus his attention on Jenny. Much like Maricel, she always treated him with the utmost respect online, never seeming to mind that he was nothing special to look at.

Tipton had no reason to think anything would change, now that they were about to meet in person. At least not on her end.

He couldn't say the same for himself. All because of Maricel...

As the pilot lowered the landing gear in preparation for landing, Ryan had a strong premonition that had he spent just one more week in Manila, he would be preparing for a more permanent future with Maricel. *Why then am I doing this?*

It was a question for which Ryan Tipton had no answer...

Cebu-Pacific Airlines flight #345 gently touched down at Mactan-Cebu International Airport, at 4:15 p.m., breaking Ryan from his reverie. The instant he was permitted to use his cell phone, he copied the text message he'd sent to Maricel a week ago and sent it to Jenny: *Just landed...The day we've both been longing for is finally upon us...See you in a few minutes! Mwah!*

Tipton sighed, feeling like a total sleazeball. *Who does such things? Apparently, I do!* He shook his head in disgust.

Walking off the plane, he was still trying to convince himself that it was okay to be there now. Aside from the purchased plane ticket, the only other logical justification he could think of was that prior to taking this trip, he wasn't 100-percent committed to any of the three women.

Judging by his lackluster past in the world of dating, how could he know for sure who, if any of them, would ultimately end up being his girlfriend?

In a way, Maricel was the one responsible for setting the stage for this way of thinking in the first place, by constantly reminding him that it all came down to meeting in person and spending quality time together. Only then would they know for sure.

This time last week, his hope was that one of the three women would like him enough to be his girlfriend.

How quickly everything had changed...

Because this was a domestic flight, there was no need to be cleared through customs this time.

In a matter of seconds, he spotted Jenny wearing a black dress and black flats looking ever so elegant, especially when compared to the rugged old blue jeans and XXL brown, long-sleeved shirt he was wearing. The smile on her face was engaging.

One thing Ryan Tipton had learned in his six months of online chatting, was that some people posted outdated photographs of themselves on their profiles. Those they met in person oftentimes came away feeling deceived by this. And rightly so.

But this couldn't be said about Maricel or Jenny. They both looked even younger and more beautiful in person.

Jenny was mindful that Ryan had spent the last night in Manila. According to him, he wanted to get a good night sleep after the long flight, so he would be well rested when they met.

Since most overseas flights landed in the Capital City of the Philippines, before connecting to various other cities, Jenny had no problem believing him.

The only red flag to go up in her mind was that her American visitor would only be staying in Cebu for four days. Other than those who took quick business trips to her country, who else flew halfway around the world for a four-day visit?

Jenny pushed that thought out of her mind. Now wasn't the time for negative thinking. "Welcome to Cebu, Ryan. Mabuhay!"

"Mabuhay, Jenny! Finally, we meet face-to-face."

They embraced. The first thing Tipton noticed was that his heart wasn't pounding wildly in his chest, like it did each time he hugged Maricel.

He blinked the comparison away. "I must say, you're even more beautiful in person!"

"Really?"

"Yes. I feel so unqualified just being here with you."

Jenny blushed. "Salamat. Did you bring my pasalubong?"

"Of course."

Jenny flashed another warm and engaging smile. "Can I see it?"

"It's in my suitcase. Can it wait until we get to the hotel?"

"Sure. I'm so excited!"

Ryan saw the duffel bag on the ground beside her and gulped hard. The thought of spending the night with someone as beautiful as her was enough to excite any man. He was equally frightened by this realization.

Not only was Jenny 18 years younger than he was, she weighed half as much as him. At least that much! This petrified him to no end, especially when considering it from a possible intimacy standpoint.

At twenty-seven, Jenny was petite and respectably attractive. What stood out most were her succulent lips. They were so luscious, they begged to be kissed. Tipton was certain that she had received many compliments on them in the past.

The prideful part of him was already high fiving himself for having what it took to snag two beautiful women in a matter of just eight days, with one more lined up four days from now.

As much as he enjoyed living on the edge of social behavior like this, thanks to the woman he'd just parted company with, he didn't feel at all victorious. He felt more like a womanizer than anything else. He hated the feeling.

Seeing Jenny staring at him quizzically, as if wondering what he was thinking, he refocused. "Are you hungry?"

"A little, I suppose."

"Where do you suggest we go?"

"There are many nice restaurants at the Waterfront Hotel, including a place with really good seafood. I forgot the name, but I ate there once. The food was delicious. The Ayala Mall also has plenty of good places to eat. It's right next to the hotel."

"Why don't we get checked in first, before we decide?"

Jenny smiled. "Sure, whatever you say…"

Walking to the baggage claim area, Tipton was tempted to reach for her hand, but at the last minute he refrained.

After the week he'd just had, the fear of rejection wasn't the reason for his reluctance. Reaching for Jenny's hand might cause his girlfriend in Manila to return to the forefront of his mind again.

How could it not, when many of his fondest memories of Maricel occurred when they were holding hands in public places? *Not good!*

They rode the shuttle bus for the 30-minute drive to the Waterfront Hotel and Casino. The long and slightly winding road leading up to the hotel's main entrance was lined with all sorts of well-manicured trees and tropical foliage.

Jenny waited in line with Ryan at the registration desk and didn't seem the slightest bit uncomfortable. She was just happy to be staying at this hotel again. The proud, almost boastful, expression on her face indicated that much. Unlike Maricel.

The front desk clerk handed him an electronic room card key, and Ryan and Jenny rode the elevator up to the sixth floor.

He placed the plastic key over the electronic receiver that was mounted on the door. A small light turned green, thus allowing them entry into the room.

They went inside.

"Nice room!" Jenny said, without a hint of anxiety in her voice.

Perspiration formed on Tipton's forehead, seeing only one bed in the room. His heart raced, and his mouth became dry as cotton. Hoping for a distraction, he pulled back the curtain exposing a sprawling view of Cebu City.

He stared out at the unfamiliar surroundings and took a few deep breaths to compose himself. "Ready for your pasalubong?"

Jenny practically jumped up and down like a little girl.

Ryan opened his suitcase, careful not to expose the second gift bag that he would give to Liezel in Davao City.

Jenny searched the contents of the bag like a child on Christmas Day. Plucking out the last of the two dresses, she said, "Which one would you like me to wear to dinner?"

"The brown one, I guess," Tipton said, his voice cracking.

Without warning, Jenny started undressing right in front of him. Ryan turned his head so fast it nearly snapped off.

Jenny got the point and went to the bathroom, or as they say in the Philippines, to the comfort room, to change.

A few moments later she emerged looking beautiful as ever in her new dress. They rode the elevator down to the lobby floor, then left the hotel for Ayala Mall.

They found a restaurant that served both American and Filipino cuisines. After the waiter took their order, Ryan excused himself and went to the rest room.

He pulled out his cell phone. After three rings he heard, "Hi, mahal ko (my love)!"

Just hearing Maricel's voice caused his heart to beat faster. Even hundreds of miles away, he could still smell her just-washed hair, and see her luminous smile in his mind.

Ryan winced. "Just landed in Tokyo. I miss you so much."

"I miss you too, sweetie. We were just talking about you."

"We?"

Instead of answering the question, Maricel activated the speaker on her phone. "Hi, Ryan!"

"Is this Typhoon Rosalyn?"

Rosa snorted a laugh. "Oo nga. Konnichiwa!"

"What in the world does that mean?"

"It's Japanese for 'Good afternoon'. I know it's evening there, but it's all the Japanese I know."

Ryan heard Maricel laughing at Rosa's comment. A strong pang of guilt attacked his insides. *If they only knew I'm not in Japan!* "I'm sure you're keeping things lively as ever in my absence."

"Of course, po," said Rosalyn.

"Hi, Ryan. How was the first leg of the flight?"

Tipton instantly recognized the voice. It was Hazel. "So far, so good," he lied. "I already miss the delicious foods you cooked."

"Come back soon and I'll cook for you again."

Tipton sighed. "I look forward to that day more than you know."

"Me too. We're praying for your safe passage home. Please let us know when you're back in the States."

"I will."

"Ingatan mo sarili mo (Take care of yourself), Ryan."

"Ikaw din (You too), Hazel."

"We love and miss you so much."

Tipton frowned. "Love and miss you too."

Maricel muted the speaker and Ryan said, "I can't stop thinking about you, baby. I knew it would be difficult, but man, oh man, I can't get you out of my head." *At least that much is true!*

"Same here," Maricel said. "Can I see you on cam?"

Tipton gulped hard. "As much as I'd love to, my phone battery's low. And I checked my battery pack into my luggage."

"It's okay. Just hearing your voice again is good enough for me. You made my day complete."

There was a brief pause. As much as Ryan wanted to bask in the pleasantness of her voice, he needed to end the call before he ran out of lies to tell her. Not only that, he didn't want to keep Jenny waiting any longer.

"Think I'll get a bite to eat and find a place to charge my cell phone before my next flight. I'll text you when I get home."

Maricel said, "Okay."

Ryan grimaced. "Sorry if we don't chat much the next couple of days. I'll be busy working double-shifts, to pay down my credit card bills from this trip."

When Maricel didn't reply, Ryan added, "But every penny spent was well worth it. Besides, look at the bright side. Thanks to social media, I don't have to worry about long-distance charges. If not for them, my phone bill might be a million dollars by now, just from calling you!"

Maricel burst into laughter. "You're so funny, Ryan."

"Instead of a bill collector they'd send a hit man to find me." *Someone should shoot me for this!*

Maricel laughed even harder.

Tipton said, "My phone battery's just about to die. Gotta go now. Mahal kita, Maricel."

"Mahal din kita, Ryan. Hope you have a safe flight home."

"Salamat, mahal ko…"

Tipton rejoined Jenny just as the waiter approached with their food. When he placed a plate full of pancit on the table, it took Ryan straight back to the homecooked meal Hazel prepared just for him.

The very thought churned his already upset stomach even more violently. *How could I stoop so low like this, and do it all so easily? Mom and Dad would be so disappointed!*

After the meal—a meal Ryan barely touched—he and Jenny went for a 30-minute walk to get some fresh air. On the way back to the Waterfront Hotel and Casino, they couldn't ignore the bright neon lights reaching skyward like a proud beacon, enticing, daring residents and visitors to come and try their luck.

Entering the hotel lobby, the fear Tipton felt building all night intensified considerably. It wasn't the same uneasy sensation that most folks walking through those doors often felt—the fear of losing hard-earned money.

Ryan wasn't the gambling type, and he had no intention of becoming one this week. What made his knees grow weak was the thought of sharing the bed with Jenny. This frightened him almost to the point of hyperventilating.

Add to that the mounting guilt and stress he felt for running around behind Maricel's back the way he was, and it was easy for anyone to understand why the man from Iowa was never more conflicted than he was at present...

10

"ARE YOU STILL AWAKE?"

Tipton had the covers pulled up to his neck. "Yes."

"Are you okay?"

"Just a little nervous, I suppose," His voice cracked.

It was just after midnight. A few faint wisps of moonlight penetrated through the curtains, providing the only source of light inside the hotel room.

But even in the darkness, Ryan was never more thankful to be wearing the button-down cotton pajamas he brought with him. They were buttoned all the way up to the neck. Even buried beneath a bed sheet and covers, he couldn't stop shivering.

But the cold room temperature had nothing to do with it. What caused his nerves to shiver more than his flesh stemmed from whatever he thought Jenny might be thinking now.

Her body movements alone told him all he needed to know; she wasn't yet ready to sleep. Not only that, she seemed ready and willing for almost anything. When she emerged from the bathroom, wearing a sexy pink lingerie with red hearts splashed all over it—flaunting her body ever so daringly—Ryan took one glance at her and quickly looked away, completely red-faced.

The more Jenny brimmed with confidence the more Tipton's heart sank in his chest. Seeing her dressed so provocatively forced Maricel's image to surface in his mind again.

It sounded judgmental, he knew, but his first thought was that his girlfriend in Manila would never prance around his hotel room scantily dressed, let alone dare sleep with him. Even more terrifying, he wasn't sure if Jenny was wearing anything now.

The restless woman tried one last time to get his attention, She inched in even closer and gently rubbed his leg with her left foot, to remind him that she was still there.

But Ryan never reciprocated. "Well, goodnight then," she said with a prolonged sigh, frustration evident in her voice.

"Goodnight Jenny. Thanks for an enjoyable evening."

"Hmm, you're welcome," came the dejected reply.

Tipton turned onto his side and his breathing slowly stabilized. Miraculously, a few moments later he was sleeping.

He woke at 4:30 a.m. and quietly climbed out of bed, careful not to wake his beautiful bed partner.

He tiptoed to the bathroom and sent a text message to Maricel: *Hi sweetie...Will be landing in Cali soon. I miss you so much :(I'll call or send another text msg when I'm back in Iowa. Wish you were with me now. Mahal kita. Mwah!*

Ryan turned his phone off. Even if lying electronically was somewhat easier to do—after all Maricel couldn't see the guilt on his face—it still wasn't right.

Ryan nearly jumped out of his skin when he rejoined Jenny to find her sitting up in bed staring at him, almost glaring, without saying a word. He didn't know how to gauge her reaction. Oddly enough, he wasn't too concerned one way or the other.

After a ten-second stare-down, Jenny laid down and rolled onto her side. A few minutes later, they both were sleeping again.

The next morning at the breakfast table, Jenny could no longer disguise her growing agitation. Sipping her orange juice, she said, "What happened last night?"

"What do you mean?" Tipton knew what she meant.

"Do you find me unattractive?"

"Of course, not! You're one of the most beautiful women I've ever met!"

"But are *you* attracted to me?"

"Of course, I am, Jenny." Ryan paused. "It's just that..."

"Just that what?"

"I'm not used to meeting women as attractive as you," he said, making sure to maintain steady eye contact with her. "I confess it was easier discussing the many possibilities with you, when I was halfway around the world. Guess I'm a little overwhelmed."

Jenny seemed satisfied with his answer for the moment.

It was time to change the subject. "I'm excited to see the Lapu-Lapu Monument and Magellan's Cross today."

"Should be fun," Jenny said, half-heartedly. Most foreigners who'd visited her in the Philippines took her to those places. As far as she was concerned, once was enough for her.

But there was one place on Mactan Island she never grew tired of visiting, the Shangri-La Resort and Spa. "After we see those things, I know the perfect place we can go to have lunch."

Ryan sipped his coffee. "Sure. Whatever you want."

Jenny smiled. *Finally, something to get excited about!*

"I look forward to going to Kawasan Falls tomorrow. Believe it or not, it'll be my first time seeing a real live waterfall."

Jenny didn't sound surprised by his admission. Nor did she seem to care. "It's a nice place for a day trip."

Ryan asked Jenny, "How many times have you been there?"

"Too many to count," she said, flatly.

Ryan was tempted to ask how many foreigners she had met in person over the years, but he let it go. But it sounded like quite a few. Ironically, it didn't bother him in the least.

Had it been Maricel, instead of Jenny, it would have pierced him all the way through to the soul.

After breakfast, they took a taxi across the Mactan-Mandaue Bridge, for the short one-kilometer ride to Lapu Lapu City.

Tipton read on the plane ride to Cebu that Mactan Island was one of Cebu's most historical places. A true lover of history, he looked forward to seeing as much of the island as he could, in the brief time they would spend there.

The first stop was the Lapu-Lapu Monument. Located a short distance from Cebu-Mactan International Airport, it was the actual site of the fierce battle between Mactan Island Chieftain Lapu Lapu and his foreign aggressor, Ferdinand Magellan.

On April 27, 1521, the local chief triumphed over the Portuguese explorer, by killing him on the shores of Mactan Island, along with several of his men.

Tipton remembered learning about Magellan in history class, way back when, but didn't remember that his final mission on earth ultimately ended in the Philippines nearly 500 years ago.

It took coming here to be reminded of it...

Using his cellphone, he took a few pictures of the 40-foot bronze statue of chieftain Lapu Lapu, holding a shield in one hand and a kampilan sword in the other. While Ferdinand Magellan and his forces used cannons and guns, these were the only two weapons the Filipino Chieftain had used on that fateful day.

Tipton wasn't surprised that the battle of Mactan was reenacted each year on the original site.

What did surprise him, however, was that the city wasn't renamed "Lapu-Lapu" until a half-century ago, back in 1961.

Prior to that, it was known as "Opon" for nearly 200 years. Tipton wondered what took them so long.

From there they visited Magellan's Cross a short distance away. Six days before the fierce battle ensued, Portuguese and Spanish explorers planted a large cross there, after Father Pedro Valderema baptized roughly 400 Filipinos into the Catholic faith.

From 1525 to 1740, Augustinian priests had built an open shrine for the cross. Many of the natives, believing it had miraculous powers, kept taking wood chips from it.

The priests, hoping to preserve it, ended up making a hollow cross out of wood, before placing the original cross inside, so it wouldn't eventually dwindle down to nothing.

The cross was later housed in a small chapel next to the Basilica Minore del Santo Niño, in front of City Hall, and mounted onto a solid marble foundation resting beneath a domed ceiling that was covered with priceless hand-painted artwork, which skillfully depicted that turbulent time in their country's history.

From there they visited the Magellan marker. Since spreading the faith was Magellan's main reason for going to Mactan Island in the first place, a monument was erected in 1886, in his honor, on the exact location where the conflict took place.

Ryan was thoroughly enjoying himself. The only drawback were the many aggressive peddlers scattered about the plaza selling food, drinks, sunglasses, balloons, and a million other things. He found them quite bothersome, especially since they kept targeting him. *Do they think I'm rich?*

Jenny was most excited when Ryan had finally had enough of sightseeing, and they took a taxi to the five-star Shangri-La Spa and Resort, for a late lunch. It was there that Ryan got his first glimpse into her exquisite taste for the finer things in life.

He silently hoped that Jenny wouldn't drain him of every peso he had in the next few days, leaving him with nothing left over for Davao City.

After lunch, they walked the impeccably maintained grounds down to the ocean pavilion and spent a few minutes by the water, before heading back to Cebu City.

They arrived back at the Waterfront Hotel just after four p.m.

Jenny said, "Why don't we go for a swim before dinner?"

"Sure, why not?" After a full day in the hot sun, the prospect of being embarrassed by exposing his overweight body to even more people, withered in favor of a refreshing swim in the pool.

Ryan and Jenny changed into their swimsuits and went down to the sprawling swimming pool area. They passed a fitness center along the way. Each window showcased motivated men and women pushing their well-toned bodies to the limit.

"When will they finally learn they're only well-formed molecules," Tipton said under his breath, taking one last glance at them. *The diet starts as soon as I get back home! Blah, blah, blah!*

After finding two chaise lounge seats poolside, Jenny took her time removing every article of outer clothing, until all that was left was a red, mini two-piece bikini.

Suddenly the main attraction, she was careful to oblige the many men and women gawking at her. Perhaps they thought she was a fashion model out on a shoot. The way she waved and smiled at everyone—like any super model would—indicated to Ryan that she clearly enjoyed having so many eyes focused on her all at once.

After taking a few selfies, she handed her phone to Ryan. "Can you take more pictures of me?"

"Sure." One snapshot turned into two, then three. Then four.

When there was finally a break in the action, Ryan went for a swim in the pool alone, doing his best not to let Jenny get under his skin. But her self-centered actions were starting to turn him off.

Maricel would never do such things!

The mental comparisons kept piling up. Two weeks ago, this sort of thing would have made him crazy jealous, but not now. Part of him wanted to pound his chest for landing a beauty like Jenny.

After a short but refreshing swim, Ryan dried himself off. "I'm heading up to the room," he said, calmly. "See you whenever."

Jenny looked up from the lounge chair she was seated on and removed her sunglasses. Squinting in the bright sunshine she watched Ryan walking away, wondering what had gotten into him.

A short while later, she went back to the room and took a hot shower before dinner.

They rode the elevator down to the lobby in silence and proceeded to Port Seafood Restaurant. Ryan wore black pleated slacks and a black and white striped button-down shirt.

Jenny wore the lavender summer dress Ryan had included as part of her pasalubong. She looked spectacular as always. So much so that, for the first time since arriving in Cebu, Ryan had a sudden urge to look beyond her self-centered antics at the pool earlier, lean across the table, and kiss those pouty lips of hers.

Jenny picked up on it and steadied herself. But to her dismay, nothing happened. Her American visitor had rejected her again. She snorted frustration. *How much more of this can I take? I should be rejecting his advances, not the other way around!*

Just as she was about to say something, the waiter approached with their appetizers. Jenny dipped a large shrimp into red cocktail sauce and studied Ryan's face very carefully.

His energy level on Mactan Island earlier reminded her of the man she admired so much online the past few months. It was the exact opposite of the man now seated across from her.

She swallowed the food in her mouth. It could wait no longer. "What's bothering you, Ryan?"

He sighed. "Guess I'm still jetlagged from all that flying."

Jenny nodded that she understood. "If you want to go up to the room and relax after dinner, that would be fine with me."

Ryan lowered his head. "Let's see how we feel after the meal."

Jenny was incredulous. This was the first time someone from the opposite sex didn't practically jump out of his skin, at the notion of spending a night in a hotel room with her. *This is crazy!*

The waiter approached with their main courses.

Without even bothering to thank God first, Tipton said, "Looks delicious. Dig in." This would have never happened in Manila.

Jenny was anxious to engage in conversation, but Ryan seemed content to eat his meal in silence.

After dinner, they strolled the casino floor.

Walking past a row of slot machines, Jenny said, "Why don't we try our luck?" *At least a slot machine will never reject me!*

"I'm not a gambler, Jenny, but if you'd like to play, feel free. I'll go for a walk outside."

"But we're supposed to be together," Jenny said. *The hits just keep on coming!*

The way she said it, so cutely, gave Ryan another strong urge to kiss her. "Sorry. Just not into slot machines. Tell you what, let me use the restroom. When I return, we can go for a walk."

"Sure. I'll wait here for you." The look on Jenny's face screamed, "Hello? I need money to gamble with!"

Ryan caught on. He reached into his pocket and gave her 2,000 pesos, which equated to just under U.S. $50. "Be back in a few minutes." He kissed her on the left cheek.

Jenny was suddenly glitzy-eyed. "Take your time."

Tipton was unsure what had caused her to light up so quickly, but he sensed the slot machine in front of her had more to do with it than anything else. Either way, he was cool with it.

Besides, he had more important things on his mind. Namely, what he would say to Maricel when he called her up in the room.

Riding the elevator up to the sixth floor, he mentally rehearsed what he would tell her, but his mind kept going blank on him.

After using the restroom, he took a deep breath and called her.

"Hi Ryan! How was the flight?"

"Well, I made it home," he lied.

"You'll never guess where I am?"

"Hmm, the Philippines?"

"Ha ha ha. Yes, but where in the Philippines?"

"Agape Coffee and Pastry Shoppe?"

With face aglow, Maricel said, "Close. I'm at Bayview Hotel with Rosalyn, having coffee. It's not the same here without you. Wanna see us on cam?"

"Wish I could, sweetie, but I woke up late. I need to take a quick shower and go to work. But please send me pics!"

"You know I will, sweetie. I was going to post them on Facebook, but didn't want to ruin the surprise."

"That's so sweet of you, Maricel." Ryan closed his eyes and shook his head in despair. He couldn't take all this lying to her. It was only day one, but it was already devouring him from within.

He needed to get off the phone before she detected something suspicious in his voice. He gulped hard. "Sorry for the short call, sweetie, but I need to get ready now," he lied. "I'll call you later."

"I understand. So nice to hear your voice again. The timing couldn't be more perfect. It's like you never left."

That's because I didn't leave! Tipton was disgusted with himself. "Tell Rosa I said hi."

"I will. I'm still clinging to your promise of visiting me again."

"Me too." Ryan sighed. "I love you, Maricel."

"Mahal din kita, Ryan."

The call ended, and Ryan rejoined Jenny downstairs in the casino where he had left her. "Did you win?"

Jenny shook her head in frustration.

Ryan's eyes widened. "You lost it all?"

"I'm about to," she barked, as the last of her credits were swallowed up by the greedy slot machine. "Grr!"

"Wow, that went fast," Tipton said, suddenly $50 poorer. He mentally chalked it up as one more steep cost of lying to his girlfriend in Manila. It was starting to get expensive.

"Sorry." Jenny seemed more disappointed that she couldn't defeat her money-sucking opponent, than she was about losing Ryan's hard-earned cash.

Tipton sighed to himself. "Ready?"

Jenny nodded yes. What she really wanted was to try her luck again on the slot machine. But Ryan's body language conveyed to her that the Bank of Ryan Tipton was closed for the night.

They walked outside the casino for fresh air, before going back to the room. When the elevator reached the sixth floor, that same anticipatory fear he had battled the night before came back with a vengeance, twisting him inside like a human pretzel.

Jenny had grown used to past visitors showering her with constant attention and affection. Many men couldn't keep their hands off her while they were in her presence. But not Ryan...

Even after practically throwing herself at him the night before, he never reciprocated. She was determined to maintain her dignity this time. *If he wants me, it's up to him to make the first move this time!* One thing Jenny wasn't, was a doormat!

When Ryan made no such move, Jenny snorted a few times in the darkness to express her displeasure, but she remained true to her commitment to not give into her fleshly desires. *This is crazy!*

A few minutes later, Tipton was sound asleep.

Jenny, on the other hand, was still awake. Quickly falling asleep, however, was the passion and tenderness she felt for Ryan.

The only thing she still clung to was that her American visitor was a kind and decent man. *But why doesn't he care for me?*

That question flooded her mind until she finally fell asleep an hour or so later...

11

THE NEXT DAY RYAN hired a personal driver to take he and Jenny to Kawasan Falls, in Badian, Cebu for a day trip.

Much like his driver back in Manila, the man named Junne was warm and friendly. Noticeably different from last week, however, was that Tipton felt entirely out of place inside the vehicle, and terribly alone, things he never felt in Maricel's presence.

It was evident that Jenny felt the same way. To prove it, the moment they left the Waterfront Hotel, she kept her face buried in her mobile phone chatting with friends on Facebook.

The silence between them left Ryan alone with his thoughts. The more they kept misfiring, so to speak, the more he longed to be back in Manila with Maricel. To make matters worse, they were three and a half hours into what was advertised as a two-hour drive, and still had thirty minutes to go, due to heavy traffic on the roads.

Ryan found himself growing increasingly frustrated but managed to keep his emotions in check. Funnily enough, had he been stuck in traffic with Maricel, they still would have enjoyed themselves. A minor inconvenience like this would have changed nothing. They would have made the best of it.

They finally arrived at Kawasan Falls at 2 p.m.

They found a cozy spot not too far from the falls and enjoyed a nice picnic together, with food Ryan had purchased at the mall next to the hotel. When they were finished eating, they climbed on board a bamboo float with ten other people, before being taken straight to the edge of the falls.

Tipton wore a yellow and blue swimsuit and yellow XXL tee-shirt. *If anyone wants me to remove it, they'll have to force me at gunpoint before I'll ever consider it.*

Jenny, on the other hand, couldn't wait to shed her clothing, exposing a bright yellow, two-piece bikini underneath. It was even skimpier than the red one she wore the day before. Some men gawked more at her than the falls. Her body language was quite flirtatious, especially toward an older foreign man who sounded Australian to Ryan. He was accompanied by a young woman half his age, but even that didn't stop him from flirting with Jenny.

Just like the day before at the pool, she handed Ryan her phone and asked him to take many snapshots of her, before she was satisfied for the moment. The more she acted like this, the more he yearned to be with Maricel back in Manila.

With this being his first waterfall experience, Ryan wished the Arcamos were here to experience it with him instead of Jenny.

If the company you keep in life was more important than the places you visit, cruel as it sounded, being at Kawasan Falls with Jenny could never compare to last week in Tagaytay, with Maricel and her family. He missed them all dearly.

After the bamboo float ride, Ryan caught Jenny off guard when he said, "What do you say we head back to the hotel?"

Jenny shot him a confused look. "So soon?"

"I've seen enough." His comment was more directed at her flirtatious ways than with the lush, tropical surroundings.

Jenny took a deep breath. "Sure, if that's what you want."

On the way back to Cebu City, Ryan became increasingly fidgety. "Jenny, I've been thinking."

Jenny raised a curious eyebrow. "About?"

"It would be better if you sleep at your house tonight."

Jenny's jaw dropped. "Why are you doing this, Ryan?"

Ryan massaged his kneecaps. "I just prefer sleeping alone."

Jenny gasped loudly and stared out the window in silence.

"I still want to spend time with you, Jenny. I just think it would be best if you went home each night." When she didn't reply, Ryan continued, "Once we get back to the hotel, you can gather your belongings. I'll ask the driver to take you home."

"Sure, whatever!" Jenny leaned back in the seat, doing her best to hold back her tears. "Actually, I think I'll hang at the Waterfront for a while…" Her tone was sarcastic.

Ryan sighed. "As you wish."

"Can I borrow some money? I want to try my luck on the slot machines again." Her eyes pleaded with him to grant her wish.

Tipton looked outside the car window, suddenly a million miles away. *Doesn't borrowing imply the intent to pay it back?*

He sighed. "Sure…" *Why can't I be in Manila now?*

TWO DAYS LATER, JENNY arrived at the Waterfront Hotel 90 minutes late for breakfast. Her attitude toward Ryan was chilly at best; her eyes were distant.

After a long silence, Tipton said, "What's wrong, Jenny?" In truth, he didn't need to ask. He already knew.

Jenny stirred creamer in her coffee. "Just tired, I guess." *Tired of feeling rejected* by you, she thought to say, but didn't. "Part of me still wonders why you're not interested in me."

"That's not true, Jenny."

Jenny raised her hands in frustration, palms out. "I felt so much closer when we were chatting online. It's like we were best friends before we met. I don't know what to think anymore. It seems even our friendship is shaky now." She took a sip of coffee, then asked, "Are you married?"

Ryan shot her a sideways look. Clearly, he was perturbed by her accusation. "Come on, Jenny, I told you about my failed marriage seven years ago."

"I know, but what am I to think? You've been acting so strangely. I'm trying to figure out who you really are. Do you have a girlfriend back in the States?"

"No, I don't," came the reply flatly.

Jenny strongly sensed that Ryan was hiding something. The fact that he was only in Cebu for four days loomed large in her mind again. No, something wasn't right. She took another small sip of coffee. "Are you taken by someone in my country?"

Ryan gulped hard. "What are you getting at?"

"Nothing. Forget it." *So that's it. Here we go again!*

"Come on, Jenny, don't be like that. Tell me."

"What's to tell, Ryan? Ever since we left Mactan Island I've felt terribly alone, especially yesterday at Camotes Island. It's like we were together, but we weren't."

Known as the "Lost Horizon of the South", Camotes Island was the perfect "stress-free" environment for anyone looking for inner tranquility. Sadly, neither one of them came close to achieving that goal.

Before boarding the fast craft boat for the 33-nautical mile trip, Brian went to Jenny's house to meet her parents. They were cordial toward him, but there was no spark between them like he felt when he met the Arcamos. Instead, there was this underlying suspicion that made him feel slightly uncomfortable in their presence.

As they toured the four islands of Camotes Island—Pacijan Island, Poro Island, Ponson Island and Tulang Island—Ryan's body was there, but his heart and mind kept drifting back to Manila, and the wonderful family who'd greatly impacted his life.

Had Maricel been with him instead of Jenny, he would have thoroughly enjoyed walking the white sandy beaches with her, while daydreaming about a possible future together.

Ryan and Jenny ate dinner at a place called Mangodlong Beach Resort. Despite the near-perfect ambiance down by the water, Ryan didn't enjoy himself. It dawned on him that while he always challenged himself to speak a few Tagalog words in their presence, he never felt inspired or encouraged to with Jenny.

Tipton's lone humorous moment happened inside a souvenir shop on the island, before they caught the last boat back to Cebu City. When he paid for two bags full of souvenirs—one for his family and friends back home, the other all for Jenny—he was comforted knowing despite what he spent on boat rides, meals and souvenirs, it was a whole lot cheaper, and far less stressful, than being near a casino with Jenny.

On his meager salary, if he gave into Jenny's every whim, he would need three jobs to pay for it all. Maricel, on the other hand, would be happy doing nothing at all, so long as they were together.

The comparisons kept piling up...

Ryan snapped out of it and refocused on the woman seated across from him. He took a sip of orange juice. "I noticed you changed your profile picture on the dating site, wearing the yellow bikini."

Jenny applied more red lipstick, then pursed her lips together to help spread it more evenly. "Yup. From Kawasan Falls."

Ryan nodded that he already knew that. "I also checked your Facebook and Instagram accounts and saw the many photographs I took of you the past three days. I noticed you didn't include me in any of the pictures. You even named the album, 'All about me.'"

Jenny gasped loudly. "What can I say, Ryan, that's how you made me feel all week. All alone by myself."

Ryan could have replied by saying she made him feel the same way, at least on some levels, but he didn't want to argue with her.

At least she was free to post whatever she wanted on social media. Ryan didn't have that luxury. The instant he did, he would have a lot of explaining to do to Maricel. This was yet another steep price he was paying for living a lie.

The regrets kept piling up...

Tipton sighed. Maricel was right all along. Most people really weren't who they proclaimed to be online. It took meeting Jenny in person to see just how self-centered and materialistic she was.

Had they not met in person, he probably would have never been exposed to this unflattering side of her. Some things could only be learned about others in person...

Then again, who was he to judge her, when he was just as flawed himself? At least she wasn't living a secret life like he was.

They spent their last full day together at the Waterfront Hotel. But "together" never happened. Ryan spent much of the day poolside, exchanging numerous messages with Maricel and Liezel, as Jenny remained inside the casino all day.

The only time she joined Ryan at the pool was when she needed more money. Each time she asked, her mood was a little more soured—his mood, too!

Thanks to her, he was already down U.S. $300, and he never pulled a single slot machine lever! Jenny's gambling losses had forced him to take a cash advance on his credit card, so he'd have enough cash for his three day visit to Davao.

But what upset him most had nothing to do with Jenny's flirtatious nature, or the lost money, even if it was money he couldn't afford to lose.

What feasted on his insides more than those things were the many lies he kept telling Maricel. Though he still had three days left in the Philippines, due to his blatant dishonesty, he couldn't spend them in Manila with the woman he believed he was in love with.

Just before midnight, Ryan was tired and wanted to rest for the evening. "Would you like me to escort you home?"

"That won't be necessary," Jenny said, halfheartedly. "But can you spare a few more pesos? I want to try my luck one last time before going home. This is the last time I'll ask, promise..."

Ryan gasped. His shoulders slumped. He wanted to say, "I'm a mall security guard, not some rich CEO!" Instead, he sheepishly caved into her self-absorbed wishes and retrieved another 2,000 pesos from his pants pocket. "Well, that's the last of it."

Jenny took the money. "Thanks Ryan. I really appreciate it."

Tipton frowned. *Did she even hear what I said?* It was the last straw. Even had he not met Maricel, he didn't need any more convincing that Jenny wasn't right for him. "You're welcome."

Jenny checked her look in the mirror, kissed Ryan on the cheek, and left his room. If he wasn't interested in her, perhaps someone down in the casino would be. Her body motion screamed, "Hey guys, I'm single and ready to mingle!"

Ryan showered, then called Maricel.

"Hello?" came the soft, sleepy voice on the other end.

"Hi, sweetie, did I wake you?"

"I was dreaming that you were still here in the Philippines."

Ryan winced. *That's because I'm still here!* "I would do anything to be with you now."

Maricel heard him sniffling. "Are you okay, Ryan?"

"I'll be fine." He had a strong urge to come clean and tell her the truth, but he couldn't bring himself to do it. "My feelings for you have only grown stronger the past few days. I can't imagine my life without you in it."

Tears formed in her eyes. "I feel the same way, Ryan."

Tipton took a few deep breaths and wiped his moist eyes. "Break time is over. I need to get back to work, sweetie. I'll call you next chance I get."

"Thanks for making my day complete. Mahal kita, Ryan."

"Mahal din kita, Maricel."

The call ended. Ryan sat on the edge of the bed and started weeping. It quickly turned into full-blown sobbing, knowing his girlfriend was safely tucked away in bed dreaming of him, yet here he was in Cebu with another woman.

Even if nothing had happened between him and Jenny, it still wasn't right. *Why did I do this to her?*

12

RYAN TIPTON WAS SEATED in row eight on a short but very full flight, to Francisco Bangoy International Airport, in Davao City.

The flight attendant just announced that they would be on the ground in less than ten minutes. It seemed they just took off, yet they were already preparing to land.

Try as he might, Ryan couldn't erase the troubling demeanor he saw riveted on Jenny's face, back at the airport. Her features weren't nearly as soft. And while there was a hint of sadness in her eyes, they were nowhere near as friendly as when he first arrived in Cebu.

Warmth was replaced with a growing skepticism that silently screamed, "I'm onto you, Ryan Tipton!" Ryan tried persuading himself that there was no reason to feel paranoid, but he failed miserably. His gut told him that Jenny knew what was going on...

His premonition was confirmed when she replied to the text message he sent on the plane, thanking her again for a good time.

Jenny replied: *You're welcome...have fun with your gf in davao!*

No further confirmation was needed. He was busted. But how in the world did she find out? What he didn't know was, thirty minutes after they said their goodbyes last night, Jenny rode the elevator up to the sixth floor, not to beg for more money, but to see if they could somehow salvage their last night together. That, plus she was exhausted, and didn't want to take a taxi home at that late hour.

Just as she was about to knock on the door, she heard him talking on the phone. Jenny couldn't make out most of the words he spoke, but she clearly heard him say, "mahal kita" (I love you), just before the call ended. It hurt. Bad.

Though her feelings for Ryan had greatly diminished, it was still painful, especially when he wept bitterly afterward. Whoever he was on the phone with was surely Filipina, and obviously someone he cared deeply about. The "mahal kita" proved that much.

Jenny lowered herself onto the floor outside Ryan's room, to hopefully prevent herself from having a full-blown collapse. She sobbed softly and quietly, causing mascara to smear on her face everywhere.

After a few torturous moments, she picked herself up off the floor and rode the elevator down to the lobby, with one thought on her mind, *Why doesn't he feel that way about me?*

Jenny arrived home at 2 a.m. and placed a frantic call to a good friend who worked for Cebu-Pacific Airlines. "I need a favor."

Joy was sound asleep when she called, "What kind of favor?"

"I need you to check on a flight for me."

"I'm not supposed to do this. I could get in serious trouble…"

"Please, Joy, I really need to know."

Joy wiped sleep from her eyes, then called a co-worker on the graveyard shift. Using Ryan Tipton's full name, he was able to confirm that the American was flying to Davao City, not Manila.

So, she lives in Davao City! Jenny's heart sank deeper in her chest. *Perhaps the next man will be the right one*, she thought, sadly.

Upon sharing the news with her parents, they refused to join Ryan at the Waterfront Hotel for breakfast, as they had planned on doing.

"When will you finally come to your senses and give up on foreigners? There are plenty of good Filipino men to love. Go find one!" her father had barked, as Jenny left the house.

When she arrived at the hotel restaurant without her parents, that was Ryan's first inclination that something was wrong. But he also breathed a sigh of relief. The last thing he needed was to feel uncomfortable in their presence again. One family member was more than enough! It was one less thing to agonize over.

Prior to taking this trip, Tipton had such high expectations with Jenny. He found it mind-numbing how four days had reduced five months of chatting—and growing feelings—down to nothing more than just a platonic friendship thing, if that.

The chemistry, or whatever it was that stirred one's feelings inside for someone else, just wasn't there. It was as simple as that.

Ryan needed a diversion from his thinking, and focused his attention on the screen before him showing the plane's flight path. He easily spotted Manila on the GPS map, and wished he could find a way to divert the plane there instead.

But how would he justify the past four days to Maricel? The answer was simple; he couldn't. If his girlfriend knew he was still in her country, she would be completely devastated, no questions asked.

In order to safeguard her heart, Ryan needed to remain incognito and refrain from disclosing his whereabouts to her, at all costs.

And this meant the lies had to continue no matter what. In a way, Tipton felt like a CIA operative traveling all throughout the Philippines, inconspicuously meeting with three different people, all of whom had no idea the others even existed.

Ryan had heard about various love triangle stories over the years, and the many dangers they presented. Now that Liezel was about to enter into the equation, the triangle was about to expand to a full-blown love square! Tipton shivered at the thought.

On the surface, to the millions of people on the planet lacking action and adventure in their lives, this sort of lifestyle might sound downright exciting. But that simply wasn't the case.

Like all other individuals in the world caught up in similar predicaments, Tipton was meeting these women under false pretenses, committing espionage of the heart at a very high level.

By playing this deadly game with the opposite sex, someone was bound to get hurt at some point. In the back of his mind, Tipton feared his dishonest actions would eventually bite him back twice as hard, and he, not them, would be hurt the most in the end.

THE PLANE TOUCHED DOWN at 3:38 p.m. Following what was quickly becoming a Ryan Tipton tradition in the Philippines, the American traveler sent a quick text message to Liezel informing her of his safe arrival. *Just landed...The day we've both been longing for is finally upon us...See you in a few minutes! Mwah!*

Tipton was disgusted with himself again, for having the gall to copy and paste the message he'd sent to Maricel and Jenny.

Yet he also felt this certain invincibility he never experienced before, when it came to meeting women. It got a little easier with each new encounter.

Part of him felt like a playboy. Hence, the soaring confidence. But because it was all being done under false pretenses it was short-lived, and always led to constant guilt on his part.

Ryan chuckled to himself. He felt like the late Chris Farley in the movie, *Tommy Boy*. After a dismal week full of constant failures, trying to save his deceased father's company, and ultimately the town in which it was located, Tommy Boy finally had a breakthrough at a restaurant somewhere in the mid-west.

Sitting across from David Spade, out of nowhere, he displayed pure salesmanship with his ability to persuade others. It began with something as basic as ordering chicken wings.

After being told by his waitress the kitchen was closed until dinnertime, Tommy Boy continued rambling on and on about how badly his week had gone, and how utterly ridiculous his life was in general. The waitress, pitying him, eventually agreed to turn on the fryers and cook chicken wings just for him.

Spade raised an eyebrow, totally blown away by what he had just witnessed. "Why can't you sell like that?" he said.

Tommy Boy nonchalantly replied, "I was just having fun. If we didn't get the wings, so what, we still got that meat lover's pizza in the trunk!" In short, he had something to fall back on, whether the waitress agreed to his self-centered wishes or not.

Spade countered by saying, "You got the wings because you were relaxed. You had confidence. And that's what it takes to sell!"

Now soon-to-be-meeting with his third woman in just eleven days, Tipton had developed that same confident mindset halfway around the world. Only in this case, he was dealing with women, not pizza or chicken wings.

He knew he was being selfish, and cruel, but he was starting to believe that he, of all people, would have little trouble meeting a different woman every day in this country, if he chose to.

Thanks to Liezel's text message, Ryan knew she was wearing denim blue jeans and a pink t-shirt. He spotted her easily and headed off in her direction.

"Welcome to my country, Ryan," she said softly, but warmly, unable to ignore Ryan's sunburned face. She silently wondered where it came from, not knowing it was on Camotes Island.

"Salamat, Liezel. Nice to finally meet you in person. Mabuhay!"

"Mabuhay!" They embraced.

The first thing Ryan noticed was that she was more wearily cautious than Maricel and Jenny were. And taller. "I must say, you're even more beautiful in person!"

"Salamat." At 5'5", Liezel was tall for a Filipino girl. Her body was lean. She had shoulder-length black hair, and possessed a youthful beauty many women in her country were envious of.

Yet, despite all that, for only being 24, she was too young to look so beaten down. Her eyes screamed, "Please love me! I'll do anything, just don't hurt me or ever leave me."

Ryan felt certain that her defeated demeanor came from being hurt by dishonest men visiting her country. *Yeah, men like me!*

For that reason alone, it was difficult maintaining steady eye contact with her. "Don't worry, I didn't forget your pasalubong."

"Salamat." Liezel seemed more grateful for the hug than the gift.

They walked to the baggage claim area mostly in silence. Where everything always seemed rushed with Jenny—the woman could never sit still—Liezel seemed the exact opposite. It went from being completely overwhelmed to underwhelmed, just like that.

But with Maricel, there was this comforting balance that never overwhelmed or underwhelmed him. If he could blink his eyes and reappear in Manila, he wouldn't hesitate to do it.

Twenty minutes after boarding, the hotel shuttle van pulled up to the Marco Polo Hotel, in Davao City. Liezel sat on a chair in the lobby as her American visitor checked into his room. Scanning the vaulted ceilings and the elegantly decorated lobby, she felt way under dressed wearing hand-me-down clothing that was given to her from her older sister, Maribeth.

Once they were inside the room on the twelfth-floor, Ryan said, "Ready for your pasalubong?"

Liezel sat on the couch and took her time pulling everything out of the pink bag, one item at a time. When she was finished, her lips pressed into a smile she couldn't contain.

"Thank you, Ryan," she said, rather warmly. But in the back of her mind she wondered what strings, if any, would be attached to accepting these gifts from him?

Would Ryan want some sort of physical retribution, like most other men traveling to her country expected? After three painful disappointments this year alone, each one causing her to do things she promised never to do with near strangers, she feared one more failure might push her to the point of no return.

Ryan appeared harmless on the surface. But with exception to the man from France, who erupted like a volcano when she rejected his strong advances and ordered her out of his room at 2 a.m., the other two men had treated her with respect.

If she rejected Ryan's advances, would he force her to walk four miles scared out of her wits, with no money in her pockets, before she finally made it home like the man from France had made her do?

Her weary heart prayed not. But one thing was certain; she was determined to remain strong this time, and protect her mind, heart, and body at all costs.

Without even asking, Ryan sensed what she was thinking. He wanted to say, "Your body's perfectly safe with me, but only you can protect your heart!" Instead, he said, "I've been thinking, perhaps it would be better if you went home each night, instead of sleeping here. I'll gladly pay your travel expenses to and from the hotel."

Whereas Jenny was offended by those very same words, Liezel was relieved to hear them.

"Hungry?" Ryan said, with a comforting smile.

Liezel folded her hands on her lap. "A little, I guess."

"The man at the check-in desk said there are five restaurants on the premises. Why don't we head downstairs for a nice meal?"

Liezel exhaled deeply. "Sounds good."

They ended up choosing the Polo Bistro. Ryan was mildly impressed when they both ordered the same things—French onion soup for an appetizer and prawns thermidor as their main course.

For dessert they shared a mango coconut creme brulee.

As the minutes passed, the warm and witty person Tipton had known online for the past five months, started materializing before his eyes. The conversation was lively and engaging.

After dinner, they went back to Ryan's room. Liezel grew anxious again. She was painfully aware that this was when most men moved in for the prize. If this was payback time, what would be his asking price? She wondered...

At least he wasn't removing his clothes or trying to force alcohol down her throat, like others had tried in the past. Even so, she was prepared to run for the door at the first sign of aggression on his part.

But it never happened. If anything, he always went out of his way to make her feel completely safe and comfortable with him.

Ryan crossed one leg over the other, and asked, "What do you suggest we do tomorrow?"

Liezel relaxed even more, then gave her best "Chamber of Commerce" speech on the city that was widely known as the 'City in Bloom'. After weighing all their options, they decided on Samal Island, followed by Eden Nature Park the following day. If all went well, Liezel would then introduce Ryan to her parents.

After four days of near-constant chaos with Jenny, this slower change of pace was quite refreshing for Tipton.

At 11 p.m., Liezel stood to leave.

Ryan asked, "Would you like me to accompany you home in the taxi?"

"That's very thoughtful of you Ryan," came the reply warmly, "but I can manage on my own."

"At least let me walk you down to your cab."

Liezel smiled at him and nodded yes.

Closing the door behind him, Ryan said, "What about your pasalubong?"

"Leave it for now. I'll bring it home with me when you leave."

Ryan shrugged his shoulders. "As you wish."

The elevator door closed. Ryan shocked himself when he reached for Liezel's hand.

After a brief hesitation, she reciprocated. They reached the lobby floor and headed outside, still hand in hand.

Ryan signaled for a driver, then gave Liezel money for cab fare.

When she lowered herself into the taxi, Ryan said, "I look forward to going to Samal Island with you tomorrow."

The comment earned him another endearing smile. "I think you'll like it there."

Tipton asked, "Can you be here at 7 a.m., so we can have breakfast together."

"Okay."

"Please call or text me when you get home," he added.

"I will. Thanks for dinner, Ryan. It was delicious."

"Having the pleasure of your company was far better than the meal. It was even better than expected!"

Liezel's face lit up. Her lips formed into another beautiful smile. "Really?"

"Yes," Tipton said, meaning it."

Liezel blushed when her American visitor leaned inside the cab and kissed her softly on the right cheek. She glanced up at him in a futile attempt at nonchalance.

Perhaps he really is different, after all, she thought, as the driver pulled away.

Tipton went back up to his room, with a warm feeling inside, something he never felt in Jenny's presence.

Ryan scratched his head. Just a few short hours ago, all he wanted was to be with Maricel again. Now he wasn't so sure. The stakes had just risen to a whole new level.

Now more than ever he knew he was playing a dangerous game of Russian Roulette in the Philippines. The question was who would still be standing in the end?

What in the world am I doing? he asked himself, for the millionth time.

13

THE NEXT DAY

AFTER BREAKFAST, RYAN AND Liezel boarded a motorized outrigger boat for the one-hour ride across the Davao Gulf, to the white sandy beaches of Samal Island. The diesel engine powering the 30-foot vessel across the relatively calm waters was so loud at times, it was difficult for them to hear each other speak.

To compensate for this, Ryan held Liezel's hand much of the way. This silent form of affectionate communication served to weaken her defenses all the more. Anticipation kept building.

"Welcome to fabulous Samal Island, the Philippines' best place for snorkeling and scuba diving," the boat captain declared, docking at Pearl Farm Beach Resort. "Before this place became a world-class resort, it was an authentic pearl farm, famous for its white-lipped oysters harvested from the Sulu Sea."

Pausing to draw much-needed oxygen into his lungs, the man with the enthusiastic voice went on, "The quaint houses you see on either side of the dock are actually patterned after the stilt houses Samal tribes lived in way back when.

"While they never got to enjoy the accommodations guests enjoy today, some of their traditions are still recognized. Most notably are the jars of water placed outside the entrances of each house accompanied by coconut shell dippers, so guests can wash sand off their feet before entering inside. Many still believe this gesture represents a cleansing of the spirit."

Pausing again to take another deep breath, he finished his memorized speech by saying, "If you're fortunate to be staying at this fine resort, I assure you that you won't be disappointed! But even if not, I hope you all enjoy everything this beautiful island has to offer. Thanks again for traveling with us. Please be careful disembarking. Mabuhay!"

As tempting as scuba diving and snorkeling sounded, those things weren't on the agenda for Ryan and Liezel. Aside from taking an afternoon boat ride, to explore underwater coral gardens and colorful marine life known to these waters, they had no other plans but to take it easy and enjoy each other's company.

While disembarking, everyone was greeted warmly by a Caribbean-style steel drums musical group. Local tribal dancers, dressed in full traditional costumes, welcomed each new visitor as they swayed to the rhythmic beat. Thousands of colorful fish swam in the crystal-clear water surrounding the small dock.

The ambiance was so alive, so festive, that even the most stressed-out minds on the planet would have no choice but to relax.

Tipton took a deep breath and exhaled. Entertaining three women in two weeks wasn't an easy thing to do. It was starting to make him crazy. Hopefully, this place would offer him the mental release he desperately needed. "Piña colada?"

Liezel smiled. "Sure."

They found two open seats at the nearby octagon-shaped tiki bar. A bartender approached.

"May we please have two piña coladas?"

"Yes sir, coming right up!" The bartender filled a blender with ice, rum, pineapple juice and coconut cream, blended it all together then poured the concoction into two tall glasses.

Tipton surveyed the tropical scenery all around him. The Samal huts towering above the water like bungalows on stilts were soothing to gaze at. Finally, his eyes rested upon Liezel. "You look so beautiful in your new dress."

"Thank you, Ryan," she said shyly, wondering if her ship had finally come in. It sure felt that way. Excitement kept building.

They finished their drinks and went to the aqua sports center, to purchase tickets for the boat soon departing for the underwater coral gardens. Upon arriving there, both were pleased that it was as beautiful as advertised.

Liezel took plenty of scenic pictures and selfies of the two of them. A palpable sense of optimism was in the air.

She was really enjoying herself. So far, so good!

They arrived back at the resort two hours later, happy to find two unoccupied chaise lounge chairs by the pool, which they quickly claimed. Conversation remained lively and engaging.

There wasn't a single thing Tipton didn't like about Liezel. She was warm and caring, adorable really. So much so that he hardly thought about Maricel all day. "Would you like to go for a walk on the beach before dinner?"

"Sure," the 24-year-old woman replied, smiling cutely.

Ryan reached for Liezel's hand and helped her out of the lounge chair. They strolled the beach at a leisurely pace. After roughly a quarter mile, Ryan turned to face her. A gentle breeze was blowing, sending wisps of her shoulder-length hair flying in all directions.

Placing a hand on each of her shoulders, Ryan gazed deep into her gorgeous eyes and was completely swallowed up by her stark beauty. He inched in a little closer to make his intentions known.

A girlish smile curled on her lips. *Go with this*, Liezel thought, coaxing herself. She gulped hard, greatly anticipating his next move.

Whatever it was, she was ready for it. And willing.

Ryan moved in closer until their lips were mere inches apart. He could feel her soft breath on his face. His heart pumped wildly in his chest; nothing seemed to register in his head.

That is, until he looked down and realized he was wearing the same jeans and Hawaiian shirt he wore to Maricel's house, on the day they shared their first kiss. He silently gasped. *What am I doing?*

As much as he wanted to kiss Liezel on the lips, he couldn't do it. He hugged her instead. "Why don't we eat now, so we don't miss the last boat back to the city."

"Okay," came the reply. *He's even more shy than me...*

They ate freshly caught seafood at Maranao Pavilion. After a scrumptious meal, they shared a plate full of exotic fruits that were grown locally on a plantation across the gulf in Davao.

This was Tipton's first-time ever trying durian, green mandarin, and mangosteen. He took one whiff of the durian and nearly choked. "You expect me to eat that?"

Liezel burst into laughter. "Just try it. It's so yummy."

"Okay, but I'm only doing it for you." Ryan held his nose and placed the raunchy-smelling fruit inside his mouth. "Hmm, I must say, once you get beyond the nasty smell, it's quite tasty."

This was a near-perfect moment for Liezel, a much-needed reprieve from her oftentimes struggle-filled life. The cloud of grief that had followed her around all this time had slowly lifted, allowing her lonesome heart to explore the possibilities again.

They made it back to the dock just in time for the 4 p.m. sailing. If Ryan had one regret, it's that he didn't get to see Pearl Farm Beach Resort lit up at night. It looked spectacular online.

Ryan couldn't speak for Liezel, but had he stayed any longer, he would be powerless from overcoming the strong temptation he'd battled all day, no matter how hard he fought against it.

When they arrived back to Davao City, Ryan insisted that he escort her home in the taxicab.

Liezel accepted his kind and caring offer this time.

Upon arriving at her house, Ryan escorted Liezel to her front door. "Thanks, again, for the pleasure of your company."

"I had a wonderful time, Ryan. Wish it didn't have to end."

"Me too." Ryan inched in closer, never once breaking that penetrating gaze of hers, until their lips practically touched. But once again, thoughts of Maricel invaded his mind. He kissed her gently on the cheek. "See you in the morning for breakfast."

Liezel blushed. "I look forward to it." She wasn't concerned that Ryan didn't kiss her. If anything, it was refreshing to finally meet a true gentleman for a change. *An extremely shy gentleman,* she thought, entering the house, *but a gentleman, nevertheless.*

THE NEXT DAY AFTER breakfast, they boarded a charter bus bound for Eden Nature Park. Thanks to Jenny, Ryan couldn't afford a personal driver this time. He was in serious budget mode.

Ninety minutes later, they arrived at the mountain resort 3,000 feet above sea level, situated just below the foot of Mount Apo, which was the highest mountain range in the Philippines.

Since some areas couldn't be reached by foot, it was highly recommended for all first-time visitors to take a guided shuttle tour of the park, in vehicles specifically designed to navigate the many steep slopes and rugged terrain.

For what equated to less than U.S. $2 per person, it was a bargain. The first stop on the tour was at a colorful flower garden located at one of the park's highest peaks.

A faint but spectacular view of the Davao City landscape and the Davao Gulf could be seen out in the distance. After taking a few selfies together, they moseyed inside the store.

Ryan purchased a bouquet of fresh-cut orchids for Liezel. Seeing how pleased she was, Tipton had another strong urge to kiss her on the lips. He knew she wouldn't object. Her eyes begged him to plant one on her. She was more than ready.

He was too. Then he saw the zip line out in the distance and was brought back to last week in Tagaytay. Despite his best efforts his mind wouldn't allow him to forget about the Arcamos.

The guilt he had suppressed for much of the past two days came back with a vengeance. Like a tidal wave, it nearly knocked him over, especially seeing Liezel's hand resting in his.

It worsened considerably when the friendly female tour guide on the bus proudly declared, "For many years, Eden Nature Park has become the perfect place for nature trippers and honeymooners…"

The young woman rambled on about hiking and horseback riding along the mountain nature trail, but after hearing the word, *honeymooners,* Ryan tuned her out, not wanting to hear anymore.

His stomach churned violently. He felt nauseous to the point of vomiting, but somehow managed to control himself.

The second stop on the tour was at an open-air exhibit of the indigenous people who once inhabited the area. The little huts resembled the ones they saw at Pearl Farm Beach Resort.

The tour guide was quite knowledgeable of this integral, yet nearly forgotten, part of her country's history.

Said she, "The indigenous people of the southern part of the Philippines, or Lumad, as they prefer to be called, are a colorful and diverse group of peaceful citizens, who tragically are in danger of disappearing someday. In a hopeful attempt to preserve their culture, we remain dedicated to never stop telling their story to all visitors to this place."

The last stop was at a garden that grew a wide assortment of herbs, fruits, and vegetables, using state-of-the-art hydroponic technology. Essentially, this technology allowed crops and plants to grow virtually in the air without the use of soil or pesticides. Much of what was grown here was served in the park's restaurants.

After the tour, Ryan purchased souvenirs to take back to the States, and matching his and her T-shirts for himself and Liezel.

The expression on her face projected someone who'd just found the missing piece to making her life complete.

Her escalating jubilance caused even more guilt to snake through him. *Why am I doing this to her?* Ryan needed a diversion. "Let's eat, shall we?"

Liezel nodded yes.

They ambled inside Vista Restaurant for a buffet lunch. They filled their plates at the salad bar with lettuce and vegetables that were organically grown on the premises, then ventured outside to eat their meals. Peacocks and other birds roamed the grounds freely, taking scraps of food from anyone seated outside kind enough to feed them.

After they finished eating their salads, they moved onto the main course, and helped themselves to a variety of Asian dishes. A wide array of desserts completed their meal, from cakes to fresh fruit.

Just as Tipton was slowly pulling himself together, the family seated next to them started raving about how much they enjoyed the zip line. Ryan lowered his head in shame, as everything came crashing down on him again.

Liezel was one of the kindest, sweetest individuals he ever had the privilege of meeting. But the love he felt for Maricel was so strong, he could no longer fight it. Nor did he want to.

Absence really did make the heart grow fonder. Whether he was high up in the mountains or down by the water's edge, he couldn't stop thinking about his girlfriend in Manila. He yearned to see her again. *But how?*

If there was one thing Tipton learned on this trip to the Philippines, it's that all the money in the world couldn't compare to having the right person by your side.

When someone took the place of that special person, even someone as lovable as Liezel, it was impossible to feel anything close to completion.

Ryan did a little mental calculating and realized that at 45 years of age, he had been alive on this planet for roughly 2,340 weeks, and counting. Though only one of those weeks was spent with Maricel Arcamo, apparently it was enough, because she was suddenly the most important person in his universe.

Normally it took many weeks, months or even years to decide on a lifetime partner, but not this time. Maricel was the one...

"Are you okay, Ryan?"

Ryan snapped out of it. "I'm fine. Why do you ask?"

Liezel frowned. "You seem troubled. Did I do something to upset you?" She appeared to be on the verge of tears.

"Of course not." The puzzled look on her face ripped into Ryan deeply. He looked down at the table, unable to maintain steady eye contact with her. Because his heart burned so feverishly for Maricel, it ached for Liezel with the very same intensity.

Had he not gone to Manila first, he very easily could have fallen in love with her. Liezel was everything a man could want in a woman. In short: she was beautiful inside and out.

Ryan thought back to the few occasions in Cebu when he wanted to pound his chest for capturing someone as vivacious as Jenny. He didn't feel this way with Liezel.

If anything, he wanted to protect her now. The last thing he wanted was to hurt her. Yet he was about to do just that...

He prayed this wouldn't push her straight over the edge.

On the ride back to Davao City, a pleasant scent from the orchids that Ryan had purchased for Liezel wafted in the air, filling the bus with a heavenly scent. Other than that, nothing else seemed pleasant.

There was no sweet talk or handholding. The silence between them was deafening. Even worse, the joy he saw on Liezel's face the past two days was solemnly replaced with the same weary expression he saw at the airport, when they first met two days ago.

Tipton couldn't help but wonder in the darkness if the handful of public displays of affection he had showered upon her the past two days, was his way of preemptively apologizing for the broken heart he knew she would soon suffer?

He knew the answer. By not being honest at the outset, he gave her a false sense of hope by letting her think the door to his heart was open when, in reality, it was never open to begin with.

The fact that he met Maricel first meant Liezel had no chance with him. Ryan looked out the bus window, his eyes those of a man barely in control of his emotions. He was never more ashamed of himself. A lone tear rode down his left cheek.

I shouldn't be here now!

They arrived back in Davao City just after 9 p.m.

Depression kept snaking its way through Liezel, from one part of her body to the next. *Why is Ryan losing interest in me?*

That question would keep her awake much of the night with constant heart palpitations, as she tried not hating herself for falling in love again too quickly.

AT 6 P.M. THE FOLLOWING evening, Liezel found herself growing more desperate as the minutes passed. This was supposed to be the day that Ryan met her family. But she was unwilling to introduce someone she was still unsure about to her family, especially as a possible suitor.

Though she was still eager to take the next step with him, how could she when he was acting so differently? She was confused, hurt and even a little angry, all wrapped up into one.

Liezel wanted answers, needed them, felt entitled to them, but Ryan offered her nothing in this regard.

They spent most of the day inside Tipton's hotel room. The view from the 12th floor was spectacular, showcasing Davao Gulf and the majestic mountains out in the distance.

But Liezel couldn't enjoy it. The only time she glanced outside the window, was to hide from her American visitor that she was weeping again. For the life in her, she couldn't understand why he was acting so strangely. In a few short hours, it went from unbelievably perfect to nothing again, just like that.

Most men fortunate enough to be in his position would have tried making a move on her by now, several moves, in fact! But Ryan was too kind and respectful for that, and never pushy.

It only made her love him more...

At 8 p.m., Ryan said, "If we're going to meet your parents, we'd better get a move on."

"Perhaps next time," Liezel said softly, already sensing there wouldn't be a next time. She gazed outside the window trying to still her anxious heart. New tears streamed down her cheeks.

Ryan heard her sniffling and tried to comfort her. She politely refused his hugs, like she'd done all day.

After another agonizing hour had passed, they both knew it was time to call it a night.

Ryan escorted her home mostly in silence. Upon arriving, Liezel allowed him to hug her, but only to appease her parents, who were peeking through the front window.

Yes, she did it for them.

Tipton gazed deep into Liezel's eyes. "I'm sad this is our last day together."

"Hmm," was all she could say.

Ryan didn't push the issue. This was all his fault. He brought her all this way, only to pull the carpet out from underneath her in the end. He felt like the biggest jerk on the planet, especially since she'd already fallen in love with him. He could see it in her eyes.

He wanted to tell her he could have easily fallen in love with her too, and almost did, in fact, but knew his words would do more harm than good. "So, I'll see you in the morning?"

Liezel nodded yes, but very cautiously.

Ryan placed his hands on her shoulders, and felt her body trembling, all because of him. He cleared his throat and said, "Hope you have a nice evening."

Liezel forced a smile for her parents to see, but a few inches below her smile was a heart that was completely broken. "You too, Ryan. Good night."

The defense mechanism she had used to safeguard from another painful heartache had failed her again. She had fallen too hard and too fast this time. She felt completely gutted.

Everything inside told her to give up and just forget about Ryan Tipton, and dating altogether, at least for the time being. Yet when the sun rose, she knew she wouldn't hesitate to venture back to his hotel.

On the way back to the Marco Polo Hotel, Tipton felt like the worst person on the planet. The guilt he felt was excruciating. He was a breath away from completely coming apart at the seams.

He called Maricel back at the hotel. In the 20 minutes they spent on the phone, his heart raced so much, he thought it would burst out of his chest and find its way to his girlfriend in Manila, without the rest of his body.

He took a hot shower and settled into bed. If anyone needed sleep, it was him.

But sleep would come hard this night for Ryan Tipton…

14

AT 3 A.M., RYAN still couldn't sleep. How could he when his mind kept torturing him without a hint of mercy?

He climbed out of bed, got dressed, then rode the stealthy elevator down to the hotel lobby, where he paced the spacious lobby floor at a feverish pace—back and forth, back and forth he went, a restless spirit leading the way.

"Is everything okay, sir?" asked the late-night shift manager.

"I honestly don't know how to answer that question," Tipton replied somberly. "But thanks for the concern. I appreciate it."

"You're welcome, sir. Hope everything turns out okay."

"Me too." Ryan knew if he kept these thoughts of shame and despair all to himself, he might implode. He reached inside his pants pocket for his cell phone. To his surprise, the business card advertising *Agape Coffee and Pastry Shoppe* was stuck to the back of it.

Out of sheer desperation, Tipton placed a frantic call to Ernesto Angeles at his home.

"Hello?" The coffee shop owner's voice was groggy after just being roused from a deep sleep.

"Hi, Mister Angeles. It's Ryan Tipton."

Ernesto suppressed a yawn. "Hi, Ryan. Funny you should call. Gloria and I prayed for you before going to bed. How are you?"

"I've been better. Sorry for waking you."

"Think nothing of it. I often receive calls at this late hour from those in need of prayer. So, what can I do for you?"

"I was hoping you could give me some advice."

"What exactly do you need advice on, Ryan?"

Tipton sighed. "Women, mostly."

Ernesto gently rubbed the sleep build-up from his eyes. "Ahh."

"I also want you to know I'm still in the Philippines."

Ernesto couldn't contain the shock on his face, even if Ryan couldn't see it. "I thought you went back to the States last week?"

Tipton gasped into the phone. "Maricel doesn't know I'm still here."

Ernesto thought back to how strangely Ryan had acted last week before leaving for the airport. *Thank You, Father, for this wonderful opportunity to further your Mission here on earth, even at this late hour.* "Where are you now, Ryan?"

"The Marco Polo Hotel, in Davao City."

"Nice place. Gloria and I stayed there a few years ago."

"Yes, but in truth, it's impossible to enjoy the beauty of your country, after what I did to Maricel."

"Are you visiting another woman there?"

Ryan took a deep breath and exhaled. "Yes. A girl named Liezel."

"I see." Ernesto paused, searching for the right words to say. "You seem like a nice man, Ryan. I'm sure you didn't come here to intentionally hurt anyone. But here's the problem; if you were as loving toward Liezel as you were with Maricel last week, I'm sure she's also developed strong feelings for you by now."

"You're right." Ryan let out another audible gasp. "I also met a girl named Jenny in Cebu before coming to Davao. I feel despicable."

Ernesto sat up in bed, suddenly wide awake. "Not to come across as judgmental, young man, but I would feel awful too, if I were trying to juggle three women all at once, knowing two of them will eventually get hurt in the end.

"This is a huge problem in my country. Because of the stark poverty found throughout much of the Philippines, it's easy for foreigners visiting here to meet with scores of beautiful women, with little or no strings attached.

"Many take full advantage of them, by filling their heads and hearts with promises of a better future. Many of these women end up falling for the first foreigner who shows an interest in them, and quickly pledge their undying love to that person, without first getting to know him better. This isn't always the case, but I'm afraid it's starting to become more of a frequent occurrence."

Tipton rubbed his throbbing head. "Yeah, I've noticed."

"But all too often, it turns out to be nothing more than a bunch of empty promises in the end, which always leads to heartache for so many women here."

"I see," came the weary reply.

Ernesto frowned. "Of course, I'm mindful of the growing number of Filipino women who constantly scheme up new ways to extort money from foreigners. As a Filipino, it greatly disappoints me knowing they are just as bad as some of the men traveling here.

"It's a vicious cycle that keeps repeating itself, that I would love to see broken someday. Until it is broken, instead of rushing into new relationships, youngsters need to be more patient, especially when meeting foreigners online."

Ernesto paused to take a small sip of water from the glass he kept on the end table next to his bed each night. "But I can say this; I am one-hundred percent certain that Maricel is one of the good girls."

Tipton sighed. "I knew it the moment I first met her."

"You must never forget, Ryan, that a woman's heart is so much more tender and fragile than the heart God chose to plant inside us men. It's evident to me that her heart beats strongly for you and no one else.

"I could see it in her eyes when the two of you were together. If only you'll look beyond her outer beauty and see how beautiful she is on the inside, you'll quickly realize how blessed you are to have someone like her care for you the way she does."

Ryan took a breath and exhaled deeply. "That's why I can't sleep. It's like I'm punishing these women for what other women did to me in the past. Part of the reason I was so eager to visit your country, is that I've always had difficulty meeting women in Iowa. From a physical standpoint, I'm not much to look at."

"By whose standards are you referring?"

"I can't tell you how many times I've been rejected by women in the past. Too many to count. When I joined that Asian dating site six months ago, I never expected anyone to show an interest in me, especially someone as beautiful as Maricel, not to mention the two other women I've met."

Ernesto interjected, "You mean Jenny and Liezel, right?"

"Yes."

"I feel it's always best to address people by their names. It helps us to see them more as people rather than objects."

Ryan swallowed back a pang of guilt. "You make a good point."

"Anyway, please continue, Ryan."

"Like I was saying, I was a complete nobody back in Iowa. Now this? Three beautiful women in two weeks' time? Frankly, it still boggles my mind."

Ernesto yawned into his fist. "I understand your dilemma, but do you think your past relationship struggles back home, gives you the right to take the hearts of three of our women hostage now?"

"Hmm." A stronger pang of guilt shot through Tipton's body.

"With all due respect, Ryan, I don't think it's fair to turn their lives into a contest of sorts, until you finally decide which one is right for you. Finding true love doesn't work that way. So, please, stop punishing our women like this, especially Maricel."

Ryan was taken aback by Ernesto's willingness to protect Maricel. He hardly knew the woman. "May I ask why you seem so interested in protecting her?"

"As a child of God, I feel it's my duty to do all I can to protect those in need. Besides, Maricel's worth protecting. She's a lovely young woman who's already developed strong feelings for you."

Ryan grimaced. "I have strong feelings for her too. That's why I called you."

Ernesto paused a moment and scratched his head. "Pardon me for saying this, Ryan, but if your feelings were genuine and true, you wouldn't be meeting other women behind her back. Do you think she's meeting other men now that you're gone?"

"No."

"How would you feel if she was?"

"Honestly, I wouldn't like it."

"Do you think it's fair for you to do such things, while she remains faithful to you?"

Tipton gasped into the phone, then gulped in more air. "Of course, not. I'm so ashamed of myself."

"It seems that you were caught in a trap of your own making, Ryan. Question is, what will you do about it?"

"What should I do?"

"Do you really love Maricel?"

Tipton cleared the lump in his throat. "It sure feels that way."

What kind of answer is that! "Let me ask you something, Ryan."

"Sure. Go right ahead."

"If you knew you only had twenty-four hours to live, who would you want by your side?"

"Wow! That's a deep question!"

"I want you to really think about that, young man. It's of vital importance."

Ryan rubbed his throbbing forehead again. "I need to ask again; why are you so interested in protecting Maricel? You act like you're her grandfather or something."

Ernesto chuckled. "No, I'm not her, 'lolo', as we say here in my country." He paused to take a deep breath. It was time. "I guess you could say she sort of reminds me of my late daughter, Jecelyn."

Late daughter? "I'm sorry," came the remorseful reply.

"It's okay. It happened long ago. My wife and I were blessed with four lovely children, three daughters and a son. Our son, Jason, lives here in Manila with his wife and four children.

"Our three daughters are no longer in the Philippines. Our youngest daughter, Lorelie, is happily married to a fine man from Canada. They live in Toronto and have two daughters.

"Our middle daughter, Elvie, is also happily married to a fine man from Sydney, Australia. They have five precious children and visit us once a year."

"Wow, so many grandchildren."

"We thank God each day for them." Ernesto grew more serious. He shifted his weight on the bed and went on, "Our oldest daughter, Jecelyn, well..." The old man started sniffling.

Ryan winced, fearing what would come out of his mouth next.

Ernesto said, "She took her life twenty years ago."

"Oh my!" Tipton's heart throbbed in his chest.

There was an awkward silence for what seemed an eternity, before Ernesto was finally able to speak again. "The worst part is she did it all because of a broken heart."

Tipton's heart pounded in his chest. "What do you mean?"

"My wife and I did our best to raise our four children in a Godly fashion. Of course, we had many ups and downs along the way. Like many families here, we were poor. But the love we shared for each other more than compensated for the absence of riches.

"We struggled mightily at times finding ways to clothe and feed our children. Believe me when I say, we oftentimes had just barely enough food to eat. But our house was always full of love, even despite our dire situation."

Ernesto paused a moment then said, "Needless to say, the biggest tragedy we faced as a family was coping with Jecelyn's suicide. The worst part was Gloria and I felt it was somehow our fault, that we'd failed to raise her properly. No matter how hard we tried to accept it for what it was, we kept blaming ourselves."

Ryan remained silent, so Ernesto continued.

"You need to know Jecelyn wasn't the suicidal type. She loved life! All she ever wanted was to love and be loved in return. When she was twenty-seven, she found the man of her dreams. He was an American man in his mid-forties, just like you. We liked Kevin instantly and embraced him with open arms. Everyone was convinced the love they shared was genuine and true.

"On his second trip to Manila, he came for the sole purpose of proposing to Jecelyn. It was the happiest time of her life. The day Kevin was scheduled to fly back to the States, we all went to the airport to see him off. Naturally, Jecelyn was sad. But just knowing he would be coming back soon to marry her gave her the strength to keep from falling apart.

"The following day, Jecelyn heard about a bridal gown expo at the Landmark Mall, in Makati. She practically dragged her two sisters there to help her start searching for the perfect wedding dress. That day turned out to be the worst day of her life, and ultimately the beginning of the end for my precious daughter."

Ernesto's voice quivered as new tears formed in his eyes. "As the elevator doors opened to take my three daughters down to the ground floor level, Kevin suddenly appeared inside the elevator car, with his arms wrapped tightly around another woman."

Tipton's knees started shaking. Now that he had pretty much done the same thing to Maricel, he felt an even stronger pang of guilt rising up inside. He bit his lower lip and kept listening.

"Kevin completely ignored my daughter as if she was a perfect stranger. According to Elvie and Lorelie, he left without saying a word to Jecelyn. He had a faraway expression on his face.

124

"Imagine that? The woman he was engaged to be married to? Talk about a jolt to the system! Believe me when I say, she wore that ring he placed on her finger proudly."

There was another prolonged silence. Ryan searched his mind for something to say, anything to ease the awkwardness, but found nothing. He almost didn't want Ernesto to continue. He remained silent.

"As you might imagine," the older Filipino man finally said, "my daughter collapsed to the floor. After a while, Elvie and Lorelie were finally able to help her to her feet and take her home. A few days later, she wrote us a farewell letter, and another one she asked us to mail to Kevin, along with the engagement ring he gave to her. After that, she climbed into bed and slit both of her wrists."

Ryan held his free hand up to his mouth. "Oh my..."

Tears trickled down Ernesto's sun-darkened, wrinkly face. "You've never lost a child, Ryan, so you can't begin to imagine how painful it is. It made all our past struggles my wife and I faced in our forty-eight years of marriage seem like nothing. And for what, a broken heart? How unfair is that?"

Ryan gasped into the phone again. His knees felt like jelly. "My heart aches for you all."

"I appreciate your concern, Ryan. But what you need to understand is something I've already shared with you. Jecelyn wasn't the suicidal type. Few people cherished life as much as she did. She was a hopeless romantic, and quite the adventurous type.

"She gave everything to Kevin in the form of a commitment. Yet in the end, he wasn't serious about her after all. If he was, why would he feel the need to find comfort in the arms of another woman, no less a few days after asking for my daughter's hand in marriage?"

Ernesto sighed. "As long as I live, I'll never figure that one out. Only a heartless man would ever think to do such a thing. A selfish man. Well, Kevin's cruel self-centered actions served to rid the world of a kind and beautiful soul."

Ernesto started sobbing so loudly, it roused Gloria from a deep sleep. She sat up in bed and gently rubbed her husband's back. Even 20 years later, he still trembled inside whenever he thought back to that tragic moment in time.

Ryan wanted to say something, but no words came out of his mouth. His mind was anything but silent. It raced with numerous thoughts. More than anything, he wanted to be with Maricel now.

Ernesto continued in a much softer, sadder tone of voice. "You see, Ryan, most men visiting my country are totally unaware that when Filipino women make a commitment to love someone, that commitment usually stands the test of time.

"On the flip side, whenever they suffer the kind of heartache my daughter was subjected to, each replay punctures fresh holes in their already fragile hearts, pushing some straight over the edge.

"I speak from experience when I say women tend to commit far more easily in relationships than us men. When my daughters were teenagers and started dating, they taught me so much about how women interacted with the boys they develop feelings for.

"Regardless of the length of relationship, whenever one of my daughters felt betrayed by someone, it always came as a complete shock to their system."

Ernesto sighed. "Once a woman feels she has nothing to live for, some no longer see the point of remaining on this cruel and oftentimes heartless planet. Tragically, Jecelyn became part of that grim statistic."

Tears flooded Tipton's eyes. Even though he never met Jecelyn, he felt partly responsible for her suicide. "I'm sorry, Ernesto. I don't know what to say."

Ernesto sniffled. "It's okay, Ryan. None of what I've just shared with you is your fault. Nevertheless, I feel the need to ask again; what are your true intentions with Maricel? Do you really love her? If not, please do us all a favor and be honest with her before it's too late. It's still early enough in the relationship to let her down gently.

"The last thing I want is to see her travel down the same road Jecelyn was forced to travel, all because of a broken heart. On some levels, her life is sort of in your hands. Which leads me back to my question; if you knew you only had twenty-four hours left to live, who would you want by your side?"

Maricel! "You're absolutely right, Ernesto! I really am blessed to have someone like her love a man like me."

"If you really mean it, you must come clean and tell her that you're still in the Philippines. No more lies. She deserves to hear the truth from you, from this point forward."

Ryan's eyes doubled in size. "Right now?"

"Of course, not at this late hour. But I believe you should tell her before you leave for America."

"What if she ends up hating me and never speaks to me again?"

"At this point, it's a risk you must be willing to take. If it's meant to be, it will be. If not, she never was yours to begin with, right?"

"Hmm."

"Do you respect Maricel enough to be honest with her?"

"Yes. I'm only afraid of what may follow. The last thing I want is to hurt her."

Ernesto glanced over at his wife. "I'm happy to hear you say that, Ryan. Perhaps you really do love her after all."

"I do. Your question merely confirmed what I've felt all week. If I only had twenty-four hours left to live, I would want Maricel by my side, no one else. Thanks for making it crystal clear to me."

"Gloria and I think you make a nice couple. If you're able to overcome this obstacle, I believe your relationship has a chance to blossom into something special, despite your recent actions. But first things first. You must tell her the truth. It won't be easy, young man, but just know we'll be praying for you."

"Thanks for all the good advice you gave me."

"My pleasure, Ryan. Let me know how things work out."

Tipton frowned. "I will."

"Hope you have a safe flight back to the U.S. for real this time," Ernesto said, trying to lighten the mood a bit. "Stop by the coffee shop whenever you're in Manila."

"I'll be sure to do that."

"May God continue to richly bless you."

"You, as well, Ernesto."

At that, the call ended. Tipton rode the elevator back up to his room on the 12th floor. With so much guilt and shame carving away on his insides, he was surprised he could still walk.

He sat on the bed and grimaced. *This won't be easy...*

15

RYAN TIPTON WAS AWAKENED by the soft knocking on his hotel room door. At first, he thought it was housekeeping.

He pried open his left eye and glanced at the clock: 7:57 a.m. *Too early for housekeeping.*

When the banging persisted, Tipton lowered his feet onto the floor and wrapped a bed sheet around himself to conceal that he was wearing boxers only. He felt hung over, mostly due to sleep deprivation.

You know you're in for a rough day when you wake up already feeling completely overwhelmed. The look on his face was one of someone being dragged away to the guillotine.

He opened the door. It was Liezel. "Good morning," Ryan said wearily. His eyes were bloodshot from a severe lack of sleep. They were distant, troubled. "You're here early."

"Since it's our last day, I wanted to spend as much time with you as possible," Liezel said, nervously. The hint of a smile she'd forced onto her face quickly faded. "Am I disturbing you?"

"Not at all. Please come in," he said, rather clinically. Their eyes met but Ryan couldn't hold her gaze. He looked away and scratched his head.

Liezel took a few deep breaths and tried shrugging off her uneasiness. But how could she when Ryan didn't even offer her a hug this time? Not wanting to betray how vulnerable she felt, she needed a diversion. "May I use your shower? We don't have hot water at home."

"Sure, go right ahead."

Closing the bathroom door, Liezel's mind was haunted with one question; *what did I do that was so terrible that he no longer wants me around?* It was a question for which she had no logical answer.

With this being her fourth failed attempt with foreign men this year alone, the 24-year-old woman felt used up, unlovable. Sure, men showed interest in her all the time, but most only wanted her body, not her heart. That wasn't true love. She felt empty inside.

The moment Liezel turned the water on, Ryan reached for his phone. It could wait no longer. His limbs quaked.

"Magandang gabi, Ryan!" Maricel said, seeing his name appear on her mobile phone screen. "We're eating one of the pineapples we brought back from Tagaytay."

"I see," Ryan said glumly. By far, this was going to be the most difficult conversation of his life.

Maricel sensed that something was wrong. "Is everything okay, sweetie?"

"No. But I hope after we talk it will be."

Maricel's heart rate accelerated. "What do you mean?"

Tipton sighed. "I'm still in the Philippines."

There was total silence, until Maricel finally found her voice to speak. "Why are you still in my country, Ryan? I thought you went home last week. I even saw you off at the airport."

"I never went back to the States." Tipton bit his lower lip. "I went to Cebu. I'm in Davao City now."

Maricel choked back tears. "Did you visit other women?"

Ryan closed his eyes and braced himself. "Yes."

Maricel felt a sharp pain in her heart, like she'd just been stabbed with a knife. Nausea swam through her body. "Why didn't you just tell me, Ryan. I feel so stupid!" Tears streamed down her cheeks one after the next.

Hazel was in the kitchen preparing breakfast and heard her daughter weeping. Which could only mean one thing: Ryan Tipton, of all people, had been unfaithful to her.

"I'm sorry for lying to you, Maricel. I'm so ashamed of myself. I called Ernesto Angeles from Agape Coffee and Pastry Shoppe at three o'clock this morning. I told him everything."

Ryan heard her sniffling. "I know how betrayed you must feel. But if you give me a second chance, I promise I'll never do it again."

Maricel started hyperventilating. She felt her wounded heart pounding straight through her shirt. She lowered herself down onto the floor. "I feel so foolish for meeting you."

"Please don't say that. You did nothing wrong. It's all my fault."

"How could you do this to me? To us?" she cried. "I thought we had something special!" Maricel wanted to lie down on the floor, curl up and never stop crying.

Hazel stopped what she was doing to console her daughter.

Ryan's hands started trembling. "I'm sorry, Maricel."

Her sobs grew louder. Hazel sat next to her daughter and wrapped her arms tightly around her.

After a few moments of silence, Maricel said, "And to think all those times you called me, you were meeting other women. I can't believe you did this to me! Now I know why you wouldn't let me see you on camera all those times. I'm sure your phone battery was perfectly fine. I need to go. Hope you're happy together!"

Maricel ended the call. In a fit of anger, she shouted the words, "Umalis ka (Go away!), Ryan Tipton," then threw her phone to the ground hoping it would shatter to pieces. She was unsuccessful.

Without saying a word to her mother, she picked herself up off the floor and fled up the stairs to her bedroom. Locking the door behind her, she leaned against it and shook uncontrollably.

A rush of shock devoured her, wave after painful wave, seemingly changing her heartbeat in the process. She did her best to draw deep breaths. She couldn't think; she could only feel.

And what she felt was total devastation. The world suddenly seemed to be spinning the wrong way. Thankfully, her sister, Vivian, with whom she shared this room, was downstairs.

Meanwhile, Ryan stared blankly at the wall in his hotel room, trembling uncontrollably. He called Maricel's mobile phone again. As it rang, visions of last week danced inside his head, occupying every square inch of his mind; from the moment he first laid eyes on her at the airport in Manila, to meeting her wonderful family on their first full day together, which ultimately led to their first kiss.

Even the tearful embrace they shared at the airport, when he supposedly flew back to the U.S., loomed large in his troubled mind.

After four rings, it went to voice mail. "Maricel, from the bottom of my heart, I'm sorry for lying to you. Can you please find it in your heart to forgive me?" Tipton reached for a breath. "I'll be back in Manila in a couple hours and will be going to Agape Coffee and Pastry Shoppe. I'd love to see you there, so I can apologize in person for what I did. Hope to see you there. Mahal kita, Maricel. I'm one-hundred percent sure of it. Bye for now."

Liezel finished showering and rejoined Ryan. He was sitting on the edge of the bed, wiping tears from his eyes.

"Are you okay, Ryan?"

"No, I shouldn't be here with you, Liezel."

After the way he'd acted of late, she wasn't completely caught off guard by his sudden posture change. "Are you married?"

"No. But I am in love with someone. A woman I met last week in Manila."

Liezel lowered her head; her shoulders slumped.

"Sorry for my dishonesty. I'll understand if you hate me too."

Liezel's voice trembled, "I don't hate you. I'm used to it."

Her words ripped through him like a hot knife in butter. Tears filled Tipton's eyes. "You're one of the most remarkable women I've ever had the privilege of meeting. I hope you can forgive me."

Liezel clung to the plastic bag in her arms which held her dirty clothes. "I should go now."

"Can I do anything for you?"

"No. I can manage on my own."

"Don't forget your pasalubong…"

"Keep it. I no longer want it." Her shoulders slumped again.

Ryan sniffled. "I never meant to hurt you."

Liezel ignored his words and walked out the door with her head down. "Please God, no more," she cried, her lips quivering.

In the short time it took her to leave the hotel, something cold started in the center of her chest before attacking the rest of her limbs. Again.

Ryan Tipton thought he was going to die which, right now, sounded like a fair proposition; especially if it helped ease the overwhelming pain and shame he felt. "I need to get out of here!"

After a quick shower, Tipton took the shuttle to the airport. Every few minutes, like a robot obeying a command, he called Maricel. It went to voice mail each time. He also sent a few text messages, but to no avail.

Ryan also messaged Liezel, apologizing again for what he did to her. She, too, never replied.

To avoid going completely insane, Ryan called Ernesto Angeles.

"Agape Coffee and Pastry Shoppe, this is Ernesto, how can I help you?"

"Hi Mister Angeles, it's Ryan Tipton."

"Good morning, young man. How did it go with Maricel?"

"Not so good, I'm afraid. I think she hates me."

"Time will tell. At the very least, she'll need time to process it all. But just know in your heart that you did the right thing by coming clean with her. If more foreigners visiting my country were like you, life would be a whole lot easier to manage here. Let's just hope in time Maricel will come to see it that way for herself."

"Thanks for the encouraging words. But I don't feel any better."

Ernesto understood how he felt. "You'll be fine in time, young man. Have a safe flight to Manila. Godspeed."

On the flight to Manila, Tipton's mind tortured him nonstop. You spend enough time alone with your thoughts and eventually your mind turns inward and feasts on you. He couldn't help but wonder if he did the right thing by coming clean with Maricel, and telling her everything. Right now, it sure didn't feel that way.

Before he opened his big mouth, only Jenny, Liezel, his parents, and a few friends and co-workers knew he was still in the Philippines. This equated to 20 people out of 8,000,000,000. No one else on the planet had a clue. Nor would they be interested in knowing about some dishonest security guard from Iowa, having relationship problems with three women in the Philippines.

As the plane began its initial descent into Ninoy Aquino International Airport, Tipton was seized by a single thought: would Maricel end up like Jecelyn, and commit suicide all because of him? If it ever came to that, perhaps he would take his own life as well.

Tipton turned on his cell phone and called Maricel. As expected, it went to voice mail again. "Hi Maricel. Just arrived in Manila. I hope to be at the coffee shop by four. I'll need to leave for the airport no later than five-thirty. Hope to see you there. I have so much to tell you. Mahal kita."

He then called Ernesto Angeles. "Hi, Mister Angeles. Just landed a few minutes ago. I meant to ask you earlier, but would it be okay if I stopped by to see you before my flight to Tokyo?"

"Why would you ever feel the need to ask that question?"

"Normally I wouldn't, but as you can imagine, I'm not myself. I feel like the worst person on the planet."

"I understand how you feel, young man."

"I just left a message with Maricel asking her to meet me there. Do you think she'll show up?"

Ernesto scratched his scalp. "Whether she does or not, Gloria and I look forward to seeing you again."

"Good, because I really need a friend to lean on now."

"Well then, you're in luck—you have two friends here."

"Salamat, po. Hope to see you soon."

Tipton ended the call and went outside to hail a cab. The driver took one look at his new passenger and sensed he was on the verge of completely losing it. He didn't know how right he was...

16

AT 4:15 P.M., RYAN Tipton arrived at Agape Coffee and Pastry Shoppe. He did a quick scan looking for Maricel but didn't see her.

Gloria was just finishing with a customer and noticed him. It had been a while since she saw someone looking so somber stricken. The shame chiseled onto his face was unmistakable.

She greeted him with an endearing smile. If anyone needed it, it was him. "Welcome back, Ryan! How was the flight?"

Tipton took an empty seat at the small counter. "Fine, thanks. Just wish I could say the same about myself. Can't stop wondering if she'll show up."

Gloria grabbed a large foam cup and poured fresh-brewed coffee inside for Ryan. "Cream and two sugars, right?"

"Yes, please." Ryan reached into his pocket for money.

"It's on the house."

Tipton wanted to protest but knew he wouldn't win. "Salamat sa kape, Gloria. Very kind of you."

Gloria raised an eyebrow and nodded her head. "Wow! Ang galing mong magtagalog!"

"Whatever you just said, I'm afraid I didn't understand it."

"I said your Tagalog is good."

Ryan shook his head. "I wouldn't go that far. All I know are the few words Maricel taught me."

"You're off to a good start! Never stop learning."

Tipton sighed. "In all honesty, Gloria, I can't think about learning Tagalog now. I've never felt so despicable in all my life."

"Relax and enjoy your coffee. Everything will be fine in time."

"I appreciate your kindness, but I feel I don't deserve it."

Gloria smiled. "Thankfully, the God I serve is a God of second chances. And third. And fourth. And fifth."

Ryan took a small sip of his coffee. "For my sake, I hope so."

"We all fall short from time to time, and make our share of mistakes on the long and winding road called life. Which means we all need God's constant mercy and forgiveness."

Ryan frowned. "I understand all that. But when our sins end up hurting others, it's much more difficult to cope with."

"That's true, Ryan. But you mustn't forget that when we sin and hurt others, we mostly hurt God's heart. Yet, He freely forgives all who truly repent and trust in Jesus as Lord and Savior."

"I know God will forgive me. Just hope Maricel will too."

Gloria smiled faintly. "At least you admitted your wrongdoings to her *before* you were caught in the act. In my book, that's always a good first step. Even if she doesn't show up today, don't lose hope. Maricel may need a little time to come to grips with it all."

Tipton's shoulders slumped. "I sure hope you're right."

Ernesto walked through the small kitchen door carrying a tray full of just-baked cherry pastries. "Ryan! I thought I heard your voice. Welcome back! How are you holding up?"

"Not too good. Feels like I'm having a sustained anxiety attack."

The pain in Ryan's eyes was unmistakable. He was a broken man. Ernesto placed the pastries in the display case and grabbed a bottle of water. "Grab your coffee and follow me."

The coffee shop owner led Ryan to a vacant corner table.

Tipton raised his hands above his head and stretched them as high as they would go. "Sorry again for calling you so late last night, and for causing you to relive the pain of losing your daughter."

"No need to apologize. Besides, you knew nothing about that tragic time in our lives."

"Even so, it was selfish of me to call so late. Usually when it comes to love, I'm the victim. Suddenly, like you rightly said on the phone, I'm the perpetrator. I know I deserve to feel this way."

Tipton did all he could to ignore the pictures of the many happy couples hanging on the walls. Seeing them pushed him even deeper into the hole he'd dug for himself this week. Yet, despite all that, the same warm sensation he felt rising up from the floorboards on his first two visits, was just as present now.

Ryan leaned up in his chair. It could wait no longer. "Why does this place remind me more of a church than a coffee shop?"

Ernesto beamed. "You're not the first person to ask that question. This place has become a church for many over the years. Whatever one calls it, Gloria and I feel blessed that we get to fulfill our joint mission here."

"Joint mission?"

"Yes. The first part is to do all we can to help struggling young couples realize how blessed they are to have each other. The grass isn't always greener on the other side. In fact, it's often worse."

Ryan sighed, then lowered his head. "Don't I know it!"

"The second part is protecting Filipino women from becoming potential suicide victims like our precious daughter, Jecelyn. Not to sound insensitive, Ryan, but our focus is mostly on those meeting with foreigners."

Ernesto pointed to one of the walls. "As you can see, God has allowed us to positively impact many Filipino women and their foreign counterparts over the years.

"As you rightly guessed, Ryan, the coffee we serve has little to do with what you see on their faces. Funny thing is, we never asked anyone to send us photographs. But they kept coming. One turned into two, then three. Next thing you know, we had a photo album full of pictures of couples we've helped along the way.

"After accumulating fifty or so, Gloria started hanging them on that wall over there," Ernesto said, pointing to his left.

"According to her, it made no sense to keep them in envelopes or in photo albums. She eventually called it our 'International Wall of Love'.

"A few years later, it was completely full of pictures, so she started hanging pictures on that wall over there, and the name was changed to our 'International Walls of Love.'"

Tipton shook his head in amazement. "Simply incredible."

"I know it's a little outdated in this high-tech world in which we live, but it works for us."

Ryan waived his comment off. "I wouldn't change a thing."

"Now that three of our walls are full of photographs, each has a specific theme. That wall over there, for instance, is reserved for those who are happily married. That one's reserved for those who are engaged. And that one's for those who are still in the developmental stages."

Ryan flashed a weary smile. Suddenly the warm sensation intensified. It was as if Ernesto, feeling his deep pain, turned the "Love Throttle", or whatever it was, on full blast just for him.

Tipton wanted to say, "How'd you do that?" He remained silent and bathed in it.

Noticing his change of expression, Ernesto silently praised God for making His presence known, even if his American friend was still unaware of the Source.

"Long before we went into the coffee business, Gloria and I randomly visited coffeehouses, internet cafes and various hotels throughout Metro Manila, looking for opportunities to have a positive impact. Some of the couples you see on our walls we met long before we opened the coffee shop. We still maintain close contact to this day."

Ryan looked up from his coffee cup and gazed deep into Ernesto's eyes. "You and Gloria are two of the nicest people I've ever known. I wish there were more people like you in the world."

"Glory to God," Ernesto said. "After we had ample time to grieve our daughter's suicide, we realized for true healing to take place, we needed to find a purpose to Jecelyn's untimely death. Naturally, the first step was to protect our two youngest daughters to make sure they didn't travel down that same destructive path."

Ernesto took a sip of water. "Like I told you on the phone last night, our daughters are both married to foreigners. Gloria and I couldn't be happier with the faithful husbands God blessed Elvie and Lorelie with. In fact, they're the ones responsible for this coffee shop."

Ryan raised an eyebrow. "Really? How?"

Ernesto nodded at him. "When Randy and Simon, our sons-in-law, became aware of what we were doing, they both wanted to help make our wish a reality. Both called it a 'much-needed' mission in the Philippines. Quite frankly, we paid them little mind at first.

"On their next trip here, Randy and Simon said they wanted to provide funding for us to start a business in Manila, something that would allow us to interact with many people each day. They said if we impacted just one person the way we did with them, every penny invested would be well worth it."

Ryan let his eyes wander the shop again. "How right they were."

"It was an exciting time for us. Our first thought was to open an internet café somewhere in downtown Manila. After praying about it for many weeks on end, we never felt God pulling us in that direction. People go to internet cafes to chat online, not socialize. Not only that, since most people now use mobile phones to go online, internet cafés are quickly becoming a thing of the past.

"My wife suggested one day that we open a coffee and pastry shop. I immediately loved the idea. Randy and Simon did too. A few months later, even though we knew we'd face stiff competition, we retired from our jobs and Agape Coffee and Pastry Shoppe officially opened its doors to the public. That was twelve years ago."

Ryan took a sip of coffee. "Looks like business has been good."

"Indeed, it has been. But we didn't open this place hoping to become wealthy. We have meager needs and don't need much to live on. We're here for one reason—to make an impact in the lives of others, plain and simple!"

Tipton nodded his head. "It's quite a calling you have."

"Though we're never open on Sundays, Gloria and I come here each week after church for our three p.m. Bible study. Then at six p.m., we offer free character-building classes to singles in the area."

Tipton raised a curious eyebrow. "What kind of character-building classes do you teach?"

Ernesto took a small sip of water. "Basically, that in order to find the right person, they first need to be the right person. We then share Godly principles to help them become just that—the right person!"

Ryan grimaced. "I think that's a lesson everyone needs to learn. Especially me."

Ernesto nodded thoughtfully. "Mostly due to loneliness and despair, many youngsters online these days willingly lower their standards and compromise the core values they were taught growing up, just to feel loved by someone. The end result is that they usually settle for someone they know deep down inside isn't the right one for them, especially as a potential lifetime partner."

"Do you have these classes every week?"

Ernesto nodded yes. "The response has been overwhelmingly positive. So much so that attendees must reserve seats weeks in advance."

Ryan was stunned hearing this. "Wow! Really?"

"Let's face it, Ryan, pain is pain. And for most, it escalates during the holidays. Since God is in the broken business, that puts us in the broken business too. With that in mind, our doors remain open even on holidays, for those who are hurting and need someplace to escape to for a while. You'd be surprised what a few hours in a safe haven, with a hot cup of coffee or soup can do for someone."

"What can I say? I'm blown away!"

"To God be the glory, Ryan."

It was time to level with Ernesto. "I never told you this, but the first time I came here with Maricel, I felt this warm, comforting sensation washing over me. I've felt it every time since, including now. I tried telling you last time I was here, but I felt foolish. Something tells me I'm not the first person to tell you this."

Ernesto's face lit up. "You're right; you're not the first to say that. Gloria and I like to think what you're feeling is a *Trace Residue* carrying over from the Christian love that flows so freely in here each Sunday."

Ryan leaned back on his chair and stretched his hands above his head. "Well, you've certainly had a profound impact on my life."

"Randy and Simon will be thrilled to hear we have another grateful beneficiary of their kind generosity. Not only did they fund this place for us, but whenever we treat someone to coffee, bread, or pastries, they insist on reimbursing us for the cost of it.

"Even after all these years, they refuse to take no for an answer. Gloria and I couldn't imagine being blessed with two better sons-in-law. Both are remarkable humanitarians."

Ryan held out his hands in mock protest. "Don't sell yourselves short. You and Gloria are remarkable humanitarians yourselves! I'm sure you've impacted their lives even more than you can imagine. Who wouldn't want in-laws like you?"

Whenever Ernesto heard such things, another small morsel of the pain he'd carried inside his heart for 20 years was removed.

"Do you mind if I ask you something, Ernesto?"

"Sure. Go right ahead," the old man answered.

"What would you consider to be the most vital step to laying a solid foundation for any lasting relationship?"

"That's easy. Each relationship must be rooted in Christ Jesus. When couples exchange vows and become husband and wife, it isn't always easy coexisting under the same roof.

Marriage can be extremely trying at times. This includes my marriage.

"But having Jesus at the center gives us confidence that everything will be okay, despite our daily encounters. I don't know how anyone can survive a single day on this crazy planet, without trusting in Jesus to lead every step of the way. This is especially true in marriage."

Ryan shifted uncomfortably in his seat.

Ernesto noticed and asked. "Have you ever been married?"

Tipton was taken aback by the question. He gulped hard. "Yes. Many years ago. Didn't last long. Came home from work one night to find my wife in bed with another man."

Ernesto shook his head sadly. "I can only imagine how betrayed you must have felt."

"You can say that again." Tipton folded his hands on the table. "It faded in time, especially after I realized she was just using me to get her green card. She never loved me."

"Does Maricel know about this?"

Ryan nodded yes.

"Was she a Filipino woman?"

"No. She was from Colombia, South America."

Ernesto steadied his gaze on Ryan. "Like I said on the phone last night, betrayal really does go both ways, especially in this self-centered, fast-paced world we find ourselves living in. Even as we speak, there are many women out there doing all sorts of bad things to us men. Sadly, you got to experience first-hand that it happens in all countries, not only here."

Ryan nodded yes.

"But speaking to you man-to-man, in most cases, I believe men are still more to blame for the far-reaching heartache in our world, than our female counterparts. Sometimes when I'm alone, I think of the countless millions of women out there who cry themselves to sleep each night from broken hearts. It frightens me to think how many are considering ending their lives this very moment."

Ernesto looked down at the table and shook his head. "Imagine that? So many of God's cherished creations contemplating taking their lives. What could be more tragic than that? If Gloria and I can prevent just one person from going down that soul-shredding destructive path, we've done a good thing indeed."

Ryan closed his eyes and lowered his head in shame.

Ernesto noticed and backpedaled. "At least you came clean and told Maricel everything. Not only does this speak to your good character, it proves you really do care for her after all."

"I still feel despicable for what I did to her."

"Well, like I said last night, so many foreigners come here for the sole purpose of having fun with our women. Nothing more. They leave the Philippines with smiles on their faces and a trail of broken promises in their wake.

"Though you started out just like them, whether Maricel ultimately forgives you and takes you back or not, you still did the right thing by telling her the truth. I'm proud of you!"

"Thanks, Ernesto. Just hope she'll find it in her heart to give me a second chance someday."

Ernesto smiled warmly at him. "Gloria and I will surely be praying for that."

Ryan looked at the clock on the wall: 5:30 p.m. It was time to go. Maricel wasn't coming. He stood to leave; his heart sank even deeper into his chest.

The coffee shop owners walked their American friend outside.

Ernesto looked deep into Ryan's sad, troubled eyes. "Don't lose hope, Ryan. The moment you turn your back on expectation is the moment you have given up. If you really love Maricel, never give up on her. Do your best to remain patient. If it's God's will for you to be together, it will happen in His time."

Ryan smiled briefly. It quickly vanished.

Ernesto placed his hands on Ryan's shoulders, "In the meantime, it wouldn't hurt to take a personal inventory of yourself when you get home, to see what changes, if any, you might need to make in life."

"Thanks for the advice. I'll do just that." Tipton pulled 9,000 pesos from his pants pocket, which amounted to just under U.S. $200. "Can you give this to Maricel? I don't have time to exchange it back to dollars. Besides, she needs it more than I do."

The expression on Ernesto's face indicated to Ryan that he was impressed by the kind gesture. "That's very kind of you, young man. Give me her mobile number and I'll see that she gets it."

A taxi pulled over and came to a stop. "I'll text it to you on my way to the airport." Tipton became teary-eyed. "How can I ever thank you both?"

Gloria said, "You already have, Ryan, with the gift of your friendship."

Just then, a middle-aged foreigner, who appeared to be either English or American, walked inside the coffee shop, with his arm wrapped tightly around a younger Filipino woman.

Ernesto grinned from ear to ear. "I need to go. Have a safe flight, Ryan."

"Go get 'em, tiger," said Gloria, nudging her husband gently.

Ernesto chuckled, then hurried inside.

Ryan smiled wearily at Gloria, then lowered himself into the taxicab. "Would it be okay if I kept in touch with you from time to time?"

Gloria said, "We would be hurt if you didn't."

"God bless you, Gloria."

"God bless you, too, Ryan."

At that, the driver pulled away...

17

STANDING ACROSS THE STREET from Agape Coffee and Pastry Shoppe, in the pouring rain—wondering why she was even there in the first place—was Maricel Arcamo. Had it not been for the umbrella she was holding to keep herself dry, it would have been difficult to differentiate her tears from the rainwater.

Maricel was completely undone. If the line between sanity and lunacy wasn't all that thick, spying on a coffee shop in a soaking rain helped her better understand that statement.

Even from this distance, the broken expression on Ryan's downtrodden face was easily recognizable. It pained her ever so deeply to think she was the one responsible for putting it there.

But after what he did, a big part of her was glad to see him leaving her country. Yet here she was feeling tortured inside, even though it was all Ryan's fault, not hers.

As it turned out, Ryan was just like the others. Even so, crazy as it sounded, part of her wanted to be inside the taxi with him, cherishing every-last moment they had together.

But it was too late; the driver had already pulled away. Her shoulders slumped, her head fell downward, and the shedding of tears increased. She felt powerless from controlling her emotions.

Maricel couldn't help but wonder if this would be the last time that she would ever see Ryan Tipton in person...

After mulling it over in her weary mind, she dismissed the thought and finally mustered the strength to make her way home.

Try as she might, she couldn't answer the most pressing question on her mind: Was Ryan Tipton merely a player, out to collect women like the rest of them, or was this a once in a lifetime occurrence? It was her new million-dollar question...*Why does life have to be so painful and unfair at times?*

THE INSTANT THE AIRPLANE wheels lifted off the Philippine soil, Ryan Tipton buried his face in his hands, doing his best to hide from everyone else on board that he was weeping.

As the plane raced toward Tokyo, Japan at 500 miles per hour, memories of Maricel flooded his mind. Tipton couldn't help but think he was moving farther and farther away from the true love of his life. It was the worst kind of torture to finally realize beyond a shadow of a doubt who he wanted to spend the rest of his life with, only to be denied a second chance with her.

This time last week their relationship was firmly established. Then Ryan ruined everything by lying to her and meeting with two other women. Now any sort of relationship with Maricel, including friendship, seemed a distant dream.

Once the fasten seat belt sign was turned off, Tipton went to the lavatory to wash his face and stuff a few tissues in his pants pocket, in case he needed them later.

Studying his reflection in the mirror, a lump rose in his throat. His eyes grew moist and still. "Who do you think you are? How could you ruin her life like this!" Fresh tears streamed down his plump cheeks one after another. "I'm so sorry, Maricel," he said to the wounded man glaring back at him, in the small mirror.

This pain was so much worse than what he felt at the hands of his ex-wife, not to mention so many other women in the past, because *he* was the perpetrator this time. Ryan returned to his seat. There was no bounce in his step. If anything, he thought his heart would explode inside his chest at any moment.

"Where you from, man?" the Caucasian man seated next to him asked, with a nod of the head.

Ryan nearly fell into his lap climbing over him to get to his window seat. "America. You?"

"Canada. Were you in the Philippines for business or pleasure?"

"Vacation. How about you?" The smell of stale beer on his breath nearly made Tipton gag.

"Definitely pleasure, man. Had the time of my life!"

"Oh yeah? What made your trip so memorable?"

"Women!" he snickered. "Lots and lots of women!"

"I see. And just how many women did you meet this week?"

"Three weeks, bro. And I'm proud to say I slept with fifteen hotties. Some more than once. Just had my last victim three hours ago, before heading to the airport. She was a real wildcat. I have video to prove it!"

Ryan was incredulous! "You actually took video?"

"Of course, bro, I'm not stupid!" He answered the question like it was a compliment rather than an accusation. "I took video of most of my victims. Would you like to see?"

"No, I wouldn't," Ryan said angrily, doing his best to remain calm. This man of vile integrity appeared to be the same age as him.

"Whoa, take it easy man!" *Your loss!*

"Did these women know you were making videos of them?"

A victorious grin crept onto his face. "What kind of question is that? Of course, not! What they don't know won't hurt them, right?" He scratched his chin. "Actually, three of them knew, but definitely not the rest of them."

Ryan thought back to what Ernesto Angeles said earlier, about foreigners visiting his country and leaving with smiles on their faces, and countless trails of tears and heartache behind. It was materializing before his very eyes. This man was one of the many "Kevins" in the world that Ernesto had warned him about.

Ryan wanted to say, "Men like you should be banned from visiting the Philippines!" He took a deep breath. "Sadly, I also took advantage of three women when I was there. But I didn't secretly record anyone without their knowledge. Nor did I use them for sex. Unlike you, I feel terrible about the things I did."

"Why feel terrible, man?" the Canadian man said, with a cocky grin on his face that bothered Tipton. "There will never be a shortage of loose women in the Philippines to choose from. Next time I come back, there will be a whole new crop of girls waiting for me."

"How can you portray Filipino women so negatively?"

"Just speaking the truth, that's all," he said, matter-of-factly.

"Oh yeah, who's truth? Most well-mannered human beings on the planet will agree that Filipino women are known for being kind and generous and sweet in nature."

"Oh, they're sweet, alright. And the key to scoring so easily with them is simple: be just as sweet in return and tell them anything they want to hear. The rest is like taking candy from a baby."

This man sickened Ryan to no end. He became increasingly angry. "How many times have you done this?"

"This was my fifth trip. Hopefully, I'll get to go back again next year."

"I see. Were your previous trips similar to this one?"

"Yup. But I must say, I've really honed my skills over the years. My first time there, I pretty much slept with anyone who would let me. I'm so much more selective these days. I only meet the really-hot women now. And I must say, it gets easier each trip."

Ryan gritted his teeth. "Can I ask you something?"

"Shoot!"

"Have you ever thought about the psychological damage you've done to the women you've lied to all those years, whose hearts you've undoubtedly shattered in the process?"

The inebriated man with bloodshot eyes stared at Ryan, with a puzzled look on his face. Confusion quickly gave way to anger. "Are you a priest or something?"

Tipton looked puzzled. "No, why?"

"Then please stop moralizing with me!" he snapped.

"Sorry, man," Ryan sighed, then anger set in again. "Actually, I'm not sorry. I'm amazed how you can be like this!

149

My foolish actions this week cost me the love of my life. I would do anything to win her back. Yet, you could care less about the many women you've lied to. All you ever wanted was to sleep with them."

"I know. Isn't it awesome!"

Tipton glared at him. "What's wrong with you, man. All you care about is yourself! How do you sleep at night? You're pathetic!"

"Whatever! Nice talking to you," he sneered, sarcastically, turning his head and looking the other way.

Within a few minutes, the man Tipton wished he hadn't been seated next to was snoring away, without a care in the world.

Ryan turned on his laptop and logged onto the Asian dating site responsible for introducing him to Maricel. He clicked on her profile and fought back more tears. She looked so happy and full of life.

He was certain she looked nothing like that now. All because of him...Tipton clicked on the "Send Message" link on her profile and started typing:

My dearest Maricel,

I waited for you at the coffee shop for nearly an hour and a half, hoping against all hope that you would finally show up. Can't say I blame you though. I got exactly what I deserved. How could I expect you to meet me after what I did to you? It's all my fault.

Leaving the Philippines was the hardest thing I ever did in my life. I can't believe how much I'm hurting right now. Not to make excuses, but this was the first time I ever did something so foolish and stupid like this in my life.

Even so, I realize how wrong it was to allow myself to get so carried away, especially knowing there were deep feelings involved. Someone was bound to get hurt in the end. I guess the joke's on me. It feels like I'm dying a little more with each breath I take.

I want you to know my last week in your country wasn't much fun. All I did was think about you, wishing we were still

150

together. Guess you could say I would have enjoyed myself so much more had I not met you first. You changed everything!

If I could somehow find a way to turn this plane around and head back to Manila, I would do it, then camp outside your house for weeks on end, until you finally gave me another chance.

But I'm starting to feel more and more that perhaps my deceitful actions have ruined something special between us. I just hope in time you'll find it in your heart to rekindle the strong feelings you had for me, before I ruined your life.

Please believe me when I say, though we only spent one week together, it was the most remarkable week of my life. You are, without a doubt, the best thing that ever happened to me!

In closing, I want you to know that I will never give up on us, Maricel. Never! If my foolish actions cause me to lose you forever, I'll never forgive myself. I just hope in time, you'll honor me by letting me call you "sweetie" again.

There's nothing more I want right now than that. You're worth fighting for, and I'm prepared to do just that. I'll always be here waiting for you. Mahal kita, Maricel!

Sincerely yours,
Ryan

Tipton sent the e-mail, then deleted his profile without bothering to read the 14 unread e-mails in his inbox. There was no need to read them, or ever visit this site again, because he had already found the true love of his life. His days of visiting dating sites were over.

Ryan reached inside his pants pocket for a tissue and dabbed at his eyes, which resembled two faucets turned on full blast.

Thankfully, the inebriated man seated next to him was still snoring away, totally oblivious that the man seated next to him was sobbing like a baby again.

The plane landed at Narita International Airport just after midnight, leaving Ryan five hours to kill before the next flight to

San Francisco. He was completely exhausted but couldn't sit still.

Tipton walked around the terminal in a daze. He looked like a zombie. The airport wasn't crowded at this late hour, but the few happy couples he saw scattered about, walking hand in hand, tortured him inside like never before. It was as if God was further punishing him for what he did to Maricel.

The last time he was at this airport, he had so much to look forward to. He was so full of anticipation. Now everything was lost, brutally replaced with constant dread.

The last time he "proclaimed" to be at this airport, he was really in Cebu with Jenny. The very thought of it sickened him.

Unable to gain control of his emotions, Ryan found an empty seat in a vacant corner and started sobbing again.

This was heartache at its worst, not that watered-down version he'd felt so many times in the past. This was a whole new threshold of pain that Tipton wouldn't even wish upon his worst enemy.

Dabbing his tear-swollen eyes, he said, "I'm so sorry, Maricel. Please forgive me."

TWO THOUSAND MILES SOUTH of Narita International Airport, it was as if Maricel had heard Ryan's desperate plea for forgiveness. Tears streamed down her cheeks, one after the next.

The instant she was notified in her Gmail account that she had a new message from the man who'd just broken her heart, Maricel fought hard to ignore it.

But her curiosity outlasted the pain and anger she felt, and she reluctantly signed-in to the dating site and read the e-mail.

That was three hours ago...She read it a dozen times since; each recount was more gut-wrenching than the last, as evidenced by the dozens of messy tissues littering her bedroom floor.

Though Ryan never made mention of it, he apparently deleted his profile on the dating site. Maricel was confused by this and called her best friend, Rosalyn. After having a similar experience last year, with a man from Germany, Maricel felt Rosa was qualified to counsel her on the subject.

Rosalyn listened very carefully, then said, "Now that Ryan's been caught, he will do all he can to win you back. If you think he was a perfect gentleman *before* it happened, he will be on his best behavior from now on. Be careful, Sis. We all got to see how kind and generous he was. Avoid talking to him. You need to protect yourself now more than ever!"

Maricel was grateful for the advice. The only issue she had with it was that Ryan didn't get caught. He confessed everything to her, without the slightest suspicion on her part. That had to count for something, she reasoned, which only added another layer of confusion to her already over-stressed mind and heart.

She already knew the roosters would be crowing long before she fell asleep. If she fell asleep, that is...

AT 5:15 A.M., RYAN Tipton was airborne again, headed back to the United States of America, thankful to be free of the despicable man from Canada.

He landed in San Francisco ten hours later, somewhat amazed that he had managed to sleep for most of the flight back.

Drained of all emotion, he just wanted to board his last airplane, soon to be departing for his hometown of Des Moines, Iowa, so he could sleep in his own bed again.

Tipton had heard stories over the years about Americans dropping to their knees the moment they arrived back on American soil, just thankful to be back home again.

A proud American himself, prior to taking this trip, Ryan thought he'd be among those to kiss the ground upon arriving home safely. But it never happened. It wasn't that his patriotism had wavered. That wasn't it at all.

What prevented him from being so joyous was the gaping hole in his heart, that kept increasing as the hours passed.

After spending the most incredible week of his life with Maricel Arcamo, his *American Dream* would never be complete without her in it. It very much felt like half of him was missing, with thousands of miles separating both parts.

As the plane gently touched down in Iowa, Tipton knew he was in for the fight of his life. Though he couldn't predict the outcome of Round 2 in the battle for Maricel Arcamo's heart, he was fully committed to do all he could to win her back.

The first step was to heed the advice of his good friend, Ernesto Angeles, and take a complete inventory of himself to see what radical changes he needed to make in life.

If he wanted Maricel back, he first had to become the right person. After everything he put her through the past 24 hours, she deserved nothing less than his very best, from this point forward.

Waiting outside the terminal for his parents to fetch him, the vision flooding Tipton's tired and numb mind was something he wanted more than anything else in life.

That vision was to someday see a photograph of he and Maricel Arcamo hanging on the "International Walls of Love" inside Agape Coffee and Pastry Shoppe, in Manila—first on the wall reserved for those still developing healthy relationships, followed by the wall reserved for those who were engaged.

But mostly, he wanted to one day see their photograph hanging on the wall reserved for those who were happily married...

18

THREE MONTHS LATER

MARICEL ARCAMO AND HER best friend, Rosalyn, were both seated in the front row occupying two of the 64 chairs, borrowed from the 16 tables inside Agape Coffee and Pastry Shoppe. All were neatly lined up in eight rows, eight chairs per row.

Thirty more plastic chairs the Angeles' kept stacked in piles of ten inside the small kitchen closet, were also spread out wherever there was space for them. All 94 chairs were occupied, not to mention the six counter seats, equating to 100 seats.

It was nearly 6 p.m., and the Sunday night character-building class was set to begin. Everyone crammed inside the tiny coffee shop greatly anticipated what Ernesto Angeles had aptly named, "the many glaring dangers of online dating."

It was a grim title, the old man knew, but the fact that everyone in attendance was searching online for lifetime partners, made it a topic of vital importance.

In the three months since Ryan Tipton had left the Philippines, Maricel was fortunate to spend lots of quality time with Ernesto and Gloria Angeles. During this time, they became two of her most trusted advisers in life. They counseled her not only on God's Holy Word but also on matters of the heart.

What Maricel didn't know was that they were giving the very same advice to Ryan. The day after he flew back to the States, Ernesto called to inform Maricel that her American visitor had left something behind for her.

Though devastated, she agreed to stop by later that night after dinner. In the three hours she spent with them, their friendship had deepened considerably. Before leaving that night, Gloria encouraged Maricel to attend their 3 p.m. weekly Bible study that Sunday, followed by the 6 p.m. character-building session.

There was a certain glow on her face, to go along with an unmistakable twinkle in her eye, that comforted Maricel greatly, prompting her in her spirit to accept Gloria's invitation.

She hadn't missed a week since. It got to where she almost couldn't function the rest of the week without first spending a few hours at the coffee shop each Sunday, surrounded by her steadily growing number of new Christian friends.

At 6 p.m. sharp, the room grew silent as Ernesto Angeles bowed his head to open the session in prayer.

When he was finished, he began, "In this age of technology in which we live, more and more people are finding romance online. Thanks to the internet, it's never been easier to meet people from every corner of the globe.

"I'll admit it sounds exciting to turn on a computer and have the entire world at your fingertips in just seconds. I'll even go so far to confess that the thought of having so many possible suitors, with just a click of the mouse, sounds intriguing even to me.

"But if the internet is the great connector of people, my opening question to each of you tonight is, why do so many online daters struggle to find even one reliable person in the entire bunch? Have you ever given much thought to that?"

Ernesto let his question hang in the air, as his gaze wandered over the room. "Personally, I believe the reasons are many. Before I share some of them with you, let me first say that I certainly believe it's possible to find a lifetime partner online.

"How could I not, when seventy percent of the pictures hanging on our walls, are from couples who met on the internet, many of whom are now married. I expect this percentage only to increase, as time goes on.

"Having said that, when it comes to choosing a lifetime partner online, there are many pitfalls to consider. Unlike meeting offline, we never get to meet the real person behind the profile, so to speak. All we have to work with are profiles which more resemble resumes with photographs affixed to them than anything else.

"Sorry if I sound a bit insensitive, but it blows my mind just knowing that so many women are falling so easily for people they know so little about and, therefore, have no business making any sort of a firm commitment to. How can anyone choose a lifetime partner with so little to work with? At least initially...

"With marriage being one of the biggest steps anyone can take in life, I find falling in love with a profile a bit shallow. I'm afraid true companionship doesn't work that way. Don't get me wrong: since most people spend more time chatting online these days, than in person, meeting online can be a good first step."

Pointing to one of the walls, Ernesto said, "But what separates those couples from the countless millions of online daters is that they've all taken the next step by meeting in person, several times, in fact, and spending quality time together, before finally knowing for sure they were compatible for marriage.

"I know this is common sense thinking, but with the internet always moving at Mach speed, and with online profiles open for all to see, common sense is often replaced with a great sense of desperation the moment someone captures your attention, despite how little you may know about him or her.

"This reminds me of those many bachelor or bachelorette shows we see on TV, where many women compete for the heart of one man, or vice versa. Out of desperation, and fear of loss, these individuals end up saying and doing almost anything to win the heart of that person, including things they would never contemplate doing had there been no competition from others.

"The same is true with online dating. But here's what makes it worse. According to various online research groups, many who ultimately end up meeting in person usually have a delightful time together. The problem they've found, however, is after they part company, for the most part, since their profiles remain on the same dating sites, the turbulent online competition continues."

157

As Ernesto uttered those words, Maricel was reminded again that Ryan had deleted his profile the moment he left the Philippines. That had to count for something, didn't it?

Ernesto went on, "Now, speaking to the women in the room, let me just say that I believe many men go online with good intentions. Most are serious in their pursuit of finding lifetime partners.

"But after being exposed to so many women all at once, many who possess, if you'll pardon the expression, 'loose morals,' these men quickly lose focus and turn into kids in candy stores, wanting a little of this and that.

"By having so many options to exercise all at once, many men secretly stockpile dozens of vulnerable women, as if they were canned goods instead of human beings. This way, they can keep sorting until they eventually find the right one.

"In the process, women who have allowed that person to become their top priority, are ultimately treated as nothing more than options. Not all men are like this, but I'm afraid the number is increasing."

Ernesto thought about his late daughter, Jecelyn. Even 20 years later, it still saddened him to think she was nothing more than some man's option, a man who never deserved her love in the first place.

He blinked the thought away and refocused. "But I would be remiss if I didn't warn you men in the room of the growing number of women online who are just as guilty of being deceitful. They make numerous false promises to countless men, hoping they'll keep sending them money.

"Their sinful actions end up hurting so many good men each year, sometimes draining them of all their savings." Ernesto shook his head, "Some of them are even married. Hard to imagine, at least for me. Needless to say, these individuals, whether male or female, should be avoided at all costs.

"But I think what concerns me most about online dating is the growing number of women who are encouraged, and sometimes even pressured, to show certain body parts to complete strangers, sometimes in open chat rooms."

Ernesto sighed. "Let me be clear: some girls aren't pressured; they do it for their own personal benefit, whether for pleasure or financial gain. Others do it to avenge those who recently scorned them. I often wonder if these women ever consider the end result of their foolish actions...

"I hate to be the bearer of bad news, ladies and gentlemen, but even if you feel a certain sense of comfort and safety at home, how can anyone know for sure the person you see on your cellphone or laptop screen—whom you seemingly know little or nothing about—isn't secretly recording or even broadcasting you without your knowledge? Even at home we're not as safe as we think we are."

Ernesto grew more somber. "I can't begin to tell you how many horror stories Gloria and I have heard over the years, from women claiming they were secretly recorded by someone. Some even told us their naked photographs ended up on various web sites for all to see, devastating them and robbing them of their dignity as a result.

"A frightening thought, wouldn't you agree?" Judging by the looks on the faces of his many listeners, Ernesto knew he had been effective in making his point. "With so much technology at our full disposal, now more than ever, the temptation factor has risen to unprecedented heights, especially while in the confines of our own homes.

"Women, especially, tend to let their guards down at home and do things online they would never consider if meeting that person face to face. My point is, just because the internet is a virtual world, it doesn't mean our foolish actions aren't far-reaching. You've just heard how far-reaching it can be."

The Godly Filipino man searched the crowd somberly, soberly. His eyes were deeply troubled. "How could this not be considered extremely dangerous territory, my dear friends?"

Ernesto nodded at Gloria, and she grabbed the stack of papers he prepared for the lesson. "Since we all know everyone's true colors will surface at some point, whether good or bad, I strongly urge you all to take your online dating experience at a very slow and healthy pace.

"Your assignment this week, though simple enough, is designed to help you do just that. The sheet of paper Gloria is passing out has been broken into three parts. Each have three separate categories which need to be completed."

Once everyone received a copy, Ernesto continued, "To help prepare for today's lesson, with my wife's guidance, I visited a handful of online dating sites this week. While I was pleased to find a few decent ones, it seems on most sites, true love and romance have taken a backseat to profits.

"Rather than having their clients' best interests in mind, it seems to me that the very notion of 'love' is the bait creators of these sites use to rake in millions of dollars. For the most part, paying customers are nothing more than numbers to them.

"With that in mind, to help you better concentrate, I'll ask you all to power down your mobile devices. Call me old-fashioned, but in my humble opinion, I believe this assignment needs to be done far away from the speed and the constant distractions of the internet."

Eyes surveying the room, he added, "I also believe it should be done in your own handwriting. To me, typing answers onto online dating profiles seems a little too impersonal."

After the last phone was turned off, Ernesto continued, "In the first section, you'll be asked to list the seven things you absolutely *need* in a lifetime partner. Answers will be required in three separate categories. The first category will focus on his or her character and appearance.

"The second category will focus on their hobbies and interests. And the third category will be on religion and morality. Since these are your 'seven musts' for each category, they should never be compromised, no matter what.

"In the second part, you'll be asked to do the same thing, except these seven things are things you *want* most in a lifetime partner. These are your 'seven likes', and therefore can be tweaked a little here and there, so long as it doesn't end up compromising your seven *needs*.

"Finally, the last part will ask you to list the seven things you cannot tolerate under any circumstances, regardless of attraction. This should include bad habits, addictions, morals, character flaws, and things such as tattoos and body piercings.

"And since cultures are constantly merging and blending online, I think one important question all online searchers need to ask themselves is, 'Am I willing to date someone outside my religion?'"

"Can we write down more than seven?" a young man in his early twenties asked.

"Yes, of course, the more the better," came the reply.

The young man nodded. "Opo (Yes, sir)."

Ernesto cautioned them, "Consequently, this assignment doesn't provide a proven magic formula, so to speak. Its sole function is to help you remain a little more patient while searching online.

"With that in mind, I hope you'll refer to it often and use it as a trusted guide to help weed out all the bad candidates, until the person you become interested in ultimately reveals his or her true colors, allowing you to finally see exactly who you are dealing with on the other end of your phone screens. Fair enough?"

Everyone nodded yes.

"Okay, let's get started. Please don't rush this assignment. If your chief goal is to find a good lifetime partner, I want you to really think it through, especially you ladies."

At that, Gloria and Ernesto went to the kitchen.

Thirty minutes later, they returned.

Ernesto asked, "How many of you are finished?"

Nearly every hand went up.

"The rest of you should complete this assignment at home, no matter how long it takes, then keep it close to you whenever you're online. Hopefully, at the very least, it will result in less hearts being broken among you in the coming weeks and months."

Ernesto placed his notebook on the table. "In closing, let me just say that, regardless of how you choose to present yourself to the world, some will like you; others won't. If this is true, which it most certainly is, why waste a single moment trying to be someone other than yourself?

"Let's face it, the only way someone can love the real you, is if you present a true likeness of yourself online. Otherwise, you're cheating the process. Once you reveal the 'true you' to the cyber world," he said, using his fingers as quotation marks to emphasize his point, "always remain true to yourselves, no matter what, until God reveals the person He has in store for you.

"Finally, there's something I want you all to ponder as you head home tonight. Actually, it's more of a challenge." Scanning the room, he said, "My hope is that every time you go online, you'll consider the future generation of online daters, by doing all you can now to help clean up the huge mess found on most online dating sites, not to mention various social media platforms.

"The only way to accomplish this is by being the person God wants you to be online. If each of you commits to taking small steps in the right direction, we'll slowly but surely make a difference for future generations.

"And since some of them will be your siblings and even your own children, you should consider it your duty and responsibility to make this good investment in the future. I believe it's the least we can do for them. Can I get an Amen?"

"Amen," came the reply in unison.

"As always, Gloria and I thank you all for joining us tonight. We love you all and hope to see you again next week, or sometime in the future. Until then, please be careful going home. May God continue to richly bless you all!"

At that, the session was over. As usual, the Godly Filipino man gave his invited guests so much to digest.

Having two younger siblings who spent considerable amounts of time online, Maricel was touched by Ernesto's bold challenge at the end, to help clean up the internet for future generations. She only wished his message had been streamed worldwide for all to hear.

If so, she believed everyone within the sound of his voice would have been greatly impacted by it.

As a small token of appreciation for everything the Angeles' had done for her, and so many others in the community, Maricel went straight to the coffee shop the past twelve Sundays, after church, to help rearrange chairs, brew fresh coffee, and bake fresh breads and pastries, which were offered freely to everyone in attendance.

She felt it was the least she could do.

But what Maricel loved most about Sundays at this place, was what happened after both sessions ended, and the coffee shop owners kept their doors and hearts open, until all the food and drink ran out. Gloria even lovingly prepared hot soup or sinigang baboy—a Filipino favorite—on the days it rained.

Since most visitors to the coffee shop were battling broken hearts—a feeling Maricel easily identified with—the sounds of sobbing and sniffling were frequent most Sunday nights.

Some preferred to sit alone and enjoy their refreshments in silence, as they read newspapers, pocketbooks or did crossword puzzles. Others sat in small groups.

Many chatted online and played games on their mobile devices.

Some came for the sole purpose of reading one of the many Bibles the Angeles kept stashed underneath the counter, for anyone who wanted one, free of charge. Those who didn't own one were encouraged to take one home with them.

Sometimes there wasn't much for volunteers to do but wait for someone in need—either for coffee, prayer, or sometimes just a hug.

Whatever the need, Maricel loved pouring herself into others and showering them with Christian kindness. It helped her forget all about her own personal heartache, if for only one day.

"This is the only place I ever go to read God's Word," was something Maricel often heard from some of them.

Another one was, "There's just something about this place that makes me want to draw closer to Jesus."

Maricel knew exactly how they felt...

The way Ernesto and Gloria had transformed their coffee shop into a safe-haven for so many—herself included—was one more reason why Maricel admired them so much.

This was Rosalyn's third straight week attending. Like all other volunteers, she, too, had come to greatly admire Ernesto and Gloria Angeles.

The payment she received for volunteering her time could never be measured in terms of money. This was so much better than merely exchanging time for a wage.

Rosa was making an investment in the lives of those who badly needed it. And what could be better than that?

BY THE TIME MARICEL arrived home from the coffee shop, it was well after midnight. She tiptoed up the stairs to her small bedroom, hoping not to wake Vivian.

Excitement kept building with each step, knowing what was on the bureau where she'd placed it the night before; the twelfth card Ryan Tipton had sent since his departure a few months ago.

Maricel's custom was to read each correspondence on Sunday nights, when she felt the most peaceful inside.

She never told anyone, not even Rosalyn, but her heart always leapt for joy whenever a new card arrived from him.

Ryan occasionally sent her flowers and chocolates. Even despite the kind gestures—aside from the handful of offline messages she sent thanking him for the money he gave to the Angeles' to pass on to her, and for the flowers, and chocolates— Maricel had still yet to communicate with him in any capacity.

She wasn't ready to take the first step. She was still vulnerable, and needed to guard her heart, until she finally felt ready to start searching for a lifetime partner again.

Maricel changed into pajamas and climbed into bed. Sitting straight up, she placed a fluffy pillow across her lap. The card rested atop the pillow. She took a deep breath in the darkness, turned on the small flashlight, and gently tore open the envelope.

As always, Ryan's words were both thoughtful and heartfelt. It was evident he was desperate for a second chance with her.

Though the verbiage bore a similar resemblance to all past correspondences, what separated this letter from the others was the post-script beneath his signature:

P.S. I'm coming back to the Philippines next month, but only for one week this time, promise! I'm going there for one reason and one reason only—YOU!

I really can't afford to take this trip, but after what I did to you, I can't afford not to take it. You mean that much to me, Maricel.

I don't expect you to greet me at the airport when I arrive, but I hope you can find it in your heart to meet with me at some point. At the very least, I want to apologize to you face to face. You deserve that much. Hope to see you then. Mahal kita, Ryan...

For a brief moment, it felt like Maricel's heart had stopped beating before kick-starting again. Her lungs lacked oxygen. She didn't know what to make of this shocking revelation.

In the few moments it took to read that short paragraph, each of her emotions were tapped. From a psychological standpoint, uncertainty certainly wasn't the most desirable place to visit, let alone remain parked at for extended periods of time.

But for whatever reason, that's where Maricel felt most comfortable with Ryan at present.

Though she wouldn't allow herself to shut the door on him just yet, she was in no position to take him back either.

And that meant, for now, she had to keep distancing herself from the American man she knew she still loved, until she finally felt prompted to take the next step, whatever that next step might be. It was as simple as that.

But in no way was it easy…

19

ONE MONTH LATER

"RYAN? IS THAT YOU?" Gloria Angeles asked.

"It's me." Tipton smiled shyly and nodded yes.

Gloria's eyes grew to the size of silver dollar pancakes. "You look fantastic! You're so much thinner now."

"Thanks, Gloria." Ryan did a quick 360 for Gloria to see.

Gloria couldn't conceal her astonishment. This was her first time seeing him wearing anything other than denim jeans and long-sleeve button down shirts. They were replaced with tan shorts and a blue tank top. "Honestly, I didn't even notice you at first…"

"Yeah, well, last time I was here, your husband urged me to take a personal inventory and make whatever changes needed to be made. He also reminded me of just how special I really was. One in infinity, I believe he said."

Gloria shook her head. "Sounds like something he would say."

Ryan nodded agreement. "I followed his advice and took a good hard look within. I quickly realized many changes were needed. First and foremost, I had to start reading the Bible again. The more I read it, really read it, the more broken I felt before my Maker. After repenting of my sinful lifestyle—for real this time—I fully understood how truly amazing His grace really is…"

Tipton smiled. "As God started recreating me on the inside, I decided it was time to put my best foot forward and present the 'best me' I could on the outside. Been working out with weights every other day, and walking three miles each day in between."

"Good for you, Ryan! Your face is so much thinner now."

"At the outset, my goal was to lose two pounds per week. So far, I've lost just over thirty pounds. I want to lose another thirty, then maintain that weight by eating healthier and maintaining a steady exercise routine."

Gloria still couldn't believe how wonderful he looked. "You're even more pogi (handsome) now. And your new hairstyle and sporty eyeglasses make you look ten years younger. What can I say? I'm amazed!"

"Salamat, Gloria." The expression on her face satisfied Ryan immensely.

Gloria asked, "Has Maricel seen pictures of you lately?"

Ryan frowned, and shook his head no. "We haven't spoken on the phone or chatted online, since I left here four months ago."

Gloria wasn't overly surprised to hear this. "All I can say is she better claim you now, before other girls start chasing you up and down the streets of Manila."

Ryan laughed at her comment, then grew serious again. "I'm here for one woman only, and you know who it is. Just hope she'll take me back."

Tears rushed to Gloria's eyes. "Time will tell, right?"

"I'm taking a great leap of faith just by being here."

"Have you prayed about it?"

Tipton sighed. "Nonstop."

Gloria broke into a warm smile. "Well then, if it's in God's hands, let's leave it there and see what happens."

Tipton shrugged his shoulders. "I have no other choice, right?"

"Correct. Would you like coffee?"

"Are you kidding! I've been dreaming about my next cup of coffee in Manila for four months now. But I insist on paying for it this time."

Gloria nodded. "Okay, one coffee coming right up!"

"Where's Ernesto?"

"Outback receiving our weekly supplies. He's been bouncing off the walls all day waiting for you to arrive."

"Yeah, been like that all week myself. Mostly because I can't stop wondering if Maricel will meet me or not."

Gloria handed Ryan his coffee.

Tipton handed her a U.S. hundred-dollar bill.

"I don't think there's enough in the register to make change."

"I don't want change back, Gloria."

Gloria shot him a confused sideways look.

"Put it toward the Gloria and Ernesto Angeles Love Fund. It isn't much, but I wish to prepay for as many coffees as the money will allow."

"That's very kind of you, Ryan, but it isn't necessary," she said, just as Ernesto appeared from the small kitchen, carrying an invoice from the inventory order he'd just received.

"Ryan! Welcome back, my friend. Mabuhay!"

"Mabuhay! Nice to see you again, Ernesto."

The two men embraced, before Ernesto gave him a good looking over. "I see someone's been exercising."

"Yes, I have, mostly thanks to you."

"Keep it up, Ryan. You look great." He glanced at his wife and saw the hundred-dollar bill in her hand. "What's that for, dear?"

"Perhaps Ryan should tell you…"

Tipton took a sip of coffee. "M-m-m, yummy! To answer your question, I gave it to Gloria to pay for my coffee, then asked her to keep the change."

Ernesto shook his head, then raised his hands in polite refusal.

"Wait! Before you refuse to accept it, please hear me out. When I left the Philippines four months ago, as God would have it, I ended up being seated next to one of the many Kevins of the world you warned me about, on the flight to Tokyo.

"This man disgusted me. He kept bragging about the many women he'd slept with in the three weeks he was here in the Philippines." Ryan took a second to retrace his memory. "Fifteen women, I think he said. Worse, he told me he privately recorded some of their escapades, without their knowledge. To say I was sickened by this would be an understatement!"

By simply looking in their eyes, there was no denying the raw emotion there, the hurt. By violating so many Filipino women, it was as if this crude man had violated them too.

Fully mindful of their joint mission in life, Tipton was beginning to understand more and more about what these two beautiful human beings stood for, and how broken they must have felt when hearing sickening stories like this.

Ryan went on, "Now more than ever I appreciate your Mission here. If my small financial contribution helps turn one more Kevin around, it will be money well spent."

Gloria was moved to tears. "That's very kind of you, Ryan. But don't you know our sons-in-law reimburse us on each cup of coffee we give away for free in love?"

Tipton nodded yes. "Your husband was kind enough to share that with me. Even so, I insist you take it."

Gloria reached across the counter and hugged him. "Thank you, Ryan. We'll see that the funds are put to good use."

"I know you will..."

Gloria's face was aglow. "Ikaw ay may mabuting puso!"

Before Ryan could inquire, Ernesto said, "My wife said you have a good heart. I agree with her."

Tipton smirked. "I still have a long way to go before I can ever make it into your league. But I promise to keep trying."

"That's the spirit, Ryan," Ernesto declared, with a proud smile.

Tipton switched gears. "So, how's Maricel?"

"She's doing well." Gloria sighed. "Even if she doesn't speak about it, deep down inside I know she misses you."

"I'm prepared to do anything to win her back."

As appealing as the new "Ryan" looked physically, he was even more attractive on the inside. Truly, he was a changed man...

Gloria said, "You're off to a good start. It was wise not to flood her with phone calls and text messages the past four months. Take it from me; most women don't like men who smother them too much. True love is a gift that's freely given from one person to another. It can never be demanded or suffocated. When people try forcing it, it's just a matter of time before that relationship ends."

Ryan rubbed his chin. "Truth be told, I wanted to call her twenty times a day the past four months, just to remind her that I still love and miss her. Can't tell you how many times I held the phone in my hand. All I had to do was push the send button."

"But the important thing is that you didn't. The cards, flowers and chocolates you sent were more than enough."

"Just hope she ends up seeing it that way." Ryan grimaced. "Did you speak to her today?"

"She calls us every day without fail. And guess what?"

Tipton flinched in anticipation. "What?"

"She called me soon after your plane had landed."

Ryan's face lit up. "Really?"

Gloria nodded yes.

"Do you think she'll meet me?"

"Hard to say. Maricel's a woman of strong principle. But the fact that she monitored your flight is a good sign."

"I sure hope so. If it's okay with you, I'd like to stay here all day, in case she decides to show up at some point."

Ernesto said, "You're welcome to stay as long as you'd like."

"Thanks Ernesto. If you need me to clean tables or take out the trash, let me know. It will be my pleasure to help anyway I can."

"That won't be necessary, Ryan, but thanks all the same."

There was a pause in the conversation until Gloria said, "Have you considered the possibility of meeting someone else, you know, in case things don't work out between you both?"

Her words momentarily extinguished what little wind she had just blown into his sails. Ryan pulled himself together. "Absolutely not! How can I, when Maricel's the only one for me?"

"I understand." *Wow, he really does love her!*

"Besides, I'm on a tight budget. I need to pinch every penny."

Gloria was astounded. Even strapped for cash, he still gave what little he had to support their mission. Most would have kept it for themselves. She was already thinking of the best way to convince Maricel that Ryan really was a changed man for the better, and that he truly loved her. Not only that, he no doubt respected their culture more than most other foreign visitors to their country.

Ernesto said, "Relax, Ryan. Take a load off. I'm sure you're exhausted from the long flight."

Ryan took a seat at the counter. He sent a message to his parents, informing them of his safe arrival.

His heart rate accelerated when Maricel suddenly logged onto Skype. He waited a few anxious moments with bated breath to see if she would greet him, worry poking its pointy fingers in his weary heart each second. But it never happened...

He couldn't help but wonder if she was chatting with another man. Whenever he saw her online, it pained him to think she might be chatting with someone else, as she avoided him like the plague.

His jealousy flared up so much at times that he was forced to take long walks alone—oftentimes teary-eyed—painfully reliving the greatest mistake of his life, which was lying to her.

Thankfully, she never posted her regrettable experience with Ryan on *Facebook* for all her friends to read, like Tipton had seen so many others do over the years.

If anything, she handled the pain and heartache privately, with class, dignity, and grace, which only made Ryan love her more.

AT 7 P.M., AGAPE Coffee and Pastry Shoppe closed its doors for business for the day. To Ryan's great dismay, Maricel wasn't among the many patrons who came and went.

It was only day one and he was already starting to panic.

Gloria could see it in his eyes. "Perhaps tomorrow will produce a better result…"

"Let's hope so," Tipton said to his two most trusted friends in life. "Hope you both have a pleasant evening."

At that, he left for Bayview Park Hotel. Just being back in the Philippines forced so many raw emotions to resurface, especially now that he was alone.

While nothing had changed since he left, the only thing missing was Maricel. Everything else looked the same to him.

Tears flooded his eyes. She was the laughter Ryan had never known in his sterile world, the caring he'd always hungered for in the dark emptiness of his heart.

A strange moment of clarity pierced his weariness. He saw Maricel's smiling face, and the serious yet playful expression protruding from her beautiful dark brown eyes, as she took hold of his hand. Life was never too serious when they were together.

More tears flooded his eyes. Having finally found *The One*, he ruined it by lying to her. Now he was paying the ultimate price, by being forced to exist on this huge planet, without having her by his side. Each step he took toward the hotel produced constant memories—beautiful and unforgettable, painful and bittersweet.

Losing the unconditional love of a woman he barely knew, yet loved so completely, was worse than losing an arm or a leg. He felt dreadfully alone, gutted; his soul was completely shredded.

Meanwhile, Ernesto and Gloria Angeles arrived home at 8 p.m. When Ernesto went to shower, Gloria reached for the phone.

"Hello?"

"Magandang gabi, Maricel. Kumusta ka?" (Good evening, Maricel. How are you?).

"Okay lang, Gloria, ikaw?" (Okay, Gloria, and you?).

"Mabuti din, salamat. Just wanted you to know Ryan spent all day at the coffee shop, hoping you would arrive."

Maricel scratched her chin. "How is he?"

"Besides missing you terribly, he's doing remarkably well."

"I'm happy to hear that. I feel relieved, actually."

"Believe me, if you saw him, you wouldn't believe your eyes."

Maricel shot her phone a confused sideways look. "Why do you say that, Gloria?"

"Why don't you meet him and see for yourself?"

Maricel felt her heart rate accelerating in her chest. "Hmm."

Gloria pressed on, "I assure you he isn't the same person he was last time he was here," she said with conviction. "I couldn't be prouder of him. Or more amazed!"

Maricel remained silent, but Gloria knew she was listening very intently.

"Speaking to you as a woman, of course, I agree what Ryan did is totally inexcusable. But I respect that he was man enough to admit his wrongdoings to you, despite the consequences he knew would follow."

Gloria suppressed a yawn. "I'm convinced what he did was a once in a lifetime thing. I also believe if you'll just give him another chance, it will never happen again. I assure you now that his love for you is true."

Maricel started weeping softly.

Gloria paused a moment. "I didn't mean to upset you."

Maricel sniffled softly. "I need to go now."

"I understand how you feel. I just hope you can find it in your heart to meet with Ryan before he goes back to the States. Even if only as friends. He did travel all this way just to see you again."

Maricel sniffled again. "I'm still praying about it, okay?"

Gloria sighed into the receiver. "Whatever you decide to do, Ernesto and I still love you like a daughter."

"Alam ko, Gloria, at maraming salamat. Mahal din kita." (I know, Gloria. Thanks so much. I love you too.)

"Walang anuman, Maricel. Hope you have a restful evening."

"You too," she said softly. The call ended.

Maricel burst into tears. The only drawback to spending so much time with Ernesto and Gloria Angeles—either on the phone or in person—was that they were Ryan Tipton's biggest fans.

She wouldn't be surprised knowing they spent each night on their knees praying that God would heal the many wounds in her heart, so she could forgive Ryan and give him a second chance.

But a lack of forgiveness certainly wasn't the issue. Maricel forgave him weeks ago. As a practicing Christian, she knew God made it crystal clear in His Word that if she didn't forgive others, her Maker wouldn't forgive her. It was that simple!

But did that mean she had to give him another chance? She thought not. Deep down inside, she still loved him. But with her heart already many miles beyond the fragile limit, one more blow from him, or from anyone else, might damage her beyond repair.

For one exquisite week, Ryan Tipton was the light in Maricel's dark world, the reason to wake up each morning with a smile on her face. Four months of painful dreams later, the constant waking to suffocating emptiness but never entertaining another man was too much to cope with most days.

Unrelenting, merciless tension took hold of her heart, body, and soul, leaving her feeling utterly alone.

To make matters worse, the man who'd subjected her to so much torture was back in her country again. Just knowing he was a taxi ride away from her house, instead of halfway around the world, filled her with great angst.

Maricel fought constant urges all day to go to Agape Coffee and Pastry Shoppe to see if they could somehow work things out.

Back and forth she went inside her unsettled mind. As day turned into night, she kept fighting strong urges, until she finally talked herself out of it for the last time.

But the price of coming to such a decision meant another sleepless night for her. As Ryan checked into the hotel, Maricel tossed and turned on her bed, wondering why her feelings didn't come with delete buttons.

Why does being in love always have to be so difficult?

20

THREE DAYS LATER

"I DON'T KNOW WHAT to say. Maricel's like an open book with us, except when it comes to you." Gloria's voice was soft and weary.

Ryan sighed. "Just wish I knew where I stood with her, one way or the other. The more I keep waiting for her to miraculously walk through those doors each day, the more hopeless I feel."

Gloria nodded empathetically at him. "Just do your best to remain patient a little while longer."

"I'm trying my best, Gloria, but I don't know how much more I can take. I'm only here for three more days."

It was just after 7 p.m., and Agape Coffee and Pastry Shoppe was closed for business.

This was Tipton's fourth day in Manila, and he'd still yet to hear from the woman he flew 8,000 miles just to see. He was growing more desperate and discouraged as the minutes passed.

Not even the warm sensation rising through the floorboards helped. His face was somber and wrought with dejection.

"Perhaps I should take a taxi to her house. Couldn't hurt, right?"

Ernesto shrugged his shoulders and left it at that.

What Ryan didn't tell his two mentors was that he already did that, when he left the coffee shop last night. He didn't see Maricel, but he did see her parents sitting out on the front porch.

He fought strong urges to get out of the cab and apologize to Francisco and Hazel, for what he did to their daughter a few months ago, but he remained inside the cab.

Maricel had to be first...

Ernesto was also perplexed by Maricel's total silence. Though she had never promised to meet with Ryan, her total refusal wasn't very Christlike of her, especially since he traveled so far just for her. It was like she was holding the three of them hostage, Ryan especially, and now they were frantically waiting to hear her ransom demands.

Seeing the despair on her American friend's face, Gloria wanted to remind Ryan again that he still had time to meet someone in the Philippines, before he went back to Iowa.

Then perhaps he could start over again…

But he made it crystal clear that he was only interested in Maricel. And to prove it, the only thing he did since arriving in Manila, besides sleep—limited as it was—was to remain camped out at the coffee shop, day and night, until closing time.

Gloria wanted to cry for Ryan, and already had several times this week, but never while in his presence. She also shed plenty of tears for Maricel, and was both shocked and confused by her total silence, especially after their heart-to-heart talk the other night.

They were all startled when there was a light tap on the door. Then again, even with the *Closed for Business* sign posted on the door, visitors frequently knocked at all hours of the night, often times for prayer, especially when seeing lights on inside.

Ernesto excused himself to see who it was. He silently rejoiced upon seeing Maricel standing outside, looking like a scared little girl, who needed to be rescued from the cruel world outside.

The shopkeeper whispered, "Hallelujah," skyward to his Maker, then opened the door. "Maricel! What a nice surprise!" He spoke softly, not wanting to ruin the glorious surprise."

"Magandang gabi, po (Good evening). Is Ryan here?"

Ernesto nodded yes.

Maricel's body started trembling. Her pulse raced in her ears. "When he wasn't at his hotel, I figured I'd find him here with the two of you."

Ernesto chuckled softly. "Good detective work. Please come in. He's been waiting day and night for this moment to happen."

Maricel tipped her sad eyes up at him. "Yes, Gloria told me."

"Are you sure you're ready to see him?"

"Part of me wants to run away as fast as I can. But I still love him, po." Maricel sighed. "He leaves in three days, right?"

Ernesto nodded yes.

She frowned. "Well then, no time like the present, right?"

Ernesto nodded again, then whispered, "Shall we?"

She gulped hard and followed her spiritual mentor inside.

Ryan was taking a sip of coffee when Maricel suddenly appeared, wearing a white cotton dress, looking beautiful as ever. Her silky black hair flowed evenly down her back. She looked like an angel, except for the broken expression on her face.

Tipton's mouth dropped open. He was frozen in his seat. The only function he was able to perform besides breathing, shallow as it was, was to move his eyeballs. From behind his sporty new eyeglasses, his suddenly moist, unbelieving eyes followed her every move. The closer she got the more air got stuck in his chest.

He thought to himself, *Am I dreaming?*

The woman who had eluded him the past four days, the past four months, he corrected himself, sat down and adjusted her chair until their kneecaps were touching.

Ryan was certain she felt him trembling through his knees. Her very presence instantly illuminated the grimness that had followed him everywhere he went, since his last visit to this country.

"You were right, Gloria," Maricel said, without taking her eyes off Ryan. "He's even more pogi now. I'm amazed."

Ryan wanted to thank her for the compliment, but he couldn't speak. His lips were so dry they were stuck together. He was too petrified to even blink, for fear that he might blink her away.

Maricel took a deep breath and exhaled, and the words came out of her mouth calmly and smoothly. "I'm sorry for making you suffer all this time. It was wrong of me. Can you please forgive me?"

Tipton blinked hard, then shot her a quizzical look. His ears perked up like a puppy dog's. *She's asking for my forgiveness?* He was completely caught off guard by her words.

Just as Ryan was about to say something, the warm sensation intensified. All four of them felt it; they were rendered speechless by it. They remained silent for the longest time, as it washed over them. It was the most amazing sensation.

After a while, Maricel searched Ryan's eyes; a lone teardrop rode down his right cheek. She couldn't bear to see him in so much pain. She ached for him.

She gathered him in her arms and stroked his hair, as he lay on her left shoulder sobbing, trembling even more than she was.

Gloria and Ernesto were completely blown away by her godly actions. They couldn't have given her a better approach to use. It was simply perfect. Tears streamed down their wrinkled faces, as they witnessed this beautiful moment of healing in silence.

Seeing answered prayer coming to pass before their eyes was too wonderful to tell. Gloria, especially, wanted to know what would happen next. But they needed to leave Ryan and Maricel alone for a while, so they could sort things out.

Ernesto turned to his wife. "How does pancakes and sausage sound, my dear?"

Gloria's face lit up. "Sounds perfect."

Then to Maricel, "We'll lock the door, so no one disturbs you. Take all the time you need. Call us when you're ready, and we'll come back to lock up."

The grateful smile on her face was all the thanks they needed.

Before leaving the building, Gloria flicked on the switch to the ceiling lights trained on the wall proudly showcasing the many happily married couples.

Ernesto whispered into his wife's ear. "Good thinking, dear."

Maricel stroked Ryan's hair thinking, *What an amazing couple!*

After a while, Tipton lifted his head off Maricel's shoulder and removed his glasses. In a contrite voice he said, "I'm so sorry for what I did to you. Meeting with those two other women was the biggest mistake of my life. I know I caused you so much pain."

Maricel craned her neck back before realizing it was pointless. He already saw her tears. She dabbed at her eyes and remained focused on him. "I'm sorry, too."

"You did nothing wrong, Maricel. It's all my fault."

"Initially, yes, it was your fault. Even so, I could have handled the situation so much better. But truth be told, until today, I wasn't sure if I ever wanted to see you again. Still, it gave me no reason to avoid you all this time. It was wrong of me." Maricel looked down at the table and sighed. *Four days wasted because of me...*

"It's okay. In the long run, you've made me appreciate the type of woman you really are. I'm not ashamed to admit you're helping me become a better man. I mean, look at me. Do I look like the same person you saw four months ago?"

Maricel nodded no.

"Wanna know the reason for the many changes in me?

Maricel eyeballed him. "Sure…"

"Last time I was here, Ernesto challenged me to take a personal inventory of myself and make whatever changes I felt were necessary. I quickly realized there were many. First and foremost, I needed to draw closer to my Maker. After sincerely repenting of all my sins, I started reading the Word of God every day."

Ryan peered deeply into her eyes. "By so doing, I realized the close relationship I thought I had with God, wasn't so close after all. My walk with Him was superficial at best. Well, no longer. I can confidently say now that Jesus is my Lord and Savior!"

Wow! A smile curled onto Maricel's lips. "Praise God!"

"I assure you I'm not the man I used to be. While I give God all the glory, my main motivation for the many positive changes you now see, was that I wanted to become the right man for you. So, in that sense, I have you to thank for it."

Maricel became teary-eyed. "Wala akong masabi…"

"What does that mean again?"

"It means, 'I don't know what to say.'" Maricel took a moment to collect herself. She dried her eyes with a napkin. "That's the nicest thing any man has ever said to me."

"It's one-hundred percent true." Ryan paused a moment, then said, "If you wouldn't mind, I'd like to see your family before I go back to the States. I would like to apologize to them face to face."

Maricel smiled wearily. "I'm sure they would appreciate that."

Ryan reached for a breath and exhaled. "There's something else you need to know."

Maricel braced herself. "Yes?"

"I didn't have sex with those two other women."

Maricel gave Ryan a sideways look and almost didn't want to hear anymore. After a brief pause, she motioned for him to continue with a nod of the head.

"I'll admit I was tempted. But each time I felt myself getting weak, it's like God placed your image at the forefront of my mind to protect me from doing something stupid. So, in a crazy sort of way, I have you to thank for it."

After this latest confession, Maricel thought it a little odd to feel jealousy rising inside. She remained silent and listened.

"On my way back to the States last time, I met this man on the plane from Canada. From a womanizing standpoint, he was the worst of the worst. The way he degraded Filipino women was pitiful. I actually thought I was going to punch him in the face."

Ryan grimaced. "It wasn't until a few days later that I realized meeting him was sort of like looking in a mirror.

Though I never did the despicable things he did, I was just as guilty myself for taking the hearts of three women captive, including yours. I'll never do that again as long as I live."

Maricel looked deep into Ryan's eyes and half-smiled. His sincerity was palpable. She believed him.

"Jenny and Liezel—the two women I met last time I was here—are both fine women. They both deserve good men to love. But I'm *not* that man. When I got home, I e-mailed them both, apologizing for lying to them, and for wasting their time."

Ryan shook his head in shame. "I'm sure they were quite bored with me most of the time, because all I did was think about you. Yes, they know about you. They also know I'm in love with you."

Maricel blinked then looked away. It was too soon for that.

Ryan noticed her discomfort and changed the topic. *Slow down!* "So, what do we do now?"

"Perhaps a movie?" Maricel knew that's not what he meant. But given the circumstances, it was the best next step she could take with him.

Ryan's eyes widened. "Are you asking me out on a date?"

"More of a friendly date for now," came the reply. "If we leave soon, we should make it in time. Do you accept?"

"Do I accept? How could I refuse? You just made my whole trip worthwhile." A surge of happiness erupted inside of him. "I feel like the luckiest man on the planet."

Maricel reached inside her purse for her phone. "Let's call Ernesto and Gloria and tell them to come back, so we can leave."

After a topsy-turvy four days, Tipton's battered heart was finally beating normally again.

"Hi, Mister Angeles," Maricel said. "Is it possible for you to come back now?"

"Sure. Is everything okay?"

"Everything's just fine. We're going to see a movie."

"That's wonderful," the older Filipino man said, giving his wife a thumbs-up gesture. "What movie will you see?"

"Not sure. We'll find something," Maricel said, matter of factly. "But we need to hurry."

"We're just finishing our meal. Be back soon."

Not even ten minutes later, they were back. "Welcome to Agape Coffee and Pastry Shoppe. My name is Ryan, how can I help you?"

"Ha! Good one, Ryan," Ernesto said. "Nice to see your sense of humor has returned. It was sorely missed."

Ryan fist bumped Ernesto. "It's nice to be back!"

Ernesto knew what he meant.

Maricel looked at Ernesto and Gloria as tears flooded her eyes. Her lips started quivering. "I honestly think God sent you both to become guardian angels to so many of His needy people. It's impossible to fully express how blessed I feel to be one of them. I honestly don't know what I would have done the past few months without the two of you, and this wonderful coffee shop. Thanks, for everything."

As if by osmosis, Gloria became teary-eyed herself. "No need to thank us. We love you both very much and want you to be happy together."

"When I grow up, I want to be just like you, Ernesto," Ryan said, trying to be funny, before growing serious again. "I couldn't imagine my life without the three of you in it."

He glanced at Maricel. His voice grew softer. "Especially you."

Maricel lowered her head. Everyone knew she was blushing.

Ryan glanced at Ernesto. "I may not be here the next two days. But I promise to be here on Sunday, no matter what."

Ernesto replied, "There's no need for you to be here. I'm sure Maricel is eager to show you more of our beautiful city, before you go back to the States."

Maricel said, "We still didn't go to Corregidor Island."

Ryan could only smile. Her words greatly comforted him. Finally, he said, "Shall we, sweetie?"

There was total silence. His comment hung thick in the air for the longest time. Ryan was mortified, and wished he could somehow retract his words.

That is, until Maricel nodded yes, then flashed the most amazing smile she could generate. It was a smile Ryan hadn't seen in four long months. It was a smile he felt he hadn't yet earned, yet there it was. It stopped his heart from exploding inside his chest.

Ernesto opened the door for them. "Have fun at the movies."

Once they were gone, the elderly couple dashed to one of the plate glass windows and watched the young couple slowly walking away. Both were anxious to see what would happen next.

Almost immediately, Ryan reached for Maricel's hand, to which she didn't object.

"Atta boy, Ryan," Ernesto said, proudly.

"Praise God," was all Gloria could manage to say, through a new batch of tears. Though she had witnessed similar scenes with couples in the past, it never grew old. Moments like this made all her hard work worthwhile.

Why would anyone want to retire from a job like this?

To Ernesto and Gloria Angeles, it was simply unthinkable...

21

THREE DAYS LATER, RYAN Tipton and Maricel Arcamo arrived at Agape Coffee and Pastry Shoppe. It was just before one p.m., and Ernesto and Gloria Angeles were already busy making coffee and baking fresh pastries for the 3 p.m. Bible study.

"Magandang hapon, Ernesto," Ryan said.

Ernesto wiped his sweaty brow with his forearm. "Welcome back to our humble little slice of Heaven. How was church?"

"He's quite a preacher," Ryan said about Maricel's pastor.

"That's what Maricel keeps telling us."

Ryan clasped his hands together. "Still in need of volunteers?"

A grin formed on Ernesto's face. "Well, Ryan, like Jesus said, the harvest is plentiful, but the workers are so few."

"Since you put it that way, how can I help?"

The old man said, "Why don't you ask Maricel. She knows what needs to be done. You can take your orders from her."

Tipton shifted his gaze to her. "What are my orders, sweetie?"

Maricel paused a moment, then said, "You can sweep then mop the floor. I'll clean the tables and chairs. Then we can arrange them together, okay?"

Ryan saluted her. "Yes sir, ma'am."

Gloria asked, "By the way, how was the movie the other night?"

"The best ever," Ryan replied.

"What movie did you see?"

"It was some Tagalog movie. I didn't understand most of it, Gloria, but believe me when I say, it was the best movie ever."

Gloria winked. "Got it. Did you visit Corregidor Island?"

Maricel answered, "Yesterday. We had a wonderful time."

Just then, Jason Angeles emerged from the kitchen with a broom, a bucket full of hot water, and two mops.

Ernesto said, "Ryan, meet my son, Jason."

The two men shook hands. "Pleasure meeting you. I'm sure you already know you have the most amazing parents on the planet."

Jason nodded in agreement. "I couldn't be more blessed."

"Would you like me to sweep or mop?" Ryan said.

"You can sweep."

"Okay, sweep it is."

At that, everyone went to work.

At 2:30 p.m., everything was set. The rich coffee aroma and fresh-baked breads and pastries wafted in the air, just as everyone started arriving. Different from any other day at this place was that Gloria used real China cups and saucers, instead of the disposable cups they used the rest of the week. As guests helped themselves to free coffee and pastries, anticipation hung thick in the air.

At 3 p.m., the Bible study began right on time. Like all other Sundays, every seat was taken, including the six counter seats.

Those who were unable to occupy seats gladly stood just to participate. In all, there were 120 people in attendance.

Ryan Tipton felt like the luckiest person on the planet to be gathered among them. The warm sensation rising in the air was so intense everyone felt it. The only other time he felt it this strongly was when he and Maricel reconciled three days ago.

But even then, it wasn't sustained like now. It's like he could almost touch it.

As always, Ernesto opened the session in prayer. When he was finished, he looked at his son. "As we begin week three of our study of the Book of Colossians, I'll ask Jason to kindly read today's memory verses, found in Colossians three, verses twelve through fourteen…"

"Sure, Papa." Jason took a sip of water and began, 'As God's chosen people, holy and dearly loved, clothe yourselves with compassion, kindness, humility, gentleness and patience. Bear with each other and forgive whatever grievances you may have against one another. Forgive as the Lord forgave you. And over all these virtues put on love, which binds them all together in perfect unity.'"

"Thank you, son," the Godly Filipino man said, with a certain glow on his face that was contagious. Letting his gaze settle on the group before him, he went on, "Do those two passages comfort you as much as they do me?"

Many heads nodded throughout the coffee shop.

"Does anyone remember last week's memory verses?"

"I do," said Samuel, a youth pastor from a nearby church. He came most Sundays after service. From memory, he said, "Colossians chapter two, verses thirteen and fourteen: 'He forgave us all our sins, having canceled the written code, with its regulations, that was against us and that stood opposed to us; he took it away, nailing it to the cross.'"

"Thank you, Samuel," Ernesto said. "Does anyone remember the memory verses from two weeks ago, found in the first chapter of the Book of Colossians?"

Without raising her hand, Maricel recited it also from memory. "Colossians chapter one, verses thirteen and fourteen: 'For he has rescued us from the dominion of darkness and brought us into the kingdom of the Son he loves, in whom we have redemption, the forgiveness of sins.'"

Ryan glanced at his girlfriend and raised an eyebrow. He was quite impressed that she knew it.

Maricel smiled at him without taking her eyes off Ernesto.

Ernesto began, "Don't you just love the Book of Colossians? It's one of my favorite books in the Bible. It would be impossible for any fair-minded person reading those passages to deny just how much God, in all His Sovereignty, loves His children.

"Someone told me a long time ago that religion is man-made, but relationship with Jesus is God-made. His words had a profound impact on me. What he meant was, in and of itself, man-inspired religion is more focused on church doctrine, tradition, and on the performing of various works and rituals than anything else. It's also more of a group participation thing."

Ernesto frowned. "I've met too many faithful churchgoers over the years who, after receiving too strong a dose of religion and church doctrine, ended up utterly confused. Despite how often they went to church, they still felt nothing close to intimacy with God. If anything, they felt misguided to the point of disillusionment.

"Sadly, so many churches that are 'religious' or 'works-based' have pews full of people who, from a spiritual standpoint, look more dead than alive. Instead of leaning into God's limitless mercy and forgiveness, they cling too tightly to religion and are crippled by guilt as a result, thus keeping them bound and chained in spiritual darkness."

Ernesto sighed. "How can anyone rejoice under such gloomy conditions? This unhealthy mindset constantly weighs them down, by making them feel guilty and even worthless at times. It's tragic to witness. Do they even understand God's Word? I think not.

"True relationship with God, on the other hand, is deeply personal and intimate. According to Romans eight, verse one, everyone who experiences this intimacy, through a personal relationship with Christ Jesus, has eternal assurance."

Ernesto glanced quickly at Ryan. "Such individuals never need to fear eternal condemnation or separation from their Creator. How awesome is that! Performing various good works or being part of any particular church or denomination cannot bring anyone closer to God. It all comes down to His amazing grace. Nothing more."

Ernesto paused to take a sip of water. "Allow me to give you a brief demonstration to further explain the difference between

'Religion' and 'Relationship'. How many of you have children?"

Most hands went up, including a woman in her early thirties named, Anabel. The mother of two was a frequent attendee on Sundays.

"Anabel, how would you feel if you came home from work one day and Jonah and Sarah sat you down on the couch, then sang the most beautiful heartfelt song you've ever heard, a song they wrote just for you, demonstrating their undying love to you for being such an awesome mother to them?"

Tears formed in Anabel's eyes. "Wow!"

Ernesto smiled. "Would it be a life-defining moment for you?"

Anabel nodded yes.

"What if their voices were off key most of the time?"

"It wouldn't matter," came the reply, softly.

Ernesto pressed on, "What if, on the other hand, they recited some generic script they learned in class with the other students, intended for all mothers instead of you alone?"

Anabel squirmed in her chair. "Hmm."

"Exactly," he said with a clap of his hands to further demonstrate his point. "Even if the words were heartfelt and the presentation was flawless, chances are good it might sound a little too scripted, and would lack the proper emotion, right?"

"Opo (Yes sir)."

"I'm sure you would still appreciate it, but could it compete with the heartfelt song they wrote then sang just for you?"

Anabel shook her head no.

"That's because the memorized song came more from the head, and the song they wrote came more from the heart, right?"

"Opo," the mother of two said again.

The coffee shop owner let his gaze wander over the room again. "Personally, I think that's the biggest difference between religion and relationship. Religion is more from the head, like some memorized script, but relationship with God comes straight from the heart, like a beautiful song."

Confident grin on his face, he said, "Ladies and gentlemen, if there's one thing you take from this lesson, let it be this: God doesn't want your memorized prayers or pompous religious church doctrine. What He wants is one on one intimacy with you; the kind that comes straight from the heart and is up close and personal."

Anabel looked completely glazed over, after just being greatly impacted by his powerful demonstration.

She wasn't the only one.

Ernesto went on, with a razor-sharp determination on his face that Ryan Tipton had never before seen, "But I'm afraid merely understanding the difference between religion and relationship cannot save your soul. Only those who have been transformed by the power of the Holy Spirit, through regeneration, are truly born again. This is the very essence of relationship with God.

"Don't get me wrong, by no means am I suggesting that becoming a Christian is a mindless act. According to Romans chapter twelve, verse two, we need to be constantly transformed by the renewing of our minds. This can only happen by reading the Word of God, which, by the way, is the most important thing—besides prayer itself—any follower of Jesus can do. Every time we open its Divinely inspired pages, God speaks to us.

"Of course, there is no such thing as a perfect Christian." Ernesto sighed. "Sadly, even after we are saved, we continue sinning against our Maker. The Apostle Paul, who I believe was the greatest Christian who ever lived, made this crystal clear in Romans, chapter seven, when he explained about the Law and sin.

"In verse fifteen, Paul said, 'What I want to do I do not do, but what I hate I do.' He even went so far to call himself a wretched man. Imagine that? You must understand, this was recorded *after* God saved him and all his sins were forgiven, not beforehand.

191

"Paul was reminding us that, as Christians, the old man dies hard. Because of our fallen sinful nature, though we are redeemed by the blood of Jesus, our flesh will constantly be at war with the Spirit within us. But because of what Christ did on the cross, we are no longer slaves to sin, which means we are in no danger of facing eternal condemnation."

The smile on his face was so bright, it warmed each soul in attendance. "Once God saves us, He is faithful to complete what He begins in us, ultimately making us more like Christ through sanctification. In short: even when we are at our weakest, those who are truly born-again are never in danger of falling out of the arms of our loving Savior. How amazing is that!"

Many in attendance broke into the warmest of smiles.

Ernesto's smile quickly faded. "But you must understand that only Christ followers get to experience this eternal grace and forgiveness I speak of. It pains me to say this but there are many in the world, and perhaps even some in this room, who think they are going to Heaven when they die, when, in truth, they are really hell bound.

"Jesus declared in Matthew seven, verses twenty-one through twenty-three that many who think they are in relationship with Him really aren't. Many are churchgoers who think they can somehow earn their salvation. Not to sound insensitive but they are nothing more than false converts who have no understanding of the true Gospel message of Jesus Christ.

"Religious people are always disturbed to hear that their religion counts for nothing. Most want to take some credit for how close they think they are to God. They mentally log hours spent in church, not to mention the various good things they do for others, as if they are scoring bonus points with their Maker.

"When it comes to God's plan of salvation, those things count for nothing. The simple truth is the only thing any of us— me and Gloria included—can bring to our salvation is our sin which needs forgiving. Because of the corrupt sinful nature all of us inherited at birth, even the things we may perceive to be our greatest accomplishments are seen by God as filthy rags.

"The first step to receiving God's salvation is acknowledging you are a sinner, and that your sins are an affront to God's holiness. Because of this, you stand condemned before your Maker. As guilty sinners, the only solution at our disposal is to repent before God and receive the salvation He freely offers through Christ Jesus. There are no exceptions to this Gospel truth.

"Only then is anyone ever truly free of sin, guilt and oppression. Only then can they move forward with a clear conscience, without fearing eternal consequences. And it's all because of what Jesus did on the cross two-thousand years ago! Praise His holy name!"

Loud applause reverberated throughout the coffee shop.

Ernesto grew serious again. "With those eternal truths settled in your minds, let me just say that if you think you are without sin and don't need God's forgiveness, the Word of God declares that the truth isn't in you."

The room fell silent. Many leaned forward in their seats, completely breathless, desperate to hear what would come out of Ernesto's mouth next.

He continued, "Two of my favorite Bible verses are found in Psalm thirty-two, verses one and two, where King David wrote: 'Blessed is the one whose transgression is forgiven, whose sin is covered. Blessed is the man against whom the Lord counts no iniquity...'"

"Gloria and I are eternally grateful to be counted among this group. How about you? Do you know Jesus? Really know Him? In other words, if your life came to an end today, do you have absolute assurance of spending eternity in Heaven with God Almighty?"

Ernesto shook his head somberly. "Sorry to say this but, if you need to think about it, chances are you don't have such assurance. If this is you, since there are only two eternal destinations, nothing can be more important than knowing where your soul will be transported the instant your time on earth comes to an end.

"With that in mind, if you have any doubts or questions regarding God's plan of salvation, allow me the honor and great privilege of sharing it with you before you leave. Since tomorrow is guaranteed to no one, the time to draw close to God is now!"

Tipton surveyed the room, completely astonished. *This place really is a church, only it's disguised as a coffee and pastry shop!*

If churches were supposed to be in the "changing lives" business, this place was better equipped to meet that challenge than most other so-called "real" churches in the world.

The many photographs on the walls indicated that much. He was certain they were only a fraction of the lives God had changed over the years, using Ernesto and Gloria as His human messengers.

Before dismissing everyone, Gloria took prayer requests from the many gathered. One by one they made their petitions known. The coffee shop owner listened very carefully to each request—whether serious or not so pressing—and even took notes.

After the final prayer request was recorded, she bowed her head and prayed for each person with a level of genuine faith, mixed with a gentle passion, that Ryan had never been exposed to before.

The faith she demonstrated in her Creator seemed to take everyone else straight into the presence of the Most High. It was as if she knew she had God's ear, which everyone knew she most certainly did. It was remarkable.

She ended her lengthy prayer by saying, "Thank You, Father, for hearing our prayers, and for always being in our midst…"

She paused a moment, then added, "On a personal note, I wish to thank You for reconciling our dear friends, Ryan and Maricel, this week. It's only because You first loved us that we're capable of loving others so freely and offering them our forgiveness, especially those who have hurt us ever so deeply..."

Ryan reached for Maricel's hand, as Gloria finished, "We lift this beautiful couple up to You, asking Your guidance in their relationship every step of the way, from this day forward. Thy will be done, Lord, in Your precious name we pray, Amen!"

"Amen!" came the reply from the gathered crowd.

Everyone stood to leave. All but seven, that is...

Wanting that same eternal assurance Ernesto was so passionate about sharing with everyone else, they remained behind as their mentor shared the Gospel with them.

Feeling God breathing regenerating life into their souls, each repented before their Maker and trusted in Christ as Lord and Savior. By crossing over from spiritual death to life, all seven were Heaven bound when their lives on earth came to an end someday...

Gloria watched it all unfolding, with an expression on her face that only a few individuals ever got to display. Of the countless benefits the Angeles' received from owning this establishment, nothing came close to the blessing of winning souls to Jesus!

To them, it was the ultimate prize and what they constantly yearned for more than anything else, because it further confirmed that they were doing exactly what God had called them to do.

And what could be better than that?

22

WITH JUST 30 MINUTES left to clean and prepare the place for the character-building class at 6p.m., it was time to get busy again.

Because Agape Coffee and Pastry Shoppe was closed on Sundays, Ernesto and Gloria Angeles relied solely on volunteers to help them prepare each week.

Ryan wasted no time loading trays full of dirty plates, cups and silverware, before taking them to the kitchen and washing them.

Maricel wiped the countertop and all chairs with a soapy cloth.

Jason swept, then mopped the floor, then deposited all trash into the waste basket.

Gloria brewed more fresh pots of coffee. Ernesto fired up the oven to bake the rest of the pastries he had prepared earlier. He was still rejoicing after having the unspeakable privilege of sharing the Gospel with seven of his guests.

There was nothing he enjoyed doing more…

Washing the last of the dishes by hand, Tipton thought back to his first visit four months ago, when the Angeles' insisted on treating him to coffee. It occurred to him that whenever someone prayed or displayed genuine Godly love toward someone else at this most blessed place, it was then that God's presence strengthened considerably.

Now more than ever, he sensed many of the customers frequenting this place might still be lost, if not for this wonderful couple and the safe haven they provided. Ryan wished there was a place like this back in Iowa.

If such a place existed, he would no doubt be one of its most frequent customers, especially on Sundays.

He hated to think what would ever happen if this place ever closed its doors for business. *Now that would be a real tragedy*, he thought, taking a seat next to Maricel.

As the Godly Filipino couple opened the meeting in prayer, Ryan scanned the room, and saw many new faces, including a dozen or so foreigners. The crowd was noticeably younger.

Whereas Ernesto taught earlier, it was Gloria's turn now. It didn't take long for Ryan to see that she was just as passionate and articulate as her husband was. Her topic was called, "relationship earthquakes."

She began, "How can any of us know the true level of our faith in God if it's never tested? Following our daughter's suicide twenty years ago, as you might imagine, Ernesto and I were completely shattered. But even with the unrelenting pain and heartache we felt, we knew God had presented us with an opportunity to remain obedient and keep on serving Him, despite it all."

Gloria sighed. "I confess it wasn't always easy. But I also knew if I didn't take this pain and make it my purpose, it would eventually devour me from within. Thankfully, we passed God's extremely challenging test. The reward we received was that we learned how to experience lasting peace in the storms of life.

"We also learned that adversity was a bridge to deeper relationship with God. Think about it; how can any couple ever know for sure if their relationship is solid, if it's never been tested? The fact that all of us are wired so differently sets the stage for the many challenges we face from time to time. After all, if two people agree on all things, one of them is unnecessary, right?"

Laughter could be heard all throughout the coffee shop.

Gloria glanced out at everyone. "Show me a relationship that's never been tested, and I'll show you one that can't be fully trusted. I believe the key to any successful long-lasting relationship—aside from trusting in God to lead every step of the way—is how we act when those inescapable trying times invade our lives.

"Let's face it, it's easy to be happy when all is well. Where's the challenge there? Of course, it's never much fun when the ground is shaking violently beneath your feet. But that's when your true character is revealed, and everyone sees you for who you really are.

"In our case, by leaning on God's understanding, instead of our human emotion, the bond between us strengthened considerably once the storm passed. In fact, it was then that the greatest spiritual growth took place in our lives and our children's lives as well.

"By always trusting that He was in complete control, always with our best interests at heart, we came to understand what Jesus' brother James said in the Book bearing his name, 'Consider it all joy, brothers and sisters, when you meet trials of many kinds, because you know that the testing of your faith produces perseverance. And let perseverance finish its work so that you may be mature and complete, not lacking anything.'"

A warm smile crossed Gloria's face. "Words can never fully describe how incredible it feels to finally reach this level of spiritual maturity in life."

Ryan tightened his grip on Maricel's hand. Having barely survived their recent relationship earthquake—an earthquake that he himself had created—Gloria's words comforted him greatly.

Noticing Ryan's expression, Gloria said, "Despite the length of any relationship, I personally believe God allows these earthquakes to occur from time to time to shake things up. This way, the many unhealthy components that creep into most relationships are dislodged and fall through the cracks, while the important elements remain intact, strengthening the deep bond all successful relationships develop over time.

"Guess you could say this is just one of the many ways God prunes us all, whether it be a friendship, business or marriage. Sure, it hurts when God prunes us, but it's always done with our best interests at heart, which leads to the deepening of our faith..."

By the time the session had ended, it was 7:15 p.m.

"So, what did you think of my wife's presentation?" Ernesto said to Ryan.

Tipton raised his hands, palms out, as if in surrender. "What can I say, I'm beyond words."

Ernesto grinned at his reply. "Next comes phase three, catering to the many brokenhearted soon to be visiting us. Hope you can stick around for it."

"As much as I'd love to stay, I want to spend my last night with Maricel's family. I've already apologized to her parents on the phone, but I want to do it in person before heading back to the States." Ernesto was impressed hearing this. It was evident on his face. Ryan added, "But I promise to stop by in the morning, to see you both one last time before heading to the airport."

Ernesto sighed. "We'll be sad to see you leaving us again."

"At least I'm leaving on good terms this time, right?"

"Amen to that! Gloria and I really appreciate your help today."

"My pleasure. You'll never know how life-changing this has been for me, especially spiritually. By far, this was the third best day I've ever spent in the Philippines."

Ernesto shot Ryan a confused glance. "Third?"

Ryan nodded at him. "My best day was the first full day I spent with Maricel, my first time here." Ryan didn't mention the first kiss part. "My second-best day was three days ago when we reconciled our relationship."

Ryan glared intently at Ernesto. "This is my third best day. But hey, the night's still young. Perhaps it'll end up being my best day here before it's over," he said, with a nervous twitch.

Ernesto caught on to where he was going, but he decided not to press him for details. "Don't lose that confidence, young man."

"I'll try not to." There was a pause. "And guess what?"

"What?" Ernesto said, just as Gloria joined them.

"I'm one-hundred percent certain the warm sensation I feel in this place is God's Holy Spirit making His presence known to all who come to your coffee shop."

Ernesto nodded. "I knew you'd figure it out sooner or later."

"I also know the reason it's felt so strongly here is because you and Gloria love and treat each person unconditionally, just like Jesus would if He worked here. It's all about relationships here, first with God, then with others. I'm living proof."

"To God be the glory, Ryan."

"Not only did I know you'd say that, Ernesto, I wholeheartedly agree with you."

Ryan glanced at Maricel, still grateful for this second chance she was giving him. *Just hope I feel this way later*, he thought, with a sigh. "Ready, sweetie?"

"Ready," came the reply, warmly.

Gloria said, "Wait, before you go, would it be okay if I took your picture and hung it on that wall over there?"

Ryan stiffened and squared his shoulders back. "Of course, Gloria! This is a dream come true for me!"

"Me too," Maricel said softly, glowingly.

Using her cell phone, Gloria took their picture, then dashed to the small office in the back to print a copy, before hanging it on the wall featuring those still developing relationships.

Ryan and Maricel stared at each other with lovestruck expressions on their faces. After four long, uncertain months of waiting for this moment to arrive, it was finally upon them.

Though it was only step one, just seeing it hanging on one of the coveted walls of this incredible establishment filled them both with the most indescribable sensation.

After sharing a warm embrace with their spiritual mentors, they took a taxi to Maricel's house in Quezon City...

23

BY THE TIME THEY arrived at the house, it was 8:30 p.m. Hazel heard a taxi pull to a stop at the front of the house. She pulled back the curtain window. "They're here!" she yelled to her husband.

Hazel watched them getting out of the vehicle. Even though she had seen the many pictures that her daughter had posted on Facebook and on Instagram the past two days, they couldn't compare to seeing Ryan in person. He looked totally different.

She rushed to the front door to greet them. She exclaimed, "Wow, Ryan, look at you! You look like a new man!"

The excitement in her voice, without a trace of anger, indicated to Ryan that she was genuinely happy to see him again. He took a deep breath and relaxed. His inner trembling subsided. "Thanks, Hazel. It's so nice to see you again. All of you, in fact."

When Hazel and Francisco heard about how Ryan had been camped out at the coffee shop waiting for Maricel to show up, for four straight days, both were convinced Ryan was a repentant man, and that he truly loved his daughter.

Hazel said, "Let's eat while the food's still hot. I prepared only the foods you like this time."

Francisco blessed the food, and everyone dug in.

Ryan filled half his plate with rice, flattened it, then piled a heaping amount of pork adobo on top, so the juices would seep into the rice. The other half of the plate was filled with pancit.

In between bites of food, Ryan said, "It's been a while, Miguel. How's life been treating you?"

Miguel smiled warmly. "Okay lang."

"And how about you, Vivian?"

After a brief pause, she finally managed to say, "Okay lang..." Taking another nervous breath, she added, "Mama made your favorite dessert—mango float."

Ryan's heart nearly stopped beating inside his chest. *She spoke to me!* "Wow! Really?"

"Oo nga," came the reply. After a brief moment of eye contact, Vivian looked down at her feet again. It was a start.

After a delicious meal, Ryan rubbed his much thinner tummy. "I must say, if I stayed here another week, I'd easily gain back the thirty pounds I worked so hard to lose the past four months."

Miguel and Vivian both chuckled softly at his comment.

Hazel's grin covered her entire face. "Glad you enjoyed it."

"More than you know, Hazel!" It was evident to the Arcamos that Ryan was grateful for this second chance he was being given by them. It was as if the past four months had never happened...

With dinner finished, Maricel excused herself so she could shower before Rosa arrived.

When she went upstairs, in a nervous whisper, Ryan said to Francisco and Hazel, "Would it be okay if we spoke in private?"

"Why don't we sit out on the front porch?"

A moment later they were outside with refills from a delicious fruit drink Hazel had prepared for dinner. It was a family recipe that was handed down from many generations. It had a hint of coconut and pineapple juice.

Francisco called it the ultimate thirst quencher.

After taking a few sips, Tipton came to the point, "I want to take this time to reiterate what I said on the phone yesterday."

"Which part?"

"About what I did last time I was here. You took me in and accepted me for who I was, without ever judging my appearance or making me feel uncomfortable. And how did I repay you? By lying to you and nearly ruining something special..."

Ryan became teary-eyed. "When it finally dawned on me that my selfish actions not only hurt Maricel, but all of you, I felt like the worst person on the planet. The thought of losing you all was the worst kind of torture for me. It will never happen again. Promise."

Francisco leaned up in his chair and spoke calmly. "I admit the past four months have been stressful around here, but what's past is past. Just seeing Maricel happy again is all that matters to us."

Ryan cleared his throat. "I know this will sound awkward, but I want you both to know I didn't have sex with the two women I met on my last trip here. I never even kissed them on the lips."

There was no reply to his outlandish comment. But not even all the gold in Fort Knox could equal in value to what Ryan saw on their faces, Francisco's especially. It was like the head of the Arcamo family had just reactivated his full membership back into the family.

Nothing else needed to be said on the matter.

Francisco reached for his wife's hand. "We know you're a good man, Ryan. You proved it by coming all this way to win our daughter back. Maricel's feelings for you are genuine. She truly loves you. We've all come to love you, in fact."

Tipton gulped hard. "Enough to call me your son-in-law?"

There was total silence. Hazel and Francisco stared at each other blankly at first, as if they were hearing things.

Francisco blinked hard, then shifted his weight in his chair. "What are you suggesting?"

"I'm here to ask your permission, and your blessing, for your daughter's hand in marriage. That is, if neither of you object."

Francisco said, "Of course, you have our permission, Ryan, and our blessing."

Relief flooded Tipton's face. "You'll never know what this means to me. I just hope Maricel accepts my proposal."

"Us too, Ryan," said Hazel, holding back tears. "Having you as our son-in-law would be answered prayer."

With a grateful expression on his face, Ryan said. "I want you both to know that if she says yes, I'll do my very best to make sure she feels completely safe and protected in America, at all times.

"Once we're settled, I'll see that she visits here at least once a year. If I have to get a second job, I'll do it. Naturally, my hope is that God will bless us with children someday..."

Grandchildren? Hazel wiped tears from her eyes and silently prayed that her daughter would say yes to Ryan's proposal.

Maricel Tipton, hmm... Francisco liked the sound of it.

Just then, Maricel appeared at the front door, wearing pink cotton shorts and a white shirt. Her hair was still wet. She saw her mother brushing tears from her eyes. And there was this satisfied look on her father's face that was impossible to overlook.

But that's not what nearly caused her heart to jump out of her chest. That wasn't it at all. The porch light was bright enough to expose the anticipatory expression she saw on Ryan's face, as he struggled to catch his next breath.

Swallowing the hairball in his throat, he rose from the wicker chair he was seated on and met Maricel at the door. Her eyes grew wide, and she let out an audible gasp. She covered her face with her hands and closed her eyes, trying to stabilize her breathing.

When she opened them again, Ryan was on one knee gazing up at her. His palms and face were soaked with perspiration. He removed his sporty eyeglasses with one hand, reached into his pants pocket with the other, and pulled out a small box.

Maricel's trembling increased. *Is this really happening? I must be dreaming!* If she released her grip on the door handle for even one second, she felt she might float away...

Maricel Arcamo had often wondered how it would feel to be on the receiving end of a marriage proposal. This was something she'd dreamed about since her teenage years.

Like most other hopeless romantics on the planet, she envisioned being at some fancy restaurant having a candlelight dinner, or at a luxurious resort, or even at the beach, and hearing someone uttering those four words to her, "Will you marry me?"

Never in a million years did she think it would take place on her own front porch—after just showering of all things—with her family watching and listening.

But now that the moment was finally upon her, this was so much better than all those other places, because she was surrounded by those she loved most in life.

Now that it was happening for real, Maricel did the strangest thing. Perhaps it was to ease the constant anguish she'd subjected Ryan to the past four months by her total silence.

Whatever the reason, she awkwardly took a knee across from her boyfriend. Before Ryan could even ask the question, Maricel said, "Yes, I'll marry you!"

At first, Ryan blinked hard, trying to hide the quizzical expression on his face.

He glanced at Francisco and Hazel. Francisco shrugged his shoulders, as Hazel shot her daughter an inquisitive sideways look.

Ryan quickly let his gaze settle back on Maricel. "Really, you'll marry me?"

Maricel nodded then collapsed in his arms.

Miguel and Vivian joined them outside, just in time to witness Ryan putting the ring on their sister's finger.

Once it was secured in place, the newly engaged couple kissed in front of God and Maricel's family. Vivian burst into tears. She couldn't be happier for her older sister.

"NO WAY!" ROSALYN SHOUTED, seeing Ryan and Maricel on their knees embracing on the front porch. She'd just gotten off the jeepney and was 50 steps away from the Arcamo residence.

Sensing that a marriage proposal had just taken place, she crossed the street as quickly as she could, doing her best to brush back tears.

Rosa asked Hazel, "Did she just get engaged?"

Hazel nodded yes, as a stream of joyful tears streamed down her cheeks one after the next. Her face was aglow.

Just as Rosalyn was about to ask to see the ring, Ryan started praying, thanking God for this incredible moment.

To see him praying so eloquently in front of the Arcamos rendered Rosa speechless, which, in itself, was miraculous.

But even if she could speak, she wouldn't want to ruin the moment by trying to find the proper words to describe it.

Rosa plucked her mobile phone from her purse and started taking pictures. Just seeing her best friend engaged to the man of her dreams filled her with an inexpressible joy that was simply priceless.

The animosity she'd harbored toward Ryan Tipton all this time, for hurting her best friend so badly, quickly dissipated.

He turned out to be a good man after all...

24

AT 10 A.M., THE next morning, Ryan and Maricel walked inside Agape Coffee and Pastry Shoppe. They were all smiles.

"Magandang umaga!" Ryan said to Gloria, in his usual American accent. Even after all this time, he still had difficulty pronouncing the word "magandang". This was his best attempt so far.

"Keep it up, Ryan," she said, "you're improving."

Ryan glanced briefly at Maricel before refocusing his attention back on Gloria. "Now that I have a good teacher again, I plan to do just that!"

Gloria was refilling someone's coffee cup. "We're sure going to miss you, Ryan."

"Don't worry, I'll be back soon enough, Lord willing."

Maricel said, "Yesterday was such an incredible day!"

Gloria nodded in agreement. "I never grow tired of spending my Sundays here. Where else can I go to witness scenes like what happened yesterday, or the other night between the two of you? It was one of the most precious moments ever..."

Gloria watched them exchange more lovestruck glances, and it dawned on her. For a couple about to be separated for who knew how long, this wasn't normal behavior. "What's gotten into you both?"

Ryan said, "We were wondering, if you would kindly move our picture from that wall to the engaged wall?"

Gloria's jaw nearly hit the counter she was standing behind. Just three days ago, her American friend was a broken man. Now this? "Are you saying what I think you are?"

Before Ryan could answer, Maricel lifted her hand, brilliantly showcasing the ring her fiancé had placed on her finger. "He proposed to me last night at home, in front of my parents!"

Gloria let out a loud scream, startling some of her customers. "Sorry everyone, but we have another engagement to celebrate!"

The coffee shop was 70-percent full of customers. Most of them applauded enthusiastically.

Gloria wrapped her arms around the newly engaged couple. "Praise God for answered prayer!"

Ernesto was back in the kitchen washing dishes and heard the loud commotion. "Is everything okay, dear?"

"Come here, honey. Ryan and Maricel just arrived. They have exciting news to share."

Ernesto cleaned his hands and quickly joined them. Without even asking, he knew what was happening. His premonition last night was correct after all. It was written all over the young couple's faces. "Did he propose to you, Maricel?"

"Opo," Maricel said joyously.

"Mind if I take a look?"

Maricel held out her left hand, so Ernesto could inspect the diamond ring his new hero had placed there last night.

Ernesto whistled through his teeth. "I see someone has good taste in diamonds. Job well done, Ryan!"

Tipton was all aglow. "Salamat, Ernesto. Turns out yesterday really was my best day in the Philippines after all."

"I should say so. As you take this next big step in life together, our prayer will be that God will guide every step along the way."

Gloria said, "Any details yet of your upcoming wedding?"

"No dates have been set yet," Ryan replied, "but we plan on having two weddings—one here and one in the U.S. Truth be told, after my first failed marriage, my parents aren't too thrilled at the prospect of me marrying another foreigner. But once they meet Maricel, they'll have a quick change of heart."

"I agree, wholeheartedly, young man," Ernesto said.

"Soon as we iron out all the details, you'll be the first to know, especially since I want you to be my best man in the Philippines."

Ernesto lowered his head. "I said I wouldn't let myself get emotional, yet here I am about to start sobbing like a baby..."

Ryan asked him. "Does that mean you'll accept?"

Ernesto tipped his head up. "I wouldn't miss this opportunity for anything in the world. I'm honored that you would even ask."

"The honor's all mine, dear friend."

Maricel then reached for Gloria's hand. "I've already asked Rosalyn to be my maid of honor, and my sister, Vivian, to be one of my bridesmaids. Would you like to be my other bridesmaid?"

Gloria enthusiastically nodded yes. With tears in their eyes, the two women embraced again.

Ryan hated to break the moment, but time was of the essence. "As much as we'd love to stay, we're on our way to visit Maricel's pastor to get his blessing, before heading to the airport..."

Maricel interjected, "As you can imagine, I'm eager to show off my ring to everyone I can before Ryan leaves."

"We understand," the old man replied. "Go now. Enjoy yourselves. And have a safe and pleasant flight back to the States, young man."

Maricel said, "Wait! We need to move our picture first..."

All eyes were fixed on Ryan and Maricel as they removed their photograph from the "still developing a relationship" wall and secured it tightly to the "engaged only" wall.

"Let me officially present to you our newly engaged couple, Mister Ryan Tipton and Miss Maricel Arcamo," Ernesto declared, to a rousing ovation from everyone.

Maricel ducked her head at the sudden burst of attention. But even with the many joyful tears streaming down her cheeks—one after the next—nothing could erase the smile from her face.

Ryan placed one hand on Ernesto's right shoulder and another on Gloria's left shoulder. "I will cherish the day I met you both for the remainder of my life."

Ernesto replied for the both of them, "Likewise, Ryan."

Before coming to the Philippines, Tipton had heard of the word "agape", but only had a vague understanding of its meaning.

But after his life was profoundly impacted in a place bearing that name, he Googled the word "agape" when he got home, and learned it represented God's divine, unconditional, self-sacrificing, ongoing love.

Many Bible scholars believed the best definition of agape love was found in John 3:16: *For God so loved the world that he gave his one and only Son, that whoever believes in him shall not perish but have eternal life.*

While it was impossible for humans to fully express that same self-sacrificing love that was focused solely on the well-being of others, Ernesto and Gloria Angeles came very close to hitting that mark.

The proof was that, after everything he did on his first visit to their country, they still loved him unconditionally.

To be in their presence now, presenting Maricel Arcamo as his fiancée, was simply too awesome to put into words.

It was priceless...

After sharing one last heartfelt embrace, the newly engaged couple left Agape Coffee and Pastry Shoppe, eager to tell the world—at least Maricel's world—about the wonderful news...

25

TWO YEARS LATER

"AGAPE COFFEE AND PASTRY Shoppe, this is Ernesto, how can I help you?"

"Hi Ernesto. It's Ryan."

"Hi Ryan! Gloria and I were just talking about you on the way to work. How's everything with you and Maricel?"

Maricel was listening on Ryan's speaker phone. "Fine, po, and you?"

"What can I say? I'm as blessed today as the day I married Gloria."

"Aww, that's so sweet." Maricel never grew tired of hearing her spiritual mentor say that.

"I must say, Maricel, though you are greatly missed here on Sundays, Miguel and Vivian have become quite capable volunteers in your absence. Rosalyn too, for that matter. You would be so proud of them."

Even though Ernesto couldn't see it, the comment earned him a smile. "Mama and Papa told me Vivian's really coming out of her shell. She even talks to Ryan on Skype now."

Ryan chimed in, "Yeah, talk about a miracle!"

Ernesto laughed at his comment. "When you come back to the Philippines, you'll see just how much progress she has made. It's been a remarkable transformation to say the least."

"That's one of the reasons we're calling, actually," Ryan said. "Is Gloria busy?"

"We're baking pastries. Let me put you on speaker phone."

"Good evening, Mr. and Mrs. Tipton," Gloria said cheerfully, just as the baby woke up. "Is that a baby I hear crying?"

"That's the reason we're calling, to inform you both of the good news—Maricel and I are proud parents!"

Gloria felt a lump in her throat. Her head started spinning. "But we never even knew Maricel was pregnant..."

Ernesto knew his wife was hurt. This sort of thing happened on occasion with couples they'd helped over the years, but Ryan and Maricel were like family to them.

He cupped the phone with his hand and whispered to his wife, "There must be some logical explanation..."

Ryan sensed their uneasiness. "Once you hear what we have to say, you'll understand things more clearly..."

"We're listening..." said Ernesto cautiously.

"We wanted to tell you the day we learned Maricel was pregnant, and many times after that, but we ultimately decided against it. And once she started showing, we purposely stopped video chatting with the two of you. We also instructed Miguel, Vivian, and Rosalyn not to tell you about the pregnancy."

Ernesto raised an eyebrow. Now he, too, felt hurt. *I was your best man!* "And why is that, Ryan?"

"Before I answer that, we first want to inform you that we'll be in the Philippines six months from now. We wanted to come sooner, but we decided to wait a few months for the baby's sake."

"That's terrific news!" Ernesto said with much less enthusiasm than he was known for. *What in the world is going on?*

Gloria rose above her hurt feelings enough to say, "Did you have a boy or girl?"

"A beautiful baby girl." The exhaustion from giving birth the other day was evident in Maricel's voice.

Ernesto asked, "Are mom and child in good health?"

"We are, praise God," said Maricel.

"When was she born?"

"Three days ago, po."

"Congratulations to you both!" Gloria said. "I can't wait to hold her in my arms."

"Check your phone. I just sent a picture of the three of us."
Gloria reached for her mobile phone.

Ryan looked at Maricel and nodded. "By the way," she said, "we hope you don't mind that we named our daughter, Jecelyn, to honor your late daughter's memory."

There was silence. Shock filled their faces, as the Godly couple wept tears of joy...

The Tiptons remained silent, savoring this precious moment.

After a while, Gloria was finally able to speak. "Nothing can ever compare to this incredible gift you've just given to us. If we ever needed to mark an occasion to signify our outreach ministry has finally come full circle, this would be that defining moment. How can we ever thank you both?"

"By becoming Jecelyn's godparents. Honor us by accepting."

There were more tears. "Of course, we accept! We'd be proud and honored to be her ninong and ninang," Gloria said, staring at the picture on her phone screen. "I see Jecelyn now. What a beautiful baby girl!"

Maricel interjected, "The moment we knew we were having a girl, which is what we were praying for all along, there was no need to wrack our brains senseless trying to come up with the perfect name. We believe God wanted to use this special occasion in our lives as a fitting tribute to you both, for being His faithful servants for so long."

Ernesto wiped his moist eyes and spoke ever so softly. "I don't know what to say. Words fail me. But now that you're raising a daughter in this oftentimes crazy world, you'll need God's Handbook for humanity now more than ever. Otherwise, how can you lay a proper foundation in her life?"

"We read the Bible every day, without fail. And I want you to know I haven't forgotten something you said on my first trip to Manila, that all men should be blessed to raise at least one daughter in their lifetime. I'm sure Jecelyn will help make me a better man."

"You can count on that, Ryan."

Maricel said, "As her ninang and ninong, we hope you'll get to teach her the many life lessons you've taught so many, including us, but never got to finish teaching your daughter."

Ernesto didn't reply. He couldn't. This was one of the most gratifying moments of his life. Not counting when God saved his soul from hell more than a half-century ago, or his lifelong marriage to Gloria and bringing four beautiful children into this world, this was the greatest gift he ever received in life.

When Maricel went to nurse baby Jecelyn, Ryan said, "Oh, there's one more thing; remember my uncle Floyd?"

Ernesto replied, "Are you referring to the one who was stationed here during the second world war?"

"Yes." Ryan paused. "He recently died."

"Sorry to hear that, Ryan," Gloria said.

"Thankfully, Maricel got to meet him before he passed. Uncle Floyd was quite fond of her."

"That doesn't surprise us," Gloria said in reply.

"Yeah, he assured us both on his deathbed that he had eternal assurance, and that he was ready to go Home to be with Jesus."

"Hallelujah!"

"He also left me a seventy-five-thousand-dollar inheritance."

Ernesto whistled through his teeth. "That's a lot of money, Ryan. Perhaps you can start a college fund for Jecelyn with it." He was already thinking about the goddaughter he never met, but already loved completely.

Ryan answered, "I appreciate your wise counsel, Ernesto, but we're thinking of using it for something entirely different."

Gloria asked, "Are you moving back to the Philippines?"

Ryan chuckled. "Not exactly, Gloria. But with the bitterly cold temperatures we've had this week, it's not a bad thought."

Gloria sat up more erectly in her chair. "What is it then?"

Ryan waited for Maricel to return with the baby, then said, "Now that your outreach ministry has come full circle, as you

214

said, I guess we're wondering if we could help make it international, like your three walls proudly boast."

Ernesto rubbed his forehead. "What are you getting at?"

"Would it be okay if we opened an Agape Coffee and Pastry Shoppe here in Iowa?"

"Seriously?" The look on Gloria's face mirrored her husband's.

"Totally serious, Gloria. The safe haven you've both created in Manila needs to be experienced worldwide."

Ryan kissed Maricel's left cheek and went on, "Of course, we're only talking about one location for now. Perhaps in time, with your permission, we can expand operations, including more locations in the Philippines. But for now, we'd like to take the first step by duplicating your efforts here in America."

Ernesto glanced at his wife. She nodded enthusiastically. "Of course, you have our permission…," he said.

"Great! We want to mirror the way you do business there, including the Sunday Bible studies and character-building classes you offer. Naturally, we'll need your help until we get our feet beneath us, so to speak, especially with the Bible studies."

"We'll do anything we can to help you both," said Ernesto.

"You realize this means waking up early in the morning— three a.m. to be exact—and teaching our customers online? Would that be asking too much of you, Ernesto?"

"I recall someone contacting me not too long ago at that hour, seeking my advice on something. Was I alert enough back then?"

The way his mentor said it made Ryan laugh. "Absolutely."

"Well then, count us in." A surge of energy raced through Ernesto. "I'm excited just thinking about it."

Ryan replied, "Hopefully when we're there, we can pick your brains and learn all we can about the coffee business."

Maricel added, "But mostly we want to introduce you to your precious goddaughter."

"We'll be counting the days." Gloria almost sang her reply.

Ernesto looked at the clock on the wall. "I hate to end this incredible moment, but people are already waiting outside for our doors to open."

Ryan said, "We understand completely."

Gloria replied, "Let us know the moment you set a date, so we can plan accordingly. We can't wait to see baby Jecelyn!"

"You got it, Gloria," Ryan said. "Can't wait to have my next cup of coffee in Manila."

Gloria took a deep breath and exhaled. "Thanks for making this one of the most unforgettable days of our lives. We love you both and miss you so much."

"Love and miss you too," said Maricel in reply. "See you soon."

The call ended.

For Ernesto and Gloria Angeles, this was the phone call of all phone calls. Try as they might, they couldn't control their emotions. Tears fell freely down their cheeks, one after the next.

Twenty-two years had passed since they were forced to lay their precious daughter to rest. Call it discernment from above, but the coffee shop owners had an overwhelming premonition that this would be their first full day of complete healing.

And to prove it, for the first time since opening their doors for business 14 years ago, God turned the *Love Throttle* on full blast just for them, removing every-last trace of pain they'd carried in their hearts for nearly a quarter-century, replacing it with His peace that surpassed all understanding.

Wave after wave of gratitude washed over them both...

The circle of life had finally come full circle for them in one sense; what began with bringing their precious daughter, Jecelyn, into the world 49 years ago, only to have her taken away from them far too soon, ended with the birth of their goddaughter bearing the same beautiful name.

The coffee shop owners opened their doors to their waiting customers, eager to share the wonderful news with them. Not only was Agape Coffee and Pastry Shoppe about to expand internationally—God had also blessed them with a beautiful goddaughter who just happened to be named after their beloved daughter, Jecelyn...

Yes indeed, life was good! *Hallelujah!*

It can happen to you too.

But if you want to find

the right person,

you first need to be

the right person!

Thanks for taking the time to read *Coffee in Manila*.
I would be most grateful if you shared your thoughts on Amazon.
Even a short review would be appreciated.
May God continue to bless and keep you.

About the Author:

Patrick Higgins is an Amazon bestseller and award-winning author of the end times prophetic series, *Chaos In The Blink Of An Eye.* The "CHAOS" in our present world is well documented in this timely series, which won the Radiqx Press Spirit-Filled Fiction Award of Excellence, soon after the first installment was published. To date, more than 12,000 positive ratings/reviews have been posted on Amazon and Goodreads, on the first 8 installments...and counting!

Once completed, there will be 10-12 installments...

He also wrote *I Never Knew You,* winner of the 2021 Readers' Favorite Gold Medal in Christian fiction, 2021 Independent Author Network (IAN) book of the year winner in Christian fiction, 2022 American Best Book Awards finalist in Christian fiction, and finalist in the 2021 International Book Awards), *The Unannounced Christmas Visitor*, which won both the International Publishers Awards (IPA) and the 2018 Readers' Favorite Gold Medal Awards in Christian fiction, *The Pelican Trees*, and *Coffee In Manila.*

While the stories he writes all have different themes and take place in different settings, the one thread that links them all together is his heart for Jesus and his yearning for the lost.

With that in mind, it is his wish that the message his stories convey will greatly impact each reader, by challenging you not only to contemplate life on this side of the grave, but on the other side as well. After all, each of us will spend eternity at one of two places, based solely upon a single decision which must be made on this side of the grave. That decision will be made crystal clear to each reader of these books.

Higgins is currently writing many other books, both fiction and non-fiction, including a sequel to *Coffee in Manila,* which will shine a bright, sobering spotlight on the diabolical human trafficking industry.

To contact author for book signings, speaking engagements,
or for bulk discounts, email @ patrick12272003@gmail.com.

To contact author: patrick12272003@gmail.com
Like on Facebook: https://www.facebook.com/patrick12272003
https://www.facebook.com/TheUnannouncedChristmasVisitor
Follow on Twitter: https://twitter.com/patrick12272003
Follow on Instagram: @patrick12272003

What readers are saying about Coffee in Manila:

Whew...what a love story!!! This is the best book I've ever read. As founder of an Asian dating site, I know it's possible to meet a good lifetime partner online. I'm also aware of the many dangers online dating presents. This book teaches so many valuable lessons we all need to learn, especially online daters, making this a 'must-read' story for the many millions currently searching online. We're proud to offer Coffee in Manila on our dating site, and highly recommend that each of our members will read it for themselves. It's that good! We even plan to include this amazing book as part of our gift baskets, which will also include flowers, chocolates, and teddy bears. Thanks for caring so much about my country, the Philippines...Great job!

Jhasty, Cagayan de Oro, Philippines

I am an American currently living in the Philippines. After reading this powerful book, I feel it needs to be read by all foreign men traveling here to Philippines. Perhaps the government should make it mandatory reading before issuing visas to them. More importantly, it should be required reading for all Filipinas living here, beginning at age 16 or 17, much like the US draft. It breaks my heart to see so many young girls throwing themselves at foreigners they barely even know (sometimes 40-50 years older). It happens all the time here and is starting to get completely out of control. Which is why this story is desperately needed here in the Philippines.

Scott Brown, an American currently living in Davao

Just finished reading *Coffee in Manila*. *It was very well written, with a great theme threaded throughout. It's great how the author was able to highlight a pulverizing social issue in the Philippines and more importantly introduce each reader to Jesus along the way. Loved it!*

Scott Hanzy/Founder Arise Asia

Coffee in Manila was so amazing! I read in just one night. There are so many good messages and lessons to be learned from this book. The story will make you both mad and sad, as it really brings to light the many problems which need to be solved in our society. I want to thank the author for writing this great book, and also thank God for the ministry of CIM.

Pastor Pedro M. Etabag/Bacalod, Philippines

What a blessing it was to read Coffee in Manila! This book is so captivating and heart-warming. As a pastor, I believe we need many Ernesto and Gloria Angeles in our society. We also need many 'AGAPE COFFEE and PASTRY SHOPS' all over the country, to become houses of refuge for those who are in need of guidance and direction. I believe this book will be a must-read book in this generation. What a wonderful way to share the love of God.

Pastor Danny Lagdamen - Australia - Arise Davao

When I discovered this book focuses on the exploitations of women, which currently exist and have existed forever, I was moved that the author chose such an important topic in society. Whether it be the Philippines, Thailand, etc., this is a huge problem in the world, and definitely needs the attention it deserves. I don't know if the coffee shop and its gracious owners exist or not, but I sure hope that they do. My wish is that this book travels the world far and wide, and makes a huge difference by bringing about change for large masses of people. By simply reading it, it will shed light on an area which needs so much more attention than it is currently receiving. I believe this book will end up being a real catalyst.

Dana—Florida, USA

Wow! This is the best book I've read in such a long time...so awesome! I can't wait to read it all now. It really opened my mind and heart! Like Ryan, I realized I would want to spend my last 24 hours on Earth with my girlfriend. Please send this to her and tell her I'm changed forever after reading this. Thanks so much for opening my eyes. I mean it sincerely.

Nick Bergsman from Sweden

This touching story really made my heart cry. I believe it will make all your readers cry. They will not need a handkerchief, but a towel...hehehe! I'm sure it will be a best seller here in my country. I hope many foreign men will read this book before visiting my country. If they do, we will see immediate positive change here in the Philippines. May God Almighty continue to bless you all.

Richie Onelods - Cebu, Philippines

Wow! What an awakening this story will be for so many in my country! Reading it made my heart tremble. As a Filipino woman raising daughters, I feel it's my moral obligation to promote this book to everyone I know. It is so needed here in the Philippines!

Ruby Laurente - Manila, Philippines